UNPLEASANTNESS

GHOST STORIES FOR THE DEPRESSED

NATHANIEL A. GILES

CONTENTS

1. The Haunting of Cubicle 1134	1
2. The Witch in the Glass	34
3. Goodbye, Ghost of Columbus	77
4. The Man in the Mirror	96
5. Disappearing	133
6. The Death and Second Life of the Crow Hero	156
7. The Smallest Degree of Holiness	196
8. An Account of Some Strange Disturbances on Old Baltimore Pike	220
9. Unpleasantness	245

Copyright © 2020 by Nathaniel A. Giles

All rights reserved. No part of this publication may be reproduced in any form or by any means without the prior written permission of Nathaniel A. Giles.

First American edition published by Nathaniel A. Giles
Giles, Nathaniel A.

Unpleasantness: Ghost Stories for the Depressed

1
THE HAUNTING OF CUBICLE 1134

Silverman Schumer Pryor, LLC, established as an S corporation in 1980 and converted to an LLC in 1993, was headquartered in a severe eight-story modernist granite block on Orange Street, not far from Rodney Square and the Del Tech campus. It stood out in a neighborhood that was largely twentieth-century poured concrete or nineteenth-century red brick, but it was designed to be distinctive regardless of context. Silverman Schumer Pryor, LLC did not lease the building, they owned it; and they did not purchase it, they commissioned the Graves Architectural Group to design and build it in 1996. There was no mortgage or lien of any kind on it, and it was self-insured. SSP had offices in Fort Lauderdale, Pittsburgh, Plainfield, Irving, and San Jose, but these were satellites. The Orange Street building was the main location. The LLC was founded there, its name partners lived there, and it was said (but not substantiated) that hourly workers made more money there and that the partners protected them from layoffs there because even in lean years they wanted the building full to project a sense of abundance.

The first floor was a huge high-ceilinged granite, steel, and glass reception area with a highly polished black basalt floor, several discrete groups of six or eight big dracaenas that each looked like a little palm forest, uncomfortable high-concept furniture in the waiting area, bathrooms and conference rooms in the back, and some mysterious maintenance rooms. Somehow Alejandro Rojas, Operations Manager of Intake, got the idea that one of them was called the pump room, but he never specified which, and there were no signs. Facing the four glass entrance doors were two oblong reception desks in delta formation at an angle of about 130 degrees, each housing two beautiful receptionists—from left to right, Monica, Amelia, Karen, and Champaign (after the city, not the wine)—each with a headset and three large monitors. Mostly they fielded and transferred phone calls, accepted deliveries, and monitored the security cameras that covered the site inside and out. During audits they greeted client reps, and prior to job interviews they seated and directed candidates. They were the points of contact for outside maintenance crews, they buzzed in employees who forgot their security badges, they politely declined the advances of male colleagues who mistook their sweetness for interest, and they beamed beautiful, bright-white smiles at everybody they saw.

The second floor was mostly accounting, which had a group of real offices in addition to cubicles because there was a group of real accountants in addition to accounting assistants and operations managers. It also housed the mail room and floating offices for visiting attorneys, visiting accountants, compliance specialists, and client associates who came as often as bi-monthly to audit and schmooze.

Floors three through six were cubicles as far as the eye could see, except for the tiny clear acrylic-walled pseudo-offices clustered in the corners and inhabited by department managers. These were the dreaded, shunned floors, peopled almost exclusively by hourly workers without degree-specific vocations. Three through six excreted the most abundant product of both SSP and law in general—documents. Though they called these floors the cube farm they were more like a factory that prepared, peer reviewed, digitally executed, printed, notarized, served, filed, scanned, saved, and shredded every document for every case, from complaint to decree. The workers had no input, nor did they write anything that was ever filed in any court. Every document was generated with software that used stock language written ages ago by the senior attorneys, and had fill-in-the-blank interfaces into which workers manually typed the key particulars—dollar amounts, dates, the names and addresses of the parties and their attorneys, and sometimes pertinent parts of other documents like legal descriptions, execution dates, filing dates, and instrument numbers. Because of this mode of production, every single document of a certain type, that was bound for a certain court, looked and read exactly the same except in these details. It was tedious, hollow work that most of the employees could do in their sleep. Since they weren't permitted to sleep, they wore earbuds and listened to podcasts all day. Most viewed their phones as life-sustaining devices like pacemakers or dialysis machines, and viewed SSP as the hospital where they were kept just barely alive. One of the managers was proud of his MBA and felt like this was where he belonged, but everyone else thought he was delusional about what it meant to be where he was. No one else wanted or planned to be on these floors. It was where you wound up when you hadn't done any planning in college, and committed a few too many venal sins in the real world, and then found it was too late to repent. A terrible painting of a black dog, allegedly by a name-partner's wife, hung opposite the elevator on six and was nicknamed Cerberus.

Seven was almost all attorney offices—some spacious with secretaries out front, some as cramped and cell-like as the pseudo-offices in the corners of three through six—but with a big cluster of cubicles in the northeast corner that housed all the paralegals. There were also several cubicles occupied by people who were mysterious insofar as no one knew what they did. One was an older guy, still young looking but mostly gray-haired, who wore jeans and boots and Harley T-shirts, and had several vines of golden pothos trained around the rim of his cubicle and secured with zip ties. Another was a young, delicate-looking man who dressed in neat business casual and had thick black hair that was complexly styled, stiff, and looked like it took a lot of product and forty-five minutes or so to do. The others were less distinctive but equally mysterious. The wage workers in the cube farm speculated that they did internal audits.

Eight was strictly name partners, senior partners, and their executive assistants, so everything about eight was different. It had thick gray-and-black carpeting that gave a little under every step you took, and absorbed so much sound that as soon as the elevator doors opened you felt like someone had pressed the mute button on a TV or turned off a white noise machine. The entire floor smelled faintly of industrial disinfectant and moderately expensive men's cologne, and everything was dark—the doors and much of the furniture was walnut with oxidized brass hardware, and the chairs and couches of brown or black leather. The walls were a dignified gunmetal gray, and the ceiling maybe three shades lighter. There were no cubicles anywhere on eight, and all of the offices were dignified though they varied greatly in size. Each of the name partners got a corner office, as did the CEO. The CFO and COO were also housed here in offices that were big and nicely furnished but not corners. There was also a big break room as well as executive washrooms and the large conference room.

The people on seven and eight, having all the rights, privileges, and responsibilities of executive types, came and went as they pleased during the work day. They were often satisfied with staying on their home floors, though, because eight was so nice, and the people on seven felt connected to the status of eight. The accountants on two, who also were executive or at least professional types, but whose floor wasn't nearly as richly apportioned as the attorneys' on eight, often fled for hours at a time, especially around noon. Even though their assistants and administrators were wage workers like their colleagues on three through six, they were so close to the ground floor that it was not a big deal for them to go down one flight to get some air and take a walk—no one complained as long as they weren't excessive about it—and at lunch they would often wander down to Rodney Square and eat outside. Some of the older ladies power walked in groups. Some of the younger ladies would lie down on the grass, which the older ladies didn't really approve of but mostly kept quiet about. But generally speaking, this group was satisfied with their lot.

The hourly workers from the cube farm had more complex issues. They wanted to go to Rodney Square or at least for a walk outside, but usually didn't, fearing that, due to all the elevator and walking time, they'd spend the bulk of their thirty-minute break in transit. Even if they walked fast, they might get back a few minutes late and therefore—the horror—have to stay late. So they sat in their cubicles for nine straight hours, or ventured into the dingy break rooms on their home floors, looking frustrated, eating Lean Cuisines, mostly of the type that didn't have to be stirred after three minutes. While this is a normal circumstance of the corporate world, they saw it as a significant problem, and one of the biggest drawbacks to working at SSP. Being tied to the mostly-beige cube farm and seeing fluorescent light almost exclusively—the windows were tinted—coupled with the soul-eroding nature of their jobs made it a hateful place to many. The dreariness of their surroundings and the relentlessness of that dreariness often overcame them. And many of those people were stuck, knowing their other employment options paid less or were less stable.

Cubicles on three through six were not singles with one person, they were big square enclosures housing three people—one per corner with the entrance where the fourth corner would be. These cubicles were arranged in clusters of four, forming a grid of twelve-person mega-cubes equally spaced across the floor. For administrative purposes the cubes were numbered, and each cube had its number posted on its visible sides. Cubicle 1134, on the sixth floor, had at one time been occupied by Karla Turner and Woody Derenberger, who were both legal assistants in Litigation.

Karla's job title was *senior* legal assistant, whereas Woody was just regular legal assistant, so he thought she thought she was queen. She actually didn't do anything arrogant or act any particular way, but Woody was sort of out there in the tinfoil hat area and had mildly paranoid fantasies about almost everything.

They mostly didn't talk. Woody was quiet. Karla was stern and serious at work, as she was older and came from the *never let them see you cry, and never let them see you in a bathing suit* school of women workers who had started in the late 70s and early 80s and had fought to be taken seriously. She was better at getting everything done the right way with all i's dotted and t's crossed and had great confidence in her recall of situational protocols, relevant laws, and company policies. Woody was faster and bolder with decision making, and his judgment was usually pretty good despite his tinfoil hattish tendencies, but he made noticeably more mistakes than Karla. IT had installed that area's communal printer in the corner where there otherwise would have been a third person, so they were a duo. Each separately fantasized about the other quitting, and then having the cubicle to him or herself. Though they didn't really know this about each other, they each felt uncomfortable around other people and preferred to be alone. They each had issues. Each had been abused as children, and each had a lot of anger that they had to make a conscious effort to suppress. Neither recognized this in the other, though other workers in that area could see clearly that they were angry, unhappy people. Karla and Woody each thought the other behaved pretty much normally.

Karla died first. On August 17, 2015, she stayed fifteen minutes late to finish a batch of discovery responses. Then she clocked out, got her things together, walked all the way to the parking garage in the rain, climbed the steps to the fifth level (she was lateish that morning and felt lucky to find a spot even on the exposed roof of the garage), only to remember that she had sat her car keys down between her scanner and monitor stand that morning and never put them back in her bag. She would have to walk down five flights (the parking garage elevators were maddeningly slow), all the way back to the SSP building, take the elevator up, get her keys, take the elevator back down, walk all the way back to the garage, and climb five flights again.

She was frantic and angry on her way back to SSP. Her husband, who worked a 6:00-3:00 shift, was waiting for her at home, but she didn't actually care about that—or him anymore, really, and sometimes not even their children. She was numb and addicted to routine and pretty much desensitized to everything in her personal life. She was frantic and angry because she wanted very much to be out of this place and at home where things were clean and nice and no one could *fucking email her*, and she knew that the later she left, the worse traffic was going to be on 495. And that's what did it. Worrying about traffic and the passing of time occupied her attention. Through the worry and frustration, she barely knew what she was doing.

After she got her keys and went all the way back to the garage, she mounted the stairs. Karla was 5'1", so stairs were difficult to begin with, and they seemed bigger the second time around. Her legs hurt from all the hurrying, she was wearing heels—as she believed proper working women should—and she was slightly out of breath. The stairs were concrete with crosshatched steel nosings meant to keep people from slipping. But they didn't work. The rainwater on the rusty steel was effectively lubricant—the cross-hatching did nothing—and she slipped. As she was falling, she wasn't sure what happened. She didn't know whether she had lost her balance or slipped or broke her heel, but somehow her right shoe failed to make firm contact, and she was in the air. Everything slowed way down during the fall but that did not surprise her. She had been in several car accidents, and this was just what happened. As she waited for the impact, she wondered in a detached way how bad it was going to hurt, whether she would sustain a real injury or just a series of bruises, whether any of her things would be damaged. When she landed, her thigh hit the edge of one of the stairs with all her weight. Her femur broke right in half, severed her femoral artery, and she died of internal bleeding right there on the stairs between the fourth and fifth levels of the parking garage.

Her death was painful and took a long time. No one came to help her because she refused to recognize that her leg was broken or to call out for help to the people she heard on the levels below. She didn't want to admit to some stranger that she was so stupid that she fell, she didn't want someone calling an ambulance, she didn't want to see a doctor. She just wanted to go home. She was determined to rest a bit, get up and get to her car, recover at home that night, and be back at work the next morning—and if the pain made her limp, she'd hide it by not drinking anything so she wouldn't have to get up to pee every hour or so. But instead she slowly lost consciousness and died alone in a rust-stained concrete stairwell, suppressing moans and taking sharp breaths to dull the pain. Before she was officially found by a woman named Ruth Jones, a man named Michael Colby saw her on the steps as he was making his way up to his car. He paused briefly, not thinking anything at all, just looking to see if she moved in any way. She did not. He sort of shifted himself over to see if her eyes were open. They were not. She looked pale and was not breathing. Her left leg was swollen. He climbed over her, got in his car and left. He, too, had been late that morning and was forced to park on the roof in the rain, and here he was leaving at the worst part of the day for traffic. He didn't want to get bogged down in paperwork and police for a person already dead. Like Karla, he just wanted to go home.

Eleven days later, while working late that Friday evening, Woody Derenberger, a big, square-headed moose of a guy, got a sudden headache, stood up at his desk in cubicle 1134, and then collapsed. It was 5:53 p.m. Legal Assistant Tricia Atwood, who thought she was the last person on the floor, left at six and walked right by his cubicle on her way to the elevator. She didn't see him at his desk, his monitors were asleep, and of course there was no reason for her to check and see whether he was lying on the floor. She assumed he had gone for the day. Because of the climate-controlled conditions in which his body lay, the coroner felt confident that Woody had died between three and six Sunday morning, meaning he lay there on the floor, still alive but probably unconscious, for somewhere in the neighborhood of thirty-six hours. He was found early Monday morning by a cleaning crew, and the cause of death was later determined to be complications following a cerebral embolism.

In the days after the deaths, things on six were just sad. 1134 was right by the hall door and there was a communal printer in it, so it was a high-traffic area, even after Karla and Woody died. People walking back and forth in front of it all day were constantly reminded that two people in the same cube died eleven days apart. It wasn't quite a coincidence, and it wasn't quite a curse, but it was a bleak reminder of the random nature of the universe, and the constant presence of death within it. Somebody put flowers on Karla's desk to try to dispel the gloom, but nobody put anything on Woody's, and this made everyone feel sad about his outsider status, and how long he had lain on that floor alone, in the dark. Later, someone put a pewter beer stein there as a general sort of manly gesture, but it was removed when it came out that Woody had been in recovery for nearly a decade before his death.

Though Karla's belongings were boxed up and given to her husband, it wasn't clear to whom Woody's should be given, so they stayed where they were. Rumor had it there was no one to give them to. This was in fact true. There wasn't much there anyway. There were ear buds and a scratched, chipped, third-generation iPod in his desk drawer. There was a box of granola bars with one bar left. There was a bright yellow paperback copy of *Feeling Good* by David D. Burns, M.D., and a black-and-red paperback copy of Aldous Huxley's *The Devils of Loudun*. There was a big snake plant that actually belonged to SSP, but since he had been with the company so long and had taken it with him every time he changed desks, no one knew that anymore. Someone picked up the snake plant and put it on his desk next to a battered banker's box with the rest of his stuff. The snake plant was several feet tall and now seemed to occupy Woody's space, a bonfire of green-and-black flames like a heavy metal album cover. Both the plant and the banker's box were getting dusty.

The sleeve of The Police's last record, *Synchronicity*, was push-pinned to the wall of the cube. No one knew that was the sleeve of the very record he bought the day it came out —June 17, 1983—at the record store at Price's Corner that later became The Wall but was now a women's clothing store. Woody had loved The Police. He saw them four times. August '81 at Liberty Bell Park Racetrack, January '82 at The Spectrum, August '83 at JFK Stadium with REM and Joan Jett and some other band he could never remember the name of, and February '84 at Boardwalk Hall in Atlantic City. There was no one living who knew this about him anymore. The medical examiner noted that Woody had two tattoos on his back. On his left shoulder blade was a circle, but the ME had missed the little spot in the middle—he had mistaken it for a freckle or mole. On the right shoulder blade—much bigger, much more complex, faded and blurry and indigo blue, and probably never very clear to begin with—was what looked like a stick-figure monster strangling itself with its own hands. No one else knew about the tattoos except a couple of women he had slept with who never thought about him anymore, and a couple of old doctors who had no reason to call him to mind. The ME forgot about them after a few days and another fact disappeared from the earth.

After more than a month, SSP employees' still felt really bad about Woody and Karla, which was not normal. Co-workers do not really serve as second families and do not really love each other. That's an illusion manufactured by the producers of *The Mary Tyler Moore Show* that seeped out of television and into the world. In real life it hardly ever happens, and never at places like SSP. SSP was a low-wage and therefore high-turnover document assembly line, an intellectual mill. Most people stayed only as long as they had to. Those that stayed longer either had clawed their way into management and were reluctant to give up their single accomplishment in life or, like Karla and Woody, were the type that always had difficulty getting work to begin with. And only these latter dug in and decided that this was where they really worked and not just a stop-gap. So, people at SSP only knew each other for a year or two before one or the other moved on, and even while they worked together, they barely interacted. This kind of work—"knowledge work"—mostly involved emailing strangers in Texas or Chicago and retrofitting one document to fit case after case. These were solitary activities performed by strangers in company with strangers. There was no family at SSP and there was no love. Mourning, when it happened, was mostly a show, put on mostly by women, and was acted imperfectly and half-heartedly, not so much for the dead or even for the loss of the dead person but because thinking about death made them sad. The men stood around wearing serious-looking expressions. If they said anything, it was from the list of preapproved platitudes. But there was little in the way of real feeling behind any of this. It was mostly about reacting the way they were expected to when other people were looking so that no one thought they were sociopaths. Why the bad feelings should last so long for two—let's face it—misfits was mysterious.

Soon, people started avoiding 1134, which was no easy feat. Jamie Fink did her best to avoid the hall door, which was right behind it. In the morning, she came in that door because she didn't have any choice, but anytime she needed to use the bathroom or go to the elevator, she left through the fire exit in the back. This required that she walk down the back hallway almost the entire length of the suite, go through the fire exit, make a left, go down a short hallway, make another left, and then walk back almost the entire length of the suite, past the hall door she could more easily have used, and then another fifteen feet to the bathrooms, or thirty feet to the elevators. But the fire exit doors only opened from the inside, so she had to come back through the hall door and walk past cubicle 1134 at least once per trip anyway. She had just transferred from Intake on four to Litigation on six, but soon after Karla and Woody died she said she wanted to go back or to transfer a second time to Title Curative on five. Larissa Stupar from HR on five told her that it was against policy to transfer twice in a year and that if she wanted to claim that the move hadn't worked out and go back to Intake, she'd have to go back to her old wage. Jamie sullenly declined and stayed on six, but now sometimes she cried in the bathroom, which she didn't do before, and she drank as little water as possible.

When Sharon Whatley started with the company, Karla and Woody had already been dead for two months, and though no one told her about what had happened to them or where they sat, she found herself overcome with dread every time she had to walk past 1134. One time she even cried a little. Whenever she had to see the dusty monitors and those chairs that hadn't moved in who knew how long, she feared that management might move her to that cubicle. No one had worked in it since her start date, and the company was so big on efficiency that she couldn't imagine that space being wasted for much longer. She could imagine having to take the whole cylinder of Clorox or Lysol disinfecting wipes into the cubicle with her to clean the thick dust off the long beige desk, the keyboard with some other person's crud under the keys and dust down their graduated sides, having to get used to a new chair, and being skeeved out by the arm rests because they had so much dust on them on top of some other person's arm funk. That, combined with the fact that she would have to sit by the door and listen to it opening and closing all day, filled her with a kind of panic she wasn't used to. Her doctor put her on Buspirone, but she drank at least a little alcohol every night, and the combination made her so dizzy that she elected to stop taking it so she could keep drinking.

The bad feelings were the only issue for a while, and in all fairness, feelings are just feelings and could have been in everyone's head. But after three months, physical events started happening. First, the printer fell over and almost crushed Susan Riddley-Walker. On Wednesday, November 18, 2015—which was a client visit day, so everyone was dressed up—Susan Riddley-Walker, Paul Bostaph, Tanya Candler, Gary Holt, Lorna Elswint, Jennifer Arroyo, Trish Doan, and Jon Dette—who sat in cubicles 1132, 1133, and 1135—were all preparing notices of motions, motions, and orders approving motions, and were all a little pissy because they were uncomfortable and because no one could wear headphones due to the client visit. When Susan printed a notice of motion, motion, and order approving motion she was working on, the print job was sent to the printer in 1134, and there was a delay. Cubicle 1134 had a Brother HL-S7000DNX, which had two extra trays making it about three feet tall by itself, but it also sat on top of a cabinet on casters containing four or five reams of standard Staples Multipurpose 8 ½" x 11", and two or three of 8 ½" by 14". So the whole printing rig was just under five feet tall. Either the Brother HL-S7000DNX or Windows had this glitch where sometimes, for reasons unknown, the print job would be delayed by almost exactly three minutes, which was long enough that you were too annoyed to stand there and wait for it, but if you went back to your desk and sat down, like immediately after that it would print and you'd have to get right back up. And once you clicked *print* and then *OK* and then realized you were getting the delay, it wouldn't let you cancel the print job and send it to a different printer.

When Susan realized she was getting the delay, instead of going back to her desk, she stood there for the better part of three minutes talking with Paul. Paul was pretty much the best person who had tried to replace Dave, but it was generally accepted that Dave had been extraordinary at his job and that, while Paul was better than sufficient, he just didn't have what Dave had—and frankly, sometimes the way he wrote sounded like a mess, even though technically everything was correct and delivered exactly on time. "It's dishonest," she whispered to him over the cubicle wall. "The clients come here and we play dress up for them, but the rest of the time we look like slobs in jeans and T-shirts. Why do we have to lie to them?"

Paul didn't care that it was dishonest. "I'm just pissed that it always seems to happen on the least convenient day. Like, today the fucking rain. I got all wet on the way in here, and now I'm not only uncomfortable but I look like a douche who doesn't own an iron. And the last time [REDACTED] was here in February it fucking snowed, so I had to scrape the ice off my fucking windshield at 6:00 a.m. wearing these paper-thin dress pants and this thin shirt. Or, like, not this exact shirt, but a shirt just like this that offers no protection. You might as well have nothing on between your skin and your coat. Just for these people who *might* walk by and see us for *four* seconds."

At this point there was an odd vibration that both of them ignored, except that Susan turned around to see whether it was coming from the printer. Its LCD screen had not even lit up yet, so she turned back around.

"Shit," she said, "I have to run the document upload report."

"Sucks for you."

"Would you run it for me?"

"That's a big fat no."

"Please?"

"Under no circumstances. I have to run it tomorrow."

"I want to get out of here at a decent hour. I don't want to be stuck here at six thirty, in these clothes, uploading documents to LPS that are never going to see the light of day."

"No."

"Why does it always seem like it's my turn?"

"It's your turn now, but it'll be my turn later." Then there was a sharply drawn breath and a deep crash intermingled with the sound of Susan trying to stifle a cry.

Everyone was silent and agape—somehow the printer had tipped over and fallen off the cabinet. The top half sort of gently bounced off Susan's back, but the bottom half banged into her heel as it crashed to the floor. Everyone was astonished, but not because of the injury the thing caused or the slightly worse ones it may have caused if it fell differently. They were astonished because there was no reason it should have fallen at all. The floor, obviously, was perfectly level, and it wasn't like Susan Riddley-Walker was leaning on the printer—she was leaning on Paul's cubicle, and there was plenty of space between her and the Brother HL-

S7000DNX. Everyone attested to this, and Morgan Lander, Operations Manager of Litigation and therefore the person responsible for this part of the floor, knew it herself and said nothing to the contrary.

Ms. Silverman's assistant insisted that Ms. Silverman insisted that Susan see a doctor and have her foot x-rayed at the very least. This was said to be due to Ms. Silverman's concern for Susan—Ms. Silverman was the most visible and hands-on of the name partners and affected the most personality to the wage workers—but really everyone knew that Susan was fine and that this was for liability purposes. SSP was a law firm, after all. So, Susan went and did that on Ms. Silverman's dime, got out of work early on a client visit day, got out of running the document upload report (Paul had to do it two days in a row), and no one from management level up raised an eyebrow when Susan called out the next day. Susan felt like a bruised ankle was not sufficient reason to miss two and a half days of work, so she came back on Friday even though that was ridiculous, and Ms. Silverman called her into her office and asked about the ankle. She said it was much better, almost good as new, right in front of one of the non-name partners, who was also Director of Compliance and was sitting silently in a corner away from Ms. Silverman. But none of this was necessary. Susan didn't have the wherewithal to file suit, and she clearly didn't want to. She considered her bruise a happy accident that got her out of work for a day and a half and was not looking to cash in any further, so the matter was closed.

This being the case, the episode was resolved from a legal perspective. The thing left to reconcile was why the printer fell. No one had a plausible explanation. Gary Holt and Jennifer Arroyo spent part of Thursday the 16th floating hypotheses to each other until Lorna butted in.

"Maybe she sort of absent-mindedly kicked the printer," Jennifer said.

"With paper in it that printer has to weigh eighty pounds," Gary said. "Susan is five foot nothing and weighs three quarters of an ounce. No way she kicked it off with one of her little Tinkerbell feet. Not standing in the position she was in, facing away from it, leaning on Paul's cube wall. And how could she kick it off the cart thing *toward* herself? The cords are *behind* it, so she couldn't have gotten tangled in them. No way she kicked it over."

"Well, what was it then?"

"I don't know. But what about this—the top sort of shelf thing that the printer sits on. What if that sort of gave way under the weight of the printer?"

"It wasn't broken, though."

"Right, but check this out. I've assembled enough cheap Ikea or Office Depot or whatever furniture to know how that stuff is put together—my apartment is full of that shit. There's like a little hole in the sides of two parts that come together, and they give you a little dowel that you stick in both holes. Then you bang the sides together and the thing is together. Sometimes they're balsa wood, but sometimes the dowels are this really shitty plastic. So what if that cabinet thing wasn't rated for the weight that was on it, or was just old or something, and the dowels bent, the printer fell off, and then being relieved of the weight, it sort of snapped back into place."

"Doubt it. I feel like you're overestimating the weight of the printer. And I don't think that cabinet thing was as cheap as the shit you assemble yourself. But even if that did happen, no way could the dowels get themselves back into the holes. Or if they did, it wouldn't look perfect. You would be able to tell that something happened to it. It would be off. But I saw it before maintenance took it. There was nothing wrong with it."

Lorna Elswint, who shared cubicle 1133 with them, turned around in her chair in the way that indicated that she intended to address the cube. They each made a provisionally-willing-to-listen half-turn toward each other, but would not yet commit to the full turn. "Someone pushed it off," she said. Gary and Jennifer gave the full turn.

"*Who?*" Jennifer whispered.

Lorna shrugged. "Woody or Karla."

Jennifer looked at Gary. Gary laughed not quite obnoxiously loudly but louder than was probably strictly appropriate—the way you laugh when you suddenly realized how two things interlock. They felt like they had realized a truth. Not one they could countenance in front of other people the way Lorna was doing now but one that they could secretly believe in and occasionally whisper to each other and to Lorna about. It was immensely satisfying and entertaining to them. The days here were long and desperately uninteresting. Having this new story to contemplate and use to explain any weird thing that might happen gave them something to think about other than how slow their computers ran when it got close to three o'clock and IT started all their maintenance bullshit or whatever. Whether it was true or not, they were grateful that Lorna had given it to them.

Except for the bad feelings, the week following Susan Riddley-Walker's accident was uneventful almost all the way to the end. Jennifer and Gary listened carefully and hoped to be able to attribute noises made by the living to Woody and Karla, but every time they heard something, they poked their heads up over the cube wall and almost immediately found the source. They hoped to see things but saw nothing. They even hoped to feel bad, but they always felt bad at work, so it was difficult to determine whether it was caused by the malevolent spirits of their deceased misfit coworkers or it was just how their lives were. Their excitement about the matter cooled.

That Friday, however, Tricia Atwood was once again the last person on the sixth floor. Tricia was very businesslike and affected to have no feelings when she was at work, but of course she did have feelings, and of course she was unhappy. Not yet having heard the whispers about Lorna's story, the idea of ghosts hadn't occurred to her, but her bad feelings in and around 1134 were still very strong. She did not find this strange, as she knew that she had walked right by Woody as he lay dying and frequently thought that if she had just bothered to look, she might have seen him, called 911, and saved his life. Or even if she hadn't saved his life, she might have saved him thirty-six odd hours of pain, discomfort, loneliness, and fear. (She did not know that he was thought to have been unconscious.) She imagined herself lying on the floor, alone in the dark, for half that long and it brought her almost to tears.

Tricia clocked out at 5:53 that evening. Like Woody, Tricia had little to go home to, so she liked to get some overtime in, especially on Fridays. Though she was really just dodging an empty apartment and a dark, silent phone, she gave out that she was so busy during the rest of the week that she had things she couldn't get done at any other time. And she didn't hate staying. After everyone rushed out of the building, and it was silent but for the computer fans and the climate control vents, she felt calmer and more productive. After twenty minutes of detecting nothing, the motion sensors let the lights go out, and she sat in the glow of her monitor, working almost smugly, feeling like she must *look* like the only truly dedicated employee on the sixth floor. But really she was just cleaning up—proofreading, finally answering emails from troublemakers it was best not to communicate with in real time, making sure all the tasks due that day had not just been completed but *marked* complete, making sure there were no physical copies of sensitive documents that hadn't been scanned and shredded. But there always came a point when there was nothing else that she could do without committing to another hour or more, and that was the time to go. On this particular Friday, that time was 5:53.

On her way to the hall door, she stopped to sort through her purse and find her phone. As she was sorting, she felt a hand on her shoulder and turned. There was no one. Then the hollow, plastic, bass drum sound of an office trash can being knocked over came from 1134. She took two diagonal steps forward-left and looked over the cube wall. There was the trash can knocked over, just as it had been when the cleaning crew found Woody—and there was Woody. He did not look well. He wasn't splayed out dramatically like a corpse in a movie. He was face down, bent slightly at the waist, and his arms were under him—she could see his left hand sticking out from under his right side. It was an unplanned, chaotic position that conscious human beings never assumed. She didn't scream or move or say anything. She just continued to look until he disappeared. Then she walked very quickly out of the suite, past the elevator to the stairwell, took off her heels, and effectively *ran* down six flights of steps, silently crying.

When she reached the ground floor, she paused before the door to hyperventilate, cry audibly, and put her shoes back on. The stairwell opened on the left side of the huge granite, steel, and glass reception area, where there was no cover from inconvenient people. She didn't think she was likely to be seen at this hour, but just in case, she wiped her eyes with the heels of her hands, smoothed her hair, and planned to make a very determined-looking beeline straight to the exit to deter any person who might otherwise think to stop her. When she opened the door, the reception area appeared empty, and she thought she was in the clear, but just as she reached the outer door, one of the receptionists, Amelia, was leaving too and called out, "Hi, Tricia!" She clearly wanted to walk with her. Tricia had no choice but to stop, and it being clear that something was wrong, Tricia explained. By the following Wednesday, everyone knew what Tricia had said, which of course she didn't like. She didn't want to be called into her manager's office to be talked to about spreading rumors. Management did nothing, however, which did not change either Tricia's fear of management retaliating or her icy outward demeanor. She just had another thing to carry around with her, another thing to pretend wasn't happening.

The *next* Wednesday, just when things were calming down about Tricia's sighting (except in 1133, where everyone was still on high alert and peering over the cube wall every few minutes), there was another incident. The printer had that three-minute delay thing happening, so out of frustration people started reprinting at other printers and never picking up the copy they made at 1134, and paper started piling up. Around three forty-five, Nathan Black, the weird fat guy from Complaints, cube 1140, forgot about the delay and accidentally printed a draft of a complaint to 1134. Instead of printing to another printer, he decided to spend the three minutes sifting through the documents that were just sitting on top of the HL-S7000DNX in case any of them were sensitive and needed to be shredded. After a few seconds, he leaned over Gary and Jennifer's cube wall and dangled a piece of paper from his fingers. "Fuck's this?" he asked, genuinely puzzled.

Jennifer and Gary were not the owners, operators, or proprietors of the printer, but because they sat closest to it now, people just brought things to them—documents, problems, questions, reports about performance, and so on. Gary was irritable about it and usually said standoffish things, but Jennifer tried to be helpful, so she took it from him and looked. Though it was only text, it had been printed in landscape view and was one word: HELP in 200-point font. It took up the entire page. "Ummmm," she said, "we'll take care of it. Thanks, Nathan," and smiled that *go away now* smile that some people have mastered. Weird Nathan went away. She showed the paper to Gary. "What font is that?" she asked.

"Times. Times New Roman."

"No," Jennifer said, "Garamond." Karla used Garamond in all of her emails, including her email signature, against company policy, which was to use 11-point Arial in all email communications. Everyone knew that Garamond was a weird Karla thing.

"It's Times New Roman."

"It is *not*," Jennifer insisted. "There are differences. Like, look at the little things at the bottom of the H. Like, the little. . . things. That it stands on, that the H stands on. In Times New Roman they're perfectly flat, the edges are perfectly straight. In Garamond they're slightly arched. Same with the P. And look at the edges. They're slightly. . . wonky. Like, the lines aren't straight. If you print this out in Times New Roman, they're perfectly straight."

"The wonkiness of the lines is just from printing real big letters—that printer isn't designed to print signs, it's designed to print documents. Garamond can't have fucked up edges like that."

"I'm telling you, Gary, it does."

Gary had to be convinced, so they did an experiment. After a few minutes they figured out that it was in 200-point font and printed one landscape HELP in Times New Roman and one in Garamond. The original, which they had marked *Original* with a blue pen, matched the one they had printed in Garamond. The lines of the Times New Roman letters were exact and straight, whereas Garamond was slightly arched and wonky, just like Jennifer had said. The original was definitely Garamond.

"OK. But so?" Gary said. "Anybody could have printed that for any reason. It could have been part of a sign that took up multiple pages or something." As a further experiment they emailed the entire floor.

Hi, Everybody!

Whoever printed a HELP sign on the printer in 1134 left it on the printer. Can you please come pick it up, or let me know it's OK to throw away?

Thanks!

Jennifer Arroyo

SENIOR LEGAL ASSISTANT—SILVERMAN SCHUMER PRYOR LLC

No one responded, but that wasn't confirmation of anything. People in this office were more likely to remain anonymous than respond to an email like this—they just had too much work and too many real emails to waste time responding to frivolous ones. But it was very odd. You don't make signs with sixteenth-century serif typefaces with wonky edges, you make them with clean-looking, smooth-lined, modernist sans serif typefaces—that's what those fonts are *for*. And even though not everyone knows that, not one living soul at SSP used Garamond. Everyone except Karla followed company policy, which was Arial 11 for email and Times New Roman 12 for every legal document except in courts where other fonts or sizes were required by court rules or recommended by counsel (which was sometimes scandalous—the Superior Court of Pennsylvania issues opinions in Verdana, and Pennsylvania Rule of Appellate Procedure 124 was amended in 2013 to increase the minimum font size from 12 to 14. SSP brass decided to mirror the court, so all docs sent to the Superior Court of Pennsylvania were in 14-point Verdana, which skeeved out the entire typography nerd community at SSP).

"Of course," Gary pointed out, "this explanation implies that Karla logged into her machine—which clearly has not been physically touched for a long time as evidenced by the centimeter-thick dust all over it—opened Word, selected *Blank Document*, selected her font—Calibri is the default in Word these days—changed the print settings to *landscape*, enlarged the font to 200—which it takes a bit of experimenting to figure out is the roughly appropriate size for this purpose—clicked *print*, waited almost exactly three minutes, and then turned off her machine without anyone noticing the monitor coming on, without her mouse moving from the position it's been in since she died, and without disturbing the dust over there in any way. Or she somehow ghosted her way into someone else's machine and interfaced with it in a way that they didn't detect, or went straight into the code or something and printed it that way. Which Karla couldn't do with her hands while alive, let alone with no physical body, and of course she had zero coding or IT know-how or whatever it would take to do that. So, if we're saying she did this, which way did she do it?"

Jennifer shrugged. They looked at Lorna. Lorna half turned toward them. "Who knows what they can do?" she said seriously, with one inclined eyebrow. She slowly turned back around. When she heard them turn back around too, she smiled into her monitor. She was enjoying playing the spooky Gypsy woman.

The next incident came the following Monday. When everyone came in that morning, they found things in a general but low-key sort of disarray. No one's trash can had been emptied. Debris of various descriptions was still all over the floor, tables, and counters in the break room, and the bathrooms were as filthy as they had been on Friday evening. It turned out that Tri-State Cleaning, SSP's longtime servicer, had been fired. Things in 1134 were torn up too. There were ripped papers everywhere, the printer's drawers were all pulled out and emptied onto the floor, the trash cans and recycling bins were flipped, and both Woody's and Karla's chairs were overturned. No one else's chairs or cans or bins or printer drawers had been messed with.

Everyone was in the dark for two or three hours, but then another rumor spread through the floor. Mackenzie Stark-White had a cousin, Garrett, who was an opioid addict and had been to prison three or four times, so he couldn't get a good job even though he had a master's degree in public policy. Garrett wound up working for one of these nighttime cleaning companies and heard from a guy who had quit Tri-State Cleaning and came to his company, Schumacher Management, Inc., that in truth the cleaning crew actually sort of quit. Tri-State had come into SSP Sunday night, and in the same place where they had found a dead body in August, they now found everything moving around—paper flying, chairs moving, printer drawers being pulled out, trash cans moving by themselves—so the cleaning crew left and refused to return. When the crew went back to their office and told management, a bunch of them got fired on the spot, and Tri-State had to separate out a bunch of people from other crews to come and form a makeshift crew to finish cleaning for SSP.

When the makeshift crew went in, nothing was moving, but things were torn up, just like the original crew had said. The makeshift crew started trying to clean it up, but then things started moving *again*, and the makeshift crew left too and refused to go back. Tri-State's management was still trying to sort out the mess that morning when some of SSP's senior partners came and found that no work had been done anywhere on six, seven, or eight. They were so mad they called and fired Tri-State. So *technically* Tri-State *was* fired, but really two different crews saw what was happening in 1134 and quit. This complex story was transmitted more or less intact through the office, with some Santeria-related additions of questionable provenance appended to certain versions. Soon enough, everyone on the floor knew what had happened, and, more importantly, as they talked about it more and more, they were starting to convince themselves it was true. After all, two different cleaning crews saw it happen, and stuff in 1134 was all messed up just like they said.

At this point, people started openly avoiding 1134, which was awkward as that effectively meant that they had to avoid the front door. At first it was only Jamie Fink, but soon there were almost twenty people using the fire exit to go to the elevator or bathroom. Again, the fire exit only opened from the inside, but they solved the return issue by leaving a pencil or pen closed in the door to keep it from shutting all the way and locking them out. Eventually, there were so many people doing this that a kind of etiquette grew up around putting the pen back in the door if one fell out when you opened it, so no one would get locked out. Of course management saw what was happening and emailed the entire floor advising that the back door/fire exit was only to be used by IT or in case of fire or emergency. Certain people continued to use it until department managers whose offices were in that back hallway started intervening, which was very awkward and smacked of high school.

Also, preventative or palliative superstitions started to gel around cubicle 1134 that, whether they worked or not, made otherwise powerless people feel like they could handle the situation better. Lydia Ryder was the first to be seen sheepishly performing the little ritual that became the standard. When she had dismissals to print, and the printer in 1134 was experiencing delays, she behaved almost as though Karla and Woody were still in the cube sitting in their chairs. That is, when they were alive and Lydia entered their cube, she was polite enough to acknowledge them in whatever way was most appropriate given what they were doing at the time. Now that they were gone, she found that it made her feel better to raise her hand just above waist level and give a brief little wave—mostly just extended fingers and a controlled shake—and whisper "Hi." Though she was embarrassed about it, and it showed on her face and in the character of her whisper, she continued do this in full view of whoever was around, even the idiots who made a show of watching to see if she'd do it this time. After a few days, some of the other ladies in Original Docs started to do the same thing.

The first male to do it was Nathan Black, the weirdo. He found himself standing there, waiting out the delay, unwilling to walk back to his desk without first getting what he came for. Feeling slightly more relaxed because it was Friday, and not really knowing what to do with himself while he waited, he half sarcastically gave the little fingers-extended half-wave and the compact guy-nod, and said, "Hey. How you guys doin'?" Gary and Paul and Jen Arroyo and Trish Doan all witnessed this, and Trish couldn't help but laugh a little. Nathan had a thing for Trish and, even though he knew she was out of his league, for some reason he considered this an encouraging sign, so he made that greeting his ritual. This pretty much set the tone for the men—slightly sarcastic but never really crossing the line to disrespectful. Only once did Nathan go as far as, "Don't you guys ever dust in here?"

Whatever specific thing someone did, the ritual was to greet Woody and Karla. This became so ingrained that people started to do it unconsciously, and by March of 2016 even Morgan was doing it without a thought—sometimes even when just walking by. This seemed to calm the activity way down, and the bad feelings were pretty much defused. Some people still had them, but acknowledging that something was there, and making a gesture toward being friendly with it, seemed to make everyone feel a little better. Insofar as physical events, a few things happened after that. Lorna Elswint, who had previously grown very proud of herself for being the first to recognize that ghosts were present, one day let out a brief little chirrup of a scream and swore that she saw Woody's chair move. This was especially interesting to Jennifer Arroyo, who thought that prior to Woody's death he had shown Lorna an inappropriate amount of attention—or if not inappropriate, definitely a disproportionate amount of attention—which made it seem an awful lot like he had a thing for her. But after the brief little chirrup, no one could really tell whether the chair had been moved. Paul swore that it had been, and Gary swore that it definitely had not and that he was closer to 1134 so he should know, but either way it was a minor incident. Then there was the day that Karla's monitors were on and the lock screen was up. No one was sure whether that was scary or not because no one knew if it had been completely shut down after her death, so it was not clear whether it had been turned on supernaturally or if it had been asleep this whole time, in which case pretty much anything could have woken the monitors up. When they checked they saw that Woody's was only asleep, but that wasn't an index for Karla's. They then powered down both machines, and there were no further incidents of that sort.

Management's non-public policy on these issues had

thus far been to pretend that nothing was happening, and they would not have changed that policy but for the outcry. Everyone knew that SSP had been squeezing too many employees into too little space for too long, and being a relatively efficient company, they couldn't see leaving 1134 unoccupied any longer. Eight months had passed, which should have been more than enough for the hourly employees to mourn the strangers who once sat near them.

Two new hires were coming in to be part of the Client Communications Team. However, Client Communications was in the area by the windows on the west side of the suite, and the new hires would need to be near their team, so management decided to move two sort of satellite employees, who made up part of the highly fragmented Post Judgment Curative Team, out of that area and into 1134. One of these employees was one of this team's senior members, April "The Wig" Burgoyne, who was competent but lazy, loud, and pompous, and could not stop talking about the move. Reproducing a great deal of her dialogue here would be annoying. It is sufficient to say that most of it was dramatically performed as though it were directed to her co-worker, Kim (who silently but emphatically didn't believe in the haunting), when in fact it was designed to create the general, widespread understanding that she didn't like the decision management made to move her to 1134. It largely consisted of loud, shrill, broken sentences like, "I just can't. They just... I just can't sit there. How am I supposed to *work* there? Where that... *man* died." The idea was to make sure management knew how unhappy she was without her having to say anything directly to them and make herself seem like a complainer. And it worked, so the plan was abandoned, and other arrangements were made.

Ultimately cubicle 1134 was dismantled. The printer was carried over and pushed up against the side of 1132, having been placed, since Susan Riddley-Walker's accident, on a low, stable, stationary cabinet that held much less paper to almost everyone's chagrin. The area where 1134 had stood soon became just a series of discolorations on the carpet in the awkwardly, confusingly empty space by the door. The pieces of 1134 were brought to the supply room, where they sat for a time like disarticulated bones in a heap, being too irregular to be neatly stacked. A positive side of this was that the supply room was located in the hallway that led to the fire exit. The remains being located there had the effect of repelling all unnecessary traffic from that hallway and re-routing it out the front door, where it was supposed to go anyway. Another positive was that people who often went to the supply room to kill time or steal supplies—especially AA or AAA batteries for use in personal electronics not purchased by SSP or necessary to SSP's business—no longer went there very often. After a few months, the remains of 1134 were moved to a maintenance room that was locked and that only Nick Millett and his tattoos could access. For a while people listened for—and heard—noises coming from that room. It was almost as if the outrage of the dead workers grew rather than receded. But eventually people stopped listening at that door, and it was simply unknown whether anything was going on in there or not. Even Nick didn't know, only rarely having occasion to unlock it. Soon, enough people quit, and enough new hires took their places, that only a handful of people on six even knew the story, and whether noises came from the maintenance room didn't matter anymore. Karla and Woody were forgotten. Disappeared from the Earth.

2

THE WITCH IN THE GLASS

My mother says I must not pass
Too near that glass;
She is afraid that I will see
A little witch that looks like me,
With a red, red mouth, to whisper low
The very thing I should not know
—Sarah Piatt, "The Witch in the Glass"

Nicole was petite and dark and compelling to men. She knew this from the time she was thirteen, when a big, strange man with long hair and a leather jacket hit on her while she was at a Borders Books with her mother. Her mother had gotten angry, both with the man and with her somehow, even though she only stood there while this man spoke to her. Her mother pulled her out of the store and through the parking lot by her wrist and rebuked her in a loud, harsh whisper, as though Nicole had started the conversation or provoked it. She was a little afraid that her mother might slap her, so she said nothing and wore a neutral expression. But inside she was thrilled. A grown man had hit on her.

There had been a solicitousness in his tone that was different from the way any grown man had ever talked to her before. He took some of the bass out of his voice and was being a little too nice. He called her "hon." Before this incident she would have said that would be creepy, but she liked it a lot. He had curled his left arm around the bookshelf she was looking at, and his arm was so long that it was pretty much in front of her, as if he were preparing to hug her or sweep her up. He was tall, and he sort of bent down over her and put his other hand on the bookshelf across the aisle, as if to trap her, to hem her in. She easily could have walked away in the other direction. And even if she couldn't have, they were in a well-lit store full of people. There was no real danger. But it still gave her a little scare that she enjoyed. A cheap one, like a jump cut in a horror film, but she liked it. She was not confused about that.

He had said "Hey, hon. What's your name?" and she knew instantly that he was modulating his voice. That it was deeper than that. And he said it in a cartoonishly friendly way, like he was trying to appear harmless, but also in a hushed way, like he didn't want other people to hear what he said or was *going* to say.

She had had no experience with men or boys. No sex, not even a kiss. But she knew that men were not harmless when they wanted to appear harmless. And this man especially was not. But she still found it amusing. When he asked her name, she had to stifle a laugh. And later, when she was back home and alone upstairs, she enjoyed replaying the event in her head even though the man himself was horrible. He was too old to be dressed like that, to have long hair like that. He was ugly and fat. She hadn't smelled anything, but she assumed for some reason that he had bad breath. He was clearly preying on her because she was young, and he must have thought she wouldn't know better. But she did know better. She would never have been with him in a million years—*ew*. She simply liked the fact that this had happened, that a man had looked at her in that way. It made her feel like she would grow up to be pretty and that soon enough better men would do things like that all the time. It made her smile, half from amusement and half from genuine enjoyment. She was going to have a fun life no matter how mad her mother got.

But she did not actually have a fun life. Soon after the event at the bookstore, her father lost his job, and they lost their house. They had to live with her father's mother for a while, and once they got their own house again, it was small and ugly and old and in a bad neighborhood. Her father found that he couldn't stop drinking, and he left them there in that house, in that neighborhood. And by herself her mother couldn't even afford that, so they had to move to an apartment. The apartment was smaller still, and the building was uglier still, though the neighborhood was slightly better.

During these years, Nicole tried to have the good time she had thought she was going to have, that she was supposed to have or that she was entitled to have. But it was never very good. She was angry because of things that happened at home even now that her dad was gone, and she found that she despised "nice boys." They seemed like weaklings or cowards, so she drifted into groups with other types of boys. But they were worse than the weaklings. She convinced herself that they were going to be mean to everyone *except* her, but she was never excepted. And it usually took her a long time to realize she wasn't going to be treated as special, even though it happened repeatedly.

Eventually she started having sex, but it was awful and disappointing, painful and often degrading. And of course word got around. Other kids acted like they hated her. They laughed at her. But they were afraid of her, of her courage.

By tenth grade the things she did started getting back to her mother, and then things were even worse at home. She started smoking cigarettes and weed in boys' backyards, behind garages, in the backs of cars. In the eleventh grade she dropped out of school to work as a waitress, drank every night, and smoked too much. She dressed in black. She wore black makeup. She listened to punk rock. She got a tattoo of the Crimson Ghost just above her ass. She got roughed up and slapped around by guys, swore she would kill them if they ever touched her again, said things like "I'll cut your fucking balls off," and then got slapped around again two weeks later. She found that she had trouble respecting boys who *didn't* rough her up. She taunted them to try to make them do it and was disgusted with them if they didn't. She once spit on a guy's shoes when he wouldn't fight back. He gave her the oddest look, and she didn't understand.

She lived this kind of life for twelve years, and then her mother was injured at work. Her mother had taken a job in a warehouse where they assembled merchandise that had been manufactured in Malaysia and Vietnam before it was shipped to stores. There she fell off a stool, shattered three disks, and was in tremendous pain, for which she was given Oxycontin.

Nicole had not made good choices in life, but she was not stupid, and she knew where Oxycontin led people like her mother. And it did lead there. Like so many people, her mother got addicted to pills, then switched to heroin, and eventually overdosed and died. Shortly after that, her grandmother had a heart attack, hung on for a few months, and then she died too. And because the universe is hideous and broken, her grandmother's death precipitated the first good thing that had ever happened to Nicole, at least since her father lost his job—her grandmother left her a house.

Her grandmother hadn't actually left her a house. Nicole simply inherited the house by course of law since she was her grandmother's only living heir. And it wasn't the house that she had grown up visiting—it wasn't "grandma's house." That house had to be sold to pay off all of grandma's debts and what was left of her second mortgage. But grandma had bought a second house in 1983 as an investment property and had rented it out to various people ever since. As a child Nicole had been vaguely aware that the house existed, but she had never been there. It was now empty but was supposed to be—and in fact turned out to be—in decent shape. Nicole now owned it and grandma's car. Owned both of them outright, debt free.

The house was a simple red-brick two-story in a part of New Castle that doesn't exist anymore—at least not the way it once did—called Shawtown. Once again she wasn't in a great neighborhood. Somewhere in her head she still thought of herself as that pretty middle-class girl whose father had a good job, so every time she moved into a new place she couldn't help but feel how terrible it was, how run down or old or damaged or likely it was to have roaches. But still she was happy with this house. It was the first house she had ever lived in on her own, and although it wasn't huge or too nice, she *owned* it. That gave her a little thrill, even though she didn't really feel like a homeowner. She felt more like a renter or squatter because the place was three-quarters empty. When she moved in, she had very few belongings—a bed, a couch, a coffee table, basic kitchen stuff, a TV, a TV stand, a laptop, two floor lamps, one table lamp, one end table, basic bathroom stuff, and her clothes. That was pretty much everything besides boxes of junk. The floors and walls were bare, and most of the rooms had literally nothing in them but venetian blinds, so every noise was reflected and amplified, and the imitation wood on the floors was creaky, so every footstep reported loudly. Living alone in Shawtown wasn't the safest thing for her to do, but in a place like this, where no noise was absorbed and every movement could be heard, if someone broke in she would definitely know it. Her ambition was to find a way to get a chair and some stuff just for decoration, but for right now she was satisfied with the way things were.

The ground floor was a front porch, living room, dining room, kitchen, and bathroom. The basement was unfinished concrete and had a washer and dryer but was full of spiders, and she decided to avoid it completely until she needed to do laundry. The second floor had three bedrooms and a bathroom. Apparently there was some kind of attic, too, but given the number and size of the spiders in the basement, she was in no hurry to see it. She didn't think she could sleep on the second floor if the attic turned out to be anything like the basement.

After she had gotten everything moved in, which didn't take very long, and returned the U-Haul, she went upstairs, lay on her bed, and looked at the ceiling. She was now twenty-nine, but she felt frazzled, spent, and old. She knew that she looked older than her age from all the smoking and drinking, and she felt like her chance at a decent life was almost gone. Like another few years the way she was going would mark a sort of end point, where she was no longer a young person playing at being a certain way to piss people off but really was irreparably that way. Her mother's and grandmother's deaths had been strokes of luck that she never would have asked for, but she felt like they provided her with an opportunity to salvage her life.

She had been heading toward an even more difficult life. She was still doing drugs and drinking. She had never been with a decent man or had a decent job, and she was already starting to find that she wasn't special anymore. When she was younger she was the prettiest girl, or close to being the prettiest girl, wherever she went, and people—especially men—paid attention to her. Now that she was older and had faded a bit, she was just another mildly attractive person, and she no longer felt that she could have whatever man she chose. She was starting to fear that she might wind up with someone who was more a convenience than a match, and they'd just be two frustrated people with nothing to offer each other but half of the bills and satisfactory sex at predictable intervals.

But now, with this car and this house, she felt like she could get a better job than just waitressing because she wouldn't have to wait on the bus. And owning the house meant no rent to pay, just utilities. She could have a *decent* life. She wouldn't have to try to find a man to move in with or be found by one who needed to move in with her. She could have something nearer to the life she had thought she was going to have before her father lost his job. Not the stoned teenage sex life she had looked forward to but the life that was supposed to come after that. But she would have to change first. She wasn't even sure what the utilities would be like here (she had heard nightmare stories about heating bills), or if she could make enough money waitressing. She needed a better job before anything else, and she became at that exact moment, laying on her bed and staring at the ceiling, determined to get one.

Within four months she had one.

She had seen an ad for a receptionist at a doctor's office and applied. She figured that was a very civil job, where she wouldn't have to know anything in particular. She had a pleasant speaking voice, she was good with old people, and because she had been a waitress for so long, she knew how to be nice to people she didn't like or who didn't like her. She couldn't think of anything else she needed to qualify. The office manager, Rita, was a severe looking older lady, and after interviewing with Rita, Nicole was sure that she wouldn't get the job. She believed Rita thought that Nicole was full of herself, even though she tried to be as down to earth as she could be. There were some people who could smell you out, whoever or whatever you were, and they knew they could do it. They showed it in their attitude if you were trying to be somebody you weren't. They wanted you to know you weren't fooling them. Rita, she thought, was one of these angry mind-reading bitches.

But apparently Nicole was wrong, because she got hired, and when she came back for her first day of work, Rita was suddenly very nice. When she met the doctor, he made it clear, in a tasteful, understated way, that he thought she was attractive, which she knew would give her at least a measure of job security as long as she was nice to everyone and did her job—which was exactly what she intended to do. Within a few weeks she was used to her job and getting good at it, and she was shocked at how much her whole life had improved in just a few months. She had health insurance for the first time in eight years and was making more money than she ever had before. Not that it was a fortune, but she didn't have to buy store-brand Cheerios anymore. She *did* buy store-brand Cheerios just to cut costs, but she *could have* sprung for real General Mills Cheerios if she had wanted.

All this change cleared up some other problems for her as well. Moving into this house and getting a new job removed her physically from the places her friends were used to finding her. She wasn't at the restaurant, she wasn't at the bar, she wasn't on the bus, and she was twenty minutes by car from her old apartment complex. They couldn't get to her without making a serious effort, and they didn't do that. All her friends did was drink and get high. But now that she wasn't around them, she didn't feel endangered by that anymore. Soon after getting this new job, she quit drinking and smoking weed and was trying valiantly to quit cigarettes. And having a regular job, where she worked every day from eight to five, forced her to stop going out every night. She had to be up in the morning, and by 9:00 p.m., when she used to get off work, wired from coffee and activity, she was too tired to do anything but get undressed. Her skin started to look better. She lost a little weight. At work, lonely old ladies who weren't really sick but came in anyway told her how pretty she was, put their hands on hers, and called her "honey." They all said she reminded them of someone. They approved of her. They liked her. And she no longer felt ashamed in front of proper old ladies. As a waitress she felt like proper old ladies wouldn't even talk to her if they knew what she was like outside the restaurant. She now felt entitled to be liked by them. She was fixed now. She felt that she had been a salvage job and that she had not been salvaged but had salvaged herself. She was happy, proud, relieved, and optimistic about what might happen next.

Things went on like this for better than a year. She was now thirty. She thought her new life was great. It was not fun, but it was better. And then she found that she couldn't sleep. She had trouble keeping her eyes open around nine thirty or ten, then went upstairs to bed, got herself all arranged under the covers, finally stopped moving around, and found herself fully awake again. Then she was mad.

She had read that if you couldn't sleep, you shouldn't just lay there, you should get up and do something else and then try again later, but this strategy didn't work for her. A few times she found herself awake at 4:00 a.m. doing stupid things like cleaning the tiles in the bathroom, so she decided to just lay there, hoping to luck out and just drift off.

Sometimes it worked but she got very poor sleep. Sometimes she entered into what she thought of as a sort of trance state. She knew she was awake, knew she wasn't sleeping, but she also lost track of time thinking about nothing. When she looked at the clock and saw that more than an hour had gone by she felt as though she hadn't slept at all. There must have been some sleep in there, but it was a kind of sleep that she couldn't feel. And other times it was more like her daydreams turned into lucid dreams, which were more like a movie she was watching than anything else. She would have a strange, nonsensical dream about, for instance, men with guns forcing her to walk a long way with her hands on her head, but somehow they never got out of her backyard. And during this she would know that she was actually awake and that she was having a bad night, which made her restless even in sleep. She kept wishing that things would just go black and that she could just wake up in the morning with that beautiful feeling of not having been conscious at all for hours and hours. And it was while she was having a dream like this that she started hearing things.

She was dreaming that she was in the woods somewhere, that all the leaves on all the trees were yellow, that she was very far away from anything, and that all she was wearing was a long T-shirt. But she knew she was dreaming, so rather than trying to go anywhere she just walked around, waiting for something to happen or for the whole scene to change, as happens in dreams. Then she realized that someone was whispering. She looked around to try to see who was whispering but quickly realized it was coming from outside the dream—reality was intruding. "What the fuck is that?" she whispered sleepily, angrily, slowly opening her eyes. Although she could not make out any particular words, she was certain she heard a person whispering. As she sat up and looked around, she saw movement near the door. She was alarmed, and she sharply inhaled, waiting for the next movement, the next sound, but there was no next sound. No one turned the door handle. The door did not open. No one stepped into the room. Nor did anyone walk back down the hall. There was only that single movement and then her breathing.

She sat on the bed for the better part of a minute, just waiting. The silence was perfect but for the occasional car going by on Route 9, and eventually she was able to persuade herself that she was safe. She stood up nervously, walked to the light switch, which unfortunately was right next to the door, and flipped it on. It was clear that there was nothing in the room with her. Although she had managed to buy a chair for her living room—her fondest wish—there still was nothing in her bedroom except her bed, her clothes, and her end table that she used as a nightstand. There was certainly nothing for anyone to hide behind. The floors were still bare except for a little throw rug, and there was still nothing on the walls to absorb sound. She would have heard something, no doubt, if someone were there. She stuck her head out the door and looked, and listened, but there was nothing. She didn't understand. She had most definitely heard something and had seen something move.

She thought for a moment. Possibly it was something moving in the reflection in the mirror on the back of the door. Like maybe from the bed she could see the window in the mirror, and something moved outside or a car drove by, and she saw the light from it reflected in the mirror. She got in bed with the light still on and tried to figure out how she saw it. The movement she had seen was almost definitely right where the mirror was, but there was nothing in that reflection when she lay in bed. From that angle the mirror only reflected the blank white wall. It was odd, but she was no longer scared and was too tired to stay up any longer. She turned out the light, went back to bed, and continued to half sleep.

The next night nothing happened that she was aware of, and the night after that she had not exactly forgotten about it but had let it go and was no longer on high alert. The third night was slightly different. The third night she woke up for no reason. She simply found herself awake in a warm cocoon of covers and sheets, and though she had to be up early the next morning, it felt so good that she didn't mind at all. She lay there for a while, just enjoying this warmth and softness, when suddenly she was interrupted. She heard nothing and saw nothing but very abruptly realized that she was afraid—she had a sinking feeling in her stomach, like riding an elevator, but her heart was also racing, as if she had just barely avoided a traffic accident. Though she was young and fit and hadn't had any nicotine or caffeine for twelve hours or more, she felt so strange that she considered the possibility that she was having a heart attack. She could feel beads of sweat coming out on her forehead and upper lip, and her moistening thighs were starting to stick to the sheets and ruin the softness.

After a few minutes, she tore the comforter off herself and got up. She intended to go into the bathroom and look at herself in the mirror and possibly to take her temperature but also to cool down. But almost immediately after she stood, she became even more uncomfortable as the cool air hit the sweat on her bare skin. That feeling registered with her, and she was in the process of telling herself that she was ill when she saw it. There was a girl in the room with her. Sort of.

She looked toward the door, and there was a girl about her age there. The girl was completely naked, and she looked like Nicole in every particular, but the girl was *in* the mirror. Nicole stopped for three or four seconds and tried to work out what was happening. She wanted to make the girl her reflection, but she was across the room and felt her arms hanging by her sides. The girl was right up close to the mirror, looking out of it as though out of a window. She was bent slightly at the waist, had her arms up, her hands resting on the edges of the door, her head turned at a sharp angle, and she was looking right at Nicole. Nicole's eyes widened. The girl in the mirror had a determined look about her. She wasn't curious or lost or sad or confused. She meant business. She knew what she wanted. And the way she was looking at Nicole made her think that she herself was what the girl wanted. Then the girl started to move.

The girl slowly tapped three times on the glass with the nail of her right index finger—*tick, tick, tick*—as if Nicole's attention wasn't already focused on her, and then slowly curled that finger back over her hand to call Nicole toward her. The girl wanted her to come. Nicole let out a terrified little screech less than a second in duration and then was silent again. The girl laughed quietly, whispered something, turned her back, and walked away. As soon as the girl was out of sight, Nicole ran toward the door, flung it open, and ran downstairs. She, too, was completely naked, so she wrapped herself with a blanket on her couch, grabbed her cell phone, and prepared to run outside. But she stopped at the door. It was freezing.

Before running outside naked in December and then hanging around waiting for the police, she wanted to make sure this was real. She thought it was real, but she had just woken up. She listened. Nothing. Sound carried in this house—everything was audible from everywhere else. But she heard nothing. Cars on Route 9 shushing by. No footsteps, no floor creaks or cracks, no voices, no doors opening, closing. There was also the long-established fact that people couldn't get into mirrors. Nicole took some cautious steps back toward the staircase, and then a few more purposely loud steps up the stairs themselves, to see whether she could provoke any noise from the other person. But there was nothing. Just cars on Route 9. The heat kicked on. The stair under her foot creaked uneasily but normally.

When she got back to her bedroom she turned on the light and took a look around. Obviously there was nothing. The mirror was just a mirror, and she was just herself in it. Her heart was racing. She was still physically excited, though she was calming down mentally. She didn't bother to look for anything in the mirror because it was so evident to her now that this was an ordinary, old, and—even when it was new—low-quality mirror. And there she was in it, just as she had expected to be. She dropped the blanket she had wrapped herself in, dropped her cell phone into the nest it created, and turned back to the mirror. That was her. Her face, her hair, her tits, her stomach, her pussy, her thighs. Just Nicole. Strangely, given what had been going on, she found that she liked what she saw there in the mirror. The girl now seemed like just a dream. As she stood assessing herself, she felt like it was a shame that she mostly saw old people and other women at her job. It would be nice to have a decent person around who could touch this body. It wouldn't be this way forever. Bad things would start happening to it soon. She went back to bed and thought about asking Dr. Vinland for a prescription for Ambien.

Nicole finally fell into a profound, satisfying oblivion. A sleep in which she was not aware of anything for what seemed like quite some time. She knew this when she woke up because she had that morning feeling of complete disorientation. For a few seconds she didn't know the day or even where she was for sure. But it was not morning proper, or close to it. Though she didn't know it, it was 3:03 a.m. She was home, in bed, and very soft arms were around her, and someone was pressed up against her back. For part of a second she was calm. It felt so good, so welcome to be held. But it occurred to her in the latter part of that second that she hadn't been held in some time and had no one to hold her—and she felt breasts on her back. She shrieked, jumped up out of bed, ran to the door, and turned on the light.

The girl was there in the bed, laughing at her loudly and deeply. And the girl was *her*. Or a version of her. Nicole had lost weight since she had gotten this job at Dr. Vinland's office, quit drinking, and almost quit smoking, and her skin looked very good now. But this girl was just a touch better. A touch thinner, younger, her hair thicker, shinier, her skin clearer, pores smaller. This girl was better than good: she was *perfect*. The way Nicole used to be. And the girl laughed carelessly, as though nothing was wrong in the world, the way young people with no real problems laugh at older people with many real problems. The girl who was her said, "What's the matter, hon? Aren't you glad to see me?" and began laughing all over again.

Nicole ran downstairs as fast as she could, accidentally kicking the banister on the way. As she limped into the center of the living room, it occurred to her that she had nothing to cover herself with and had left her phone in her blanket. She held herself, her arms crossed on her chest, her eyes closed, and was very close to crying. This was not possible. She knew that. She said so out loud. She gathered herself and slowly ascended the stairs. *Nothing was happening.* She heard *nothing*. In this house, she would hear someone walking up there. There had to be nothing, she assured herself. This could only be a dream or a hallucination. Nothing else was possible. She told herself so out loud and fearfully started to climb the stairs again.

After six stairs she looked up, and there was the girl, leaning over the banister. "It's OK, hon. Really, it is. Everything is going to be better. I promise. I'll make sure it will be." And she laughed again.

Nicole shrieked and ran back downstairs. She was at the front door, ready to open it, but it was so cold out. She had no phone, no clothes, no keys. If she ran out, she would have to knock on a neighboring house, bare naked, screaming in the middle of the night. She couldn't bring herself to stay or go. For a long time she stood at the door, afraid to move. But after a while she didn't hear anything else upstairs and grew slightly bolder. She was so tired she could barely keep awake, and in a while she found the courage to slip over to the coat closet, put on her long winter coat, and lay on the couch, where she stayed until morning.

By the time the sun came up, she was already supposed to be awake. She went upstairs, completely unafraid, regarding last night as a dream or hallucination, as it *must* have been. When she saw that her alarm clock said 7:55, she was so upset that she came very near to crying. But she held it together. She told herself that she would sleep for fifteen minutes and then go into work late. Just fifteen minutes. She fumbled with the clock for a few minutes trying to change the alarm but, sure that she wouldn't sleep long anyway, eventually just lay herself down. When she woke, it was 10:48.

Nicole got out of bed as quickly as she could, as though moving fast would help her somehow, and tried desperately to locate her phone. She was halfway down the stairs when she realized that last night she had dropped it in the blanket by the door, and she turned around. When she located it, the battery was completely dead. Plugging it in brought it back to life, but the battery had somehow been drained to zero, and maddeningly the phone made her wait until the charge had reached 3 percent before she could make a phone call.

"Dr. Vinland's office." Rita herself had been reduced to answering the phone. And no doubt she was very angry about that.

"Rita, I'm so sorry. I couldn't sleep at all last night, and then when I finally did fall asleep it was very close to morning and I literally just now woke up. Calling you was the very first thing I did, and I'll be in as soon as I can get there." Nicole said all of this at top speed, the way she talked in middle school—so fast that some people couldn't understand her. She expected to be yelled at, but Rita simply said, "OK, honey, come in when you can," and hung up.

When she got to work, things were surprisingly normal. Once she took over the phones and the window, there were no problems to speak of, and Rita didn't show any anger at all, which made Nicole feel much better. She was afraid because even though this was the most money she had ever made, she was discovering it still wasn't enough. Though she had no rent to pay, only taxes and utilities, the taxes in November were four hundred and sixty dollars, which cleaned her out. Also, it had been a cold autumn, and the heating bill for November was almost two hundred dollars. And she saw no end to financial need. December so far was colder than November, so the heating bill would increase, and if her friends got sentimental and tracked her down near Christmas, she would need money for presents and food and alcohol. These would require massive chunks of cash from her, and she would not be able to absorb any more serious hits, much less spend *any* time out of work. She even considered getting a second job waitressing just to give herself some breathing room.

As it got closer to closing, Nicole kept expecting Rita to take her aside and say something about the lateness, but she never did. She kept trying to ask Dr. Vinland to write her a prescription but was too ashamed. All she could bring herself to do was look at him and grin and hope he would ask if everything was all right. But he never asked.

As she drove home in the December dark, she began to think better of her shame. Stepping out of the utterly sober reality of sick old ladies and fluorescent lights and into the parking lot that was already at this hour glistening with black ice and windshield frost reminded her that whatever was happening to her at home was not at all normal. The fact that she was seeing things that felt so real meant that there was something seriously wrong. Since she started working for Dr. Vinland, she had heard about every phantom old-lady illness in the world, and as far as she was aware, not one person had come in complaining that a younger, naked version of herself had stepped out of a mirror and into her bed. But something ate at her when she tried to explain these events as hallucinations. She felt disingenuous when she told herself that was the only explanation. Years back Nicole had done acid and mushrooms more than her share of times, and she knew that only a person who had never done hallucinogens would suggest that a flashback could account for something like this. This was not what acid was like—not even a *lot* of it—and she felt sure that no one had ever had a flashback strong enough to do this.

The closer she got to home the more upset she got. She felt thankful that she had to stop at the store because it delayed her going back to that house. When she pulled into the parking lot, it was packed and she had to park way off to one side of the grocery, practically in front of the liquor store next door. There was a blue neon sign for a particular brand of fizzy yellow American beer that she had a lot of experience with. When she was fifteen, a boy named Ricky used to steal it from his father so he could get her drunk behind the garage in his backyard. It made her remember that sometimes men touched her, and that it felt good, and that it felt good that they wanted to touch her. That there was a certain freedom in dulling her senses, and that dullness could be an important way to keep sane.

She wasn't stupid enough to think that getting drunk was good or good for you, but when she was a kid she had heard the phrase *self-medicate*. The meaning or polarity of the phrase seemed to change over her lifetime. She remembered going with her mother to see a doctor at a time when neither of them had insurance. Her mother had been treating some illness or other with pills she had gotten at the drugstore, and the doctor was talking down to her for self-medicating. *He* would treat her, and *she* would be the patient. That was the tone of the discussion. She wasn't qualified to determine what she needed or what it might do to her. She should come see *him* when something was wrong, and he would *tell* her what to take. But now, years later, working for Dr. Vinland, things were different. In his office there was a better understanding of the fact that not everyone had insurance, not everyone could hand a co-pay over to a doctor every time something was slightly wrong, and she had personally heard Dr. Vinland tell a woman who was taking three or four over-the-counter drugs, "You're self-medicating. Good."

Nicole was not aware of any over-the-counter pills she could take to make herself feel better, but she had a strong feeling that having a couple drinks would relax her in a way that she hadn't relaxed in more than a year. Just thinking about it almost gave her the cloudy, slightly less-aware feeling of a good solid buzz, and she decided that she was going to self-medicate.

She finished her shopping, put the groceries in her car, and then went into the liquor store. She was excited to see the inside of it. She had been to this one years before and noticed that more of the store's square footage was dedicated to wine than it used to be. Otherwise it looked the same, and it was like remembering a dream that she hadn't thought of since the night she had it. If she had more money, she would have made several purchases, but as things were, she knew what was best. Vodka. She went straight to the counter.

"How much is a fifth of Absolut?"

"Twenty-three ninety-nine."

"Sold." In that second, something in her clicked. She wasn't some mousy little office girl. She had a Misfits tattoo on her ass. When she was sixteen she snuck into the Pontiac Grille to see Carfax Abbey, and men bought her drinks all night until one guy pulled her outside by the wrist and tried to get her to come back to his car, and she had to take off her heels and run away. This life she had been living recently was not her life. Not yet.

"What flavor you want?"

"What flavor?"

"Yeah, what flavor. We're out of Citron right now, but we have orange, blueberry, pomegranate ... whatever."

"Uh ... vodka-flavored vodka is fine," she said.

The cashier smirked. "OK."

I don't drink girl drinks, she almost said. *I'm a professional.*

Once at home, things seemed better before she even opened the bottle. The light inside was warm and inviting, and even the spare little dinner that she made for herself seemed excellent—she had persuaded herself that frying boneless chicken breasts in olive oil was good with just a little salt and pepper—and once she started cooking, she went to the freezer, where she had stashed the bottle, and poured herself a glass. She smelled it like it was wine, and that cold, sickening, astringent taste went through her nose, into the back of her throat, even into the tops of her lungs a little bit, and made her stomach feel like she was in an elevator. She remembered this vividly and took a drink. The first sip gave her that little shiver, where it seemed like her body was trying to reject it, her esophagus was unhappy about what was traveling through it. But after that it was smooth. By the time she had eaten her miserable little chicken breast in oil and was cleaning up and washing dishes, she had the solid buzz she wanted. She wasn't going to get drunk, but she felt so much better that she decided she was going to stay like this. She would not sink below this buzz until she was ready to sleep.

Sleep.

That made her pause. She turned off the water, and once the water in the sink had settled and the drain stopped gurgling, she listened to the silence. Cars on the highway.

The heat turned off, and things got quieter still. In order to keep calm, she pretended she wasn't sure what else she was hearing, but there were footsteps on the second floor. It sounded like someone had been standing at the head of the stairs and then walked back toward the bedroom. Nicole wanted so badly to ignore this, but she also had that strange courage that only vodka gave her. She reminded herself that she had already tried running away and being scared, and that hadn't helped. What was this thing going to do to her? If it was a hallucination, nothing. If it was a ghost or something, what *could* it do? What did ghosts *ever* do except show up somewhere they were not wanted and then disappear? Even in ghost stories they didn't *do* anything other than scare some ditsy girl or some know-it-all guy who thought he was smart enough to figure everything out. And if somehow there was a real girl upstairs, who just by coincidence looked like Nicole's younger self, what was she going to do? Probably nothing. So Nicole went up there.

When she reached the top of the stairs, she turned the lights on boldly but stood quietly for a few seconds to see if she could hear any movement in response. Nothing. But then the bedroom door moved.

The door had been standing mostly open. She was sure of it. She knew its normal position. Not that she ever thought about it or left it that way on purpose, but it just seemed normal that the door would be open a certain distance every day. It would be at a certain angle. But standing there at the head of the stairs, waiting for something to happen, she was sure that she had seen it close just a little bit and that now the angle was off. Part of her entertained the notion that the girl had closed it a little bit to get *behind* it—because that's where the mirror was. But, again, she had been scared already, and being scared hadn't helped, so she went into the bedroom.

There was nothing in there. She turned the light on, looked around. She looked in the closet. She closed the door entirely, looked right in the mirror and saw nothing but herself. She touched it with her finger—solid glass. And despite that her hair wasn't in the greatest shape, she felt like she looked pretty damn good right then. Not like some little weakling, at any rate. She was a grown woman. She didn't quite have the courage to tell the girl to come out if she was in the glass, but she was satisfied that there was no one anywhere else in the room, at least. She had given the girl every opportunity to come out and do whatever she was going to do—Nicole was even slightly incapacitated by the booze, so the girl would have every advantage—and she had done nothing. Didn't even say hi.

Nicole turned off all the lights and went downstairs as bravely as she was able, though there were a few seconds where she thought she might pee a little.

When she returned to her dishes, she was much happier even than she had been. It seemed to her in some sloppy, half-thought-out way that whatever had been happening was now solved, that her attempt at confronting the thing had driven it away or proven that it had never existed in the first place. She felt excellent. As she dried the dishes and put them away, she looked carefully at her disparate kitchen collection. A coffee mug she had stolen from a Denny's. A big blue dinner plate that a former roommate had left behind in her apartment on Thorn Lane, where they kept getting mice in their closet. A small white one with green clovers around the edge that had once been part of her grandmother's matching set. A thick, heavy white one that she had stolen from the Eagle Diner.

She hadn't intended to steal that plate. The girls who worked there sometimes made themselves something to take home, wrapped it up on a plate, and brought it back the next day. She had done that, but then she missed her shift the next day and got fired. The plate was severance. She missed her shift due to a bout of day drinking with her friends Kate Marcellus and Melissa Schumacher. The three of them had scored two fifths of Stoli and started drinking while watching *Law & Order: Criminal Intent* on A&E, but it turned out there wasn't just one episode—it was one of those marathons A&E used to run. Nicole and Kate didn't have cable at their places, but Michelle could afford it because she was living with her boyfriend, Tommy Swanson, and they had two incomes. So Nicole and Kate wanted to stay and absorb as much of Vincent D'Onofrio's weird neck twisting and gravelly, high-voiced, end-of-episode questioning as they could. They had no particular intentions about what they were going to do or when it was going to end. They just didn't stop watching or drinking.

They watched in Melissa's bedroom, on her bed, so they eventually all fell asleep. Sometime after dark they woke up, and Tommy was in bed with them, wearing only his jeans— he had come home from work while they were passed out and decided they weren't going to displace him from his own bed, so he got in and went to sleep. Eventually someone realized there was a man in the bed and started screaming, and then the three of them were screaming, and then Tommy started screaming, too, just to make fun of them.

She always remembered Tommy screaming like that

and laughing afterward, and how funny his falsetto was, the faces he made, and what a huge contrast it was with his personality at other times. She had seen him mean as a snake both before and after that night, and he could be frightening.

Nicole stood at the sink laughing and laughing about Tommy and that night, but then she stopped. It sounded like her voice was echoing somewhere. And then she realized that it continued long after she had stopped. It was upstairs. By this point Nicole was really loose, and not feeling meek, so she ran up there.

"Who are you?" she shouted in a half slur. Of course there was no answer, but she heard the girl still laughing in the bedroom, so she opened the door. The girl was lying in Nicole's bed, under the comforter, just the way Nicole lay down at night, and looked just the way Nicole knew herself to look. Her nerve ended here—she wasn't *that* drunk. This was the confrontation she had been trying to provoke, and now in the midst of it she found herself unable to proceed in a meaningful way. She stood there, mouth dry, palms wet, right hand shaking nervously, rubbing her left hand against her jeans, trying to dry the increasingly wet palm. She was struggling to find something to actually *do* now that she was here, but the girl did it for her. She started giggling. Quietly at first and then louder and louder. The girl threw the comforter off her back and sat up for a few seconds before standing and taking a few steps toward Nicole. She was now only feet away.

The girl looked at her with a broad smile that looked genuinely friendly. So much so that if she hadn't been a naked stranger who gotten into her house uninvited, it wouldn't even seem creepy. The girl said, "Hi, hon. Don't you know me?"

Nicole had no idea what the girl was talking about—but she was only half listening anyway. Primarily she was concerned with the fact that on close inspection this girl was *her*. Everything was exactly right about her. She wasn't even a mirror image—everything was on the correct side. The little mole on the right side of her stomach, the scar on her right knee, the left breast slightly larger than the right. But *young*, and *perfect*. The girl very gently put her hands on Nicole's shoulders, rubbed them up and down the tiniest bit, said, "It's not you," and kissed her very softly on her cheek. "You aren't the real one." The girl smiled again, and then slapped Nicole harder than she had ever been slapped. When she hit the floor the girl was instantly on top of her, slapping her face over and over, yelling *"You aren't the real one"* in a desperate shriek.

Nicole slid out from under the girl and bolted down the stairs. She did not turn to look, but she heard the girl behind her the whole way down. Nicole had her keys in her pocket, so she flung the door open, ran to her car, and locked herself in. The girl stood laughing on the front porch. It was as though the girl was seeing her off. She even crossed her arms and leaned against the door jamb until Nicole began to back out of the driveway, and then did that little wave that people did with crossed arms. As Nicole was pulling away, the girl went back inside and shut the door behind her, like it was her house.

Nicole had no idea where to go or what to do. She desperately wanted a friend, but she had no idea what she would say happened, and anyway she felt like a hypocrite. She had made a point of avoiding all her friends since her grandmother died and had gone out of her way to not be found, to not be available for any reason. How could she show up at one of their places, drunk, in the middle of the night, with a crazy story? There was nothing for her to do. Mainly she wanted to get off the road. She couldn't get a DUI. She would lose her job. She pulled into the shopping center across the highway and slowly trolled past Walgreens toward Porto-Fino Pizza. They were still open for another couple hours. She could go there and hide out in a booth, eat something and drink some coffee, and that would sober her up. She would get a little fat eating right on top of her dinner, but she had to deal with this situation, and the very first thing she needed was to sit in a safe place and calm down.

She pulled into a parking space and checked her face and hair in the rearview. "Oh Jesus, I look like shit." Her eye makeup was smeared, and even in the hideous yellow half light of the parking lot's vapor lamps it was obvious that she had been crying. She was too humiliated to go inside. Everyone would think that some drunk man had beaten her and that she was here to get even drunker than she already was. But she had to do something, go somewhere, so she told herself that even if that was what everyone thought, they couldn't throw her out for it. She started getting herself ready. She pulled her shirt up and wiped her face off as best she could with the inside of it. It didn't make her skin look much better, but at least her face was dry. The plan was to go inside, have eggplant parmigiana, sober up, figure out what to do, who she could call, where she could sleep, and hope that at the end of that process things would be better. Then it occurred to her that she had no wallet. Her purse was at home. She almost started crying again, but she found fifteen dollars in the pocket of her jeans. That was more than enough for a small eggplant sub. She could even get a beer. Just one. Which would be fine. With the sub she'd be eating it wouldn't matter.

When she got inside there were two men at the bar and a few people eating at tables, but the restaurant was mostly empty. She sat in a booth with her left side toward the wall so she could look out the window and hide the left side of her face, which had taken the bulk of the beating and was where the redness was more apparent—and where the bruises would be tomorrow. The window had a HELP WANTED sign in the bottom right corner facing outward. Away from her. *Good.* The waitress came, and Nicole ordered the sub, which she knew cost six ninety-five, but something stopped her from ordering a beer with it. She felt like she might need the other eight dollars and was content to drink water anyway. Or so she thought. As the waitress walked away, Nicole felt like her last chance at happiness had walked away too. Soon she would eat a cheap sub without even a drink, and then she'd have to face this thing sober.

This *thing*. This thing she was singularly unprepared to deal with. Her life was a delicate balance right now, and keeping that balance was as much as she could handle. She didn't have the wherewithal to resolve any additional ridiculous situations. And it *was* ridiculous. She had never heard of anything like this in her life. There were no books or stories or movies about this that might give her a formula she could follow to make it go away or stop. She had no frame of reference for understanding it at all. She kept coming back to hallucination, but now the girl had hit her, physically touched her, and then disappeared into the mirror, and that's not what a hallucination is. It's like the girl wasn't anything. She wasn't a ghost or hallucination because she was physical, but she couldn't be physical because she disappeared into a mirror. But how could she do both? It didn't make sense. Nicole sat for a few minutes not thinking at all, just looking out over top of the HELP WANTED sign into the parking lot, trying to calm herself down. She wished her head would start hurting or she would start feeling sick or something else would go wrong that would give her an excuse to go to the ER, see a doctor, *talk to someone*. This was not a thing that she could take care of.

She was preparing to give in to her stronger urge to cry but was interrupted by the waitress.

"Hon, we're out of eggplant. Can I get you something else?"

Nicole pretended to think. When she saw that the waitress had come back empty-handed, she knew exactly what the situation was and exactly what she would do. "Could you just bring me a pitcher of Yuengling?"

"Sure."

And that was that. Her spirits rose immediately. She would keep herself *braced*. That was the word she thought of. She needed this to *brace* herself against whatever the fuck was happening. She would keep herself braced, and once she was out of beer she would either sleep in her car or go home. Sure she'd be fucked up, but home was just across the way. Turn right out of the shopping center, turn left into Shawtown, park the car. Period. The girl couldn't still be there. She never stayed around for long. And anyway she could sleep in her car if it got that bad. Things were looking significantly better.

The waitress returned. "Six fifty. Yuengling is on special."

Nicole was very happy to hear that. She started pouring.

Porto-Fino wasn't a bar. It was a pizza place with a bar in it, so it closed at eleven instead of one. But even so, it had its share of bar-type patrons. Nicole had been one herself many times in the past, so she not only knew the closing time, she also knew that the closer it got to eleven, the more bar-like the place became. The ratio of restaurant customers to bar customers would shift because it's not easy to eat heavy Italian dinners after 7:00 p.m. As it got later, and more drinkers drifted in, she began to look around hoping that someone she knew might show up, but there were only strangers. By 9:00 p.m. she was a pitcher and a half deep and very loose, which she felt was wasted on this situation. Despite the beating she took from the insane half-hallucination, she was feeling much better, like she had recovered and was in her right mind again. But she wasn't at home, she had no friends now, and she couldn't even fuck around on her phone because her battery was at 37 percent and she didn't know what might happen later. She was a friendly, gregarious girl alone in a crisis, and she just wanted to forget and have fun. She had tried to talk to the waitress who she thought was probably about her age, but the waitress could see that drinking was Nicole's only reason for being there, and she was telegraphing the fact that she was nervous about where this was going.

A few younger people had come in and then left, but they looked like high school kids to her, and she was surprised to see that they were getting served. She wondered whether the bar staff had relaxed about carding people. At around ten thirty, a man moved to a booth near her. She had seen him come in but hadn't considered talking to him. He was scary looking, *very* big, and a little older than the men she was interested in. He had a lot of gray in his beard and a long pony tail. She hadn't heard a bike pull up, but he was wearing cuts and colors. She was a little too far gone to tell, but she was pretty sure that his patches indicated that he was not to be fucked with, so she felt like she knew what he was about, and she wasn't interested in being noticed by him. But he was really nice.

"You drinking that all by yourself, hon?" he asked, gesturing toward her pitcher.

"Yeah. I've had a bit to drink." She was smiling though she didn't want to be. Couldn't imagine wearing a leather vest with a patch on the back that said "Property of Mickey," or whatever this guy's name was. But despite his size and outward prickliness, he was being really sweet.

"You know who you look like?"

"No."

"Liz Taylor. With a black eye. Who put his hands on you like that?"

"Just somebody." Nicole didn't know who Liz Taylor was, really, but she knew that she had been an actress and that she was supposed to be beautiful. She tried to hide her smile.

"What's your name?"

"Nicole."

"I'm Rick."

"Rick? That's it? I thought you'd have a, like a nickname, like a colorful name like you guys have."

"I do. Maybe I'll tell it to you sometime."

"Oh yeah? When?"

"I'm around here a lot. I'll be looking out for you."

"Well you're seeing me now. I'm, like, right here."

"I know that. But right now I have to talk business with someone, and he's going to be here soon, so I'm going to have to ask you to move to another booth."

"Really?"

"Yes, really. But I'll be more polite the next time I see you, Nicole."

When she stood up, she realized exactly how perilous things were for her in terms of drunkenness. There was no chance she was driving home, and in fact she might not make it out of the restaurant. She had had this desperate feeling before, where things were moving too fast, and she knew that sometimes this ended with a cool rush of air and abrupt contact with the floor. She used the ladies' room one last time, and while she was washing her hands she noticed how horrible she looked in the mirror. She *did* look beaten up. And awful. How Rick thought she looked like some beautiful dead girl was beyond her.

Instead of going to another booth, she did her best not to stumble out of the restaurant. She wanted to move quickly but not fast enough to cause herself to fall, which she felt she was likely to do if she didn't find a place to sit soon. She made her way to her car, got inside, and suddenly regretted her previous determination to sleep here. It was cold, and she didn't know whether it was OK to leave a car running all night. This was only the second car she had ever owned, and she had never had occasion to try that. Her current vehicle wasn't in any condition to pass an endurance test, so she decided to leave it off. She figured her clothes would keep her warm enough.

At first she felt like the best place to sleep would be in the back seat until she climbed back there and lay down.

She had forgotten that hump in the middle. No matter how she arranged herself, it felt like that thing was situated right at the small of her back, and her upper body seemed to be sloping downhill. She wisely surmised that might lead to vomiting, so she got into the driver's seat and put the seat back all the way down. She was still pretty uncomfortable, but it wasn't as bad as the back seat, and she was about as intoxicated as she could be, so she quickly sank into the void.

Several hours later—she didn't know how long—she woke up freezing with a desperate need to piss. One that could not be ignored. She was so cold that she was shivering violently and realized immediately that shivering like this could most definitely cause her to pee herself if she wasn't careful. She started the car and turned on the heater, but it had been sitting for hours and the fan was just blowing cold air at her, which only made things worse. She knew that she was going to have to go outside, which was a problem because there was nowhere for her to hide. Her car was now the only one in the parking lot, and the whole lot was lit up, so anyone driving by on Route 9 would likely see her. But holding it any longer was not an option, so she had to just go ahead with it. She got out of the car and walked around to the side that was hidden from the road. Of course, that made it the side that faced every single storefront in the shopping center, but it was very late, and she decided to take it on faith that no cars in the lot meant literally no people in the stores, so this was somewhat better than facing the road.

She so loathed the idea of pulling her pants down in the freezing cold that she was almost afraid. She even cried a little. But she did it, got down, and promptly got a significant amount of piss all over her pants and underwear. She didn't realize exactly how much she had gotten on her clothes until she pulled her pants back up, but when she did she stood there and cried for almost ten seconds before getting back into the car, which was still ice cold. Her wet pants had already lost the residual body heat they had absorbed, and she knew there was no way she would be able to spend the night in the parking lot now, so she started preparing herself to drive. She put the seat up, arranged herself in it, and tried to get herself together. She was still drunk but not as dramatically as she had been. All she had to do was make a right out of here, drive a short distance, then make a left, drive another short distance, and then park. That was it. She would go slow. She would be careful. She would get home.

Nicole pulled out of her parking space, trolled slowly along the storefronts, stopped an unnecessarily long time at the light, made a right turn, and then went exactly thirty-five, which she knew was the speed limit. She was in sight of her street, where she would make the left turn and be virtually home, when the blue and red lights started flashing behind her. She let out a brief shriek and, in the process of pulling over, turned too far and hit a telephone pole.

Luckily she was too drunk to remember much of her night in jail. She only remembered being put in the cell, lying down, blackness, and then being woken up. The morning went by quickly. She was given a court date and released, then got her car from the impound lot. The front end was damaged, but it was still drivable. By the time she got home it was 11:35 a.m.

Nicole was so hung over that, even though she had at one time been very good at calling out of work, she handled it all wrong this morning. She told Rita that she didn't come in because she had been arrested for driving under the influence. She was too ashamed to mention that she had spent the night in jail wearing urine-soaked clothing, which might have garnered her a bit of sympathy, but after an opening like that it might not have mattered. A clear-headed Nicole wouldn't have said any of that. She would have said that she had gotten into an accident late last night and then either admitted to the DUI or not, depending on how the questioning went. But Rita showed no mercy.

"Alright. Well, we're going to have to let you go."

"Rita, *please* give me another chance. I won't be able to pay my bills. I'll lose my *house*. I can't. . ." Nicole burst into tears.

"Come on, honey. It's time to be a big girl. You've got two no-call no-shows. It's standard to fire you at this point. There are some discrepancies in your time card too. I wasn't going to mention them yet, but now you didn't show again. We can't have this." Rita hung up without saying goodbye.

Nicole was now in tears, still in last night's clothes, hung over, unemployed, broke, and alone with an impending court date. Next week would be Christmas, and by then she would have no money to buy food. Her mother and grandmother were dead, and the house she could no longer afford to keep and the car she had wrecked were all that they had left her. Everything, her whole life, was in ruins. She cried for some time before she heard herself walking around upstairs. It made her whole body go numb.

Even though she didn't feel any better, after a little while the crying stopped, as if her body had just had enough of it. She got up, stripped off her clothes, put them directly into the washing machine, started it, and went upstairs. She didn't care about what might happen when she got up there—she needed to shower, and that girl wasn't going to stop her. But Nicole didn't find her there. She could hear the girl from time to time, something that sounded like a whisper or a footstep, but she didn't see anything. She took a shower, blew her hair dry, and went to bed.

It was late when she woke up, so the light had that ugly yellow evening tinge that she hated. Even so, she felt fortunate to have that light because the sun was setting earlier and earlier, and most of the days this month had been overcast and colorless, like black and white TV. She opened the curtains and pulled up the blinds to let as much of it in as she could and saw that the sun was so low that in just a few minutes it would dip behind the house across the backyard, and then things would be as gray as they had been all month. She stood there in the window, directly in the sun, for as long as it was visible, surprised at how cold she was even with those strong evening rays hitting her directly.

She wanted coffee but discovered that she had very little left. Her impulse was to go to the store, but then she remembered that she also had very little money left, and even that would be gone soon. The question of whether she needed coffee or whether it was a luxury quickly exhausted her, so she decided to put it out of her mind and sat on the couch instead.

Nicole spent the next several hours crying and applying for jobs on the internet. When she was done she closed her laptop. Inside and outside, her house was completely dark. She sat for a time listening to the cars in the neighborhood that together caused a sort of white noise background. One of the jobs she applied for was just like her current job—or the job she had just lost—and she allowed herself to feel hopeful about it. Exact same type of work. Probably paid about the same. It was much farther away, but it was still something that she could do to make decent money, and she knew better than to be choosy. People had to commute. That was life. The other jobs she had applied for were long shots, but she felt like she had to apply or she would lose her mind, and it paid off. She felt like she had made some progress.

After a while she got up and turned on the lights. She was calm. She had been in bad situations before, and she wasn't the only person who had ever been fired. The world hadn't ended. She still had a house and a car and 224 dollars in the bank. She would get another job eventually. Maybe even that one at the doctor's office she had just applied for.

By this point she hadn't eaten in almost twenty-four hours, so she felt like she couldn't go without food any longer, and she was getting so cold that she was starting to shiver. She thought about turning the heat up, but now that she was going to have to do without for a little while, she decided she would put some proper clothes on instead. She was still in the shirt that she had slept in, so she had to go upstairs. She climbed the stairs, paused at the landing, and listened. Everything came back to her. So many things were happening in her head while she was filling out those online applications that she had virtually forgotten about the girl and all the chaos she had caused. But standing here at the top of the steps, hand on the newel post, just listening, she felt almost like none of that was real. And she heard nothing. Cars on the highway. The heat kicked on. So she went into her bedroom and got dressed.

Nicole made herself dinner—one chicken breast, oil, salt, pepper—and spent a few hours watching TV in the dark before she thought about the bottle of vodka that was still in her kitchen. She had nothing to do right now, and since she had nowhere to go in the morning, she figured she could actually drink the rest of it and it would make no difference. Unless she got a call back from one of the jobs she had applied for today. She spent a few minutes fighting with herself about whether she needed to stay sober, and then another few minutes thinking about rationing the vodka over the next couple of days, before she realized what kind of discussion she was having with herself. She didn't want to be this person. Drunk all the time, making rules about drinking, setting limits, as if that would make her OK. She went into the kitchen, poured out the entire bottle, threw it in the trash, and went back to watching TV. She wasn't going to drink anymore. That was the end of it. Drinking had cost her her job. She had wrecked her car, she was certain to be convicted of DUI, and she might even have her license suspended. Where would she be then? She wanted to be a different kind of person.

At around nine thirty she realized that she was tired enough, so she went back to bed for the night. Everything in the bed felt warm and soft. She was pleasantly drowsy, and she fell asleep almost immediately. And then she started to come out of it. There was a strange, warm, humid feeling on the back of her neck. Why was there movement? The girl.

She was out of bed in a second, standing in the corner looking at the girl, who didn't laugh at her anymore. The girl was a woman now, strong and angry. Her hair was long and stringy and thin, and wisps of it dripped down over her shoulders. Her long, sagging breasts with hard, dark nipples swayed heavily as she approached Nicole. The woman easily knocked her down and dragged her by the wrists toward the bedroom door. The woman's grip was inexorable, unbreakable, powerful. Nicole realized quickly that the woman wasn't dragging her toward the door but toward the *mirror*. She stepped into the it and tried to pull Nicole in with her, but Nicole's head kept hitting the glass, stopping them short. She couldn't go through the way the woman could. Nicole wanted to scream as head her pounded the door over and over again, shattering the mirror in spiderweb patterns, but she couldn't make a sound. She needed her breathing to manage the pain and resist the strength of this strange person.

As if the woman realized suddenly that this was not a game she could win, she let go of Nicole and stood looking down at her through the wrong side of the glass. Nicole stood up, gripping the wounds on her head, crying silently, waiting. The woman looked her right in the eye for a long time, and then stepped back into the bedoom. Nicole finally screamed the way she had wanted to all along. The cracks in the glass striped the woman with gashes—thin, wide, long, and short—over her whole body, as though the cracks formed a web of razors she was willing to brave just to get back to Nicole. The woman fell on her hands and knees and crawled toward her.

Still screaming, Nicole shot past her, opened the door a narrow eight inches, slipped through, and flew down the stairs. She grabbed her purse from the table and ran outside. In seconds she was in her car. She started it and was quickly out of the neighborhood. Right across from where she had hit the telephone pole she smelled something familiar. It was wet, a little like mildew, a little sweet. She knew this smell but couldn't place it. She was puzzled. Even if the seals around the windows were dry rotted, no liquid could have leaked in since she had last been in the car. It was freezing outside, even during the day.

Thinking about the smell and the physical reality of her car brought her out of the dreamlike state she had been in while escaping from the house. The top of her head throbbed where it had smashed the glass, and she was sure it was bleeding. The woman had tried to drag her into that mirror. *What was going to happen in there?* Nicole's face and hands went numb, and she was so frightened that she pulled off the highway at the first possible place—River Plaza Shopping Center. As she pulled in, her engine started to knock in a strange way that she had only ever heard on TV, and the car started to shake. She wasn't even past Walgreens before steam started pouring out from under the hood, and it stopped by itself right in front of Porto-Fino Pizza. Thinking the steam was smoke, Nicole ran from the car until she reached the brick archway in front of the restaurant where she waited to see whether the car was going to catch fire or explode or do something else that cars did on TV. But soon enough the steam drifted toward her, and when she smelled it she realized what it was. It smelled just like the inside of her car, and in the glare of the sodium-vapor lamps she could see a puddle of unearthly green forming around her front tire.

Somehow things had gotten even worse. Two hundred and twenty-four dollars was all the money she had in the world. Just the cost of towing her hemorrhaging car would wipe her out. She figured it would leave her with like a hundred and sixty dollars, and there was no more money coming in. How long could she live on that? And what if the car was dead now, permanently? How would she get to a job interview? How would she get to court? Court was hell and gone from here—she had to drive for miles and get on 95. How many busses would that take? And how much did those busses cost? "Jesus," she said out loud and burst into tears.

She turned to the restaurant and pulled on the door. It was locked. She had missed 11:00 p.m. by twenty minutes. She banged on the glass, but it was one of those glass doors so solid that the heel of her hand only made a quiet thud, and knocking with her knuckles only hurt them and wasn't any louder. She couldn't see anyone inside anyway. She moved over to the dining room windows to see if anyone was cleaning up, but it was empty too. All the lights were out, and only the red and white HELP WANTED sign was clearly visible. She looked at the sign for a few seconds and then took a picture of it with her phone. She enlarged the picture so she could see the phone number clearly and saved the edit.

She sat on the curb and covered her face with her hands. There wasn't even anyone there to help her push the car out of the way. It would be towed somewhere by morning, and she'd have to pay the impound fee too. Unless she just ditched it. "Let them fucking keep it," she said unintelligibly through bitter tears.

Half an hour later she was frozen stiff, and her ass was completely numb from sitting on the curb, but at least she had stopped crying. No one had come out of the restaurant to help her. They must have gone out the back if there had even been anyone there. No one driving by had stopped to help. She felt like the last person on earth, completely alone. There weren't even any cars on the highway. Eventually she got so cold that she couldn't stand it another second. She got up and started to walk home.

Once she got out on the highway, she was scared. There was no one around, and anybody could do anything they wanted to her. She just wanted to be warm. Once again drawing about even with the telephone pole she had hit, she saw a truck coming toward her. It passed her and made a U-turn in the street behind her. She thought, *oh shit*, but she also thought she would do anything to get inside that truck and be warm. And to go somewhere other than that house. A dive. An apartment. A trailer. Anywhere was fine. Just warm, and *not that fucking house*. The truck pulled up next to her and stopped. A very large man leaned over and rolled the passenger side window down. She looked inside. He had a lot of gray in his beard and a long pony tail.

3

GOODBYE, GHOST OF COLUMBUS

I always wanted to write my ghost story down, but I never did until now because I didn't have all the information you need to make a ghost story compelling. The template of a ghost story usually goes like this: somebody who claims to be a skeptic moves into a new place and notices weird things. The weird things get progressively weirder until the person sees the ghost in a climactic scene that scares them so badly that they move out. Later they talk to the landlord/real estate agent/neighbor/person who used to live there, find out that someone matching the description of the ghost died there way back when, and become a believer. Both fictional and supposedly true ghost stories work roughly this way, and the template sort of demands that you hit most of these beats. If you don't, the story isn't compelling—it feels incomplete. And that's my story. It feels incomplete because it's missing so much of this information. It's not even so much a story as a fragment or an incident. But there's something in me that can't let it go.

Something about the fact that it's true makes it very important to me—important enough that I will be uneasy until I have recorded it. So here we are.

Before I get to the actual ghost story, I should explain my general disposition toward this kind of thing. To tell the honest and contradictory truth, I was and *am* an atheist who doesn't believe in survival of the personality, or an afterlife. That's stupid given that I'm about to tell you that I saw a ghost, and given that ghosts imply god, survival of the personality, and an afterlife. I'm not sure how to justify myself here. Maybe I can't. But people often believe contradictory or mutually exclusive things. There are both poetic and scientific names for it. George Orwell called it *doublethink*—we've always been at war with Eurasia, we've always been at war with Eastasia. When having contradictory views causes you some kind of emotional distress, shrinks call it *cognitive dissonance*. Or they used to. Since it bothers me, I guess I have something like cognitive dissonance. I can't bring myself to simply abide and believe both things, or to consider both but believe neither "without any irritable reaching after fact and reason," so I'm kind of stuck with the discord. I could try to explain my experience away by saying something like maybe I was hallucinating, but that would be a lie. I've never hallucinated. Not even when I was a drug-using teenager. The fact is that I saw a person disappear right in front of me. Since I feel sure that person was neither a hallucination nor a living physical being, I don't have any way to explain it except to call it a ghost. But there's so much unacceptable baggage that comes with that word that I simultaneously call it a ghost and don't believe in ghosts. As you can see, the whole thing is pretty muddled. *I'm* pretty muddled.

Because people who report paranormal experiences often report more than one, I also feel like I should say whether I've had other paranormal experiences, but I'm not sure how to answer. I guess the answer is yes, but it's a weak yes or a yes with very poor examples to back it up. That is, I never saw any ghosts before or after the one in this story, but I had what you might consider psychic experiences as a child and as a young man. When I was around six years old, I had some vivid dreams. I didn't take particular note of them at the time because nothing noteworthy happened in them. They weren't nightmares or anything; they were just regular dreams in which lots of mildly weird and seemingly illogical things took place. The only unusual thing about them was that they were really vivid in the literal sense of that word—they seemed alive.

After I woke up, the dreams rapidly drained from my memory until there were only two scenes left. One was almost like a tableau. There was a girl in a blue shirt standing at a chalkboard with her arm stretched up to it, but there were no words on the board, just a grid of dots. The second was more like a very short film. In this dream, or scene from a dream, I woke up in an unfamiliar bedroom, and in that foggy way that you only *sort of* know things immediately after you wake up, I knew that it was the first day of a new school year. I went out of the unfamiliar bedroom, navigated the hallway to the living room, and looked out the window *directly at the school*, which was right across the street. In reality, I didn't live anywhere near my school, and certainly not close enough to see it out the window. The strangeness of being so close was jarring and seemed almost ridiculously convenient—the kind of thing that'd make fiction unbelievable. And it didn't look like a school. It just looked like a rectangular gray block. But anyway, I looked out the window, saw the school, noticed that there was what I took to be smoke everywhere, and said excitedly, "The school is on fire! I don't have to go!" And that was it. My brain didn't store any more of the data from those dreams.

Fast-forward then to age ten or eleven, when I was in the sixth grade. I never liked school, but that year it was much worse than it had ever been, at least partly because they made us take a class called "Study Skills." The purpose of the class was to teach us how to study in a more high school–type way as we transitioned out of elementary school, and to that end they were constantly giving us bothersome little busywork assignments. And they were relentless about it—they even made us do them as homework. We had to do all kinds of pointless writing that they pretended was useful, puzzles that weren't fun, games that were embarrassing, working in groups, and during class there were always exercises at the chalkboard. That was the worst thing. I wasn't comfortable being in front of people until much later in life, so being called to the board was torture.

One day the class was called to the board row by row, and each of us had to complete an exercise in which we had to find certain coordinates in a pattern of dots and then connect them to make a line graph. I did mine at top speed, not caring whether it was right or wrong, preferring the private ignominy of a low grade to the public humiliation of standing at the board for one second longer than I had to. When I got back to my seat, I started to check my work, which I had time to do because the other kids in my row weren't finished. So I looked down at the directions for the assignment and then up at my line graph. It looked right, or close enough to right, as far as I could tell. Then I looked over at the student who had been next to me at the board, a girl named Lisa Schneider. She was wearing a blue shirt, and she was reaching up with the chalk in her hand, not having drawn a line yet, but getting ready to connect some dots—and it was *exactly* the tableau I had seen in my dream five years earlier. Every particular was the same—her shirt was the right shade of blue, her hair was the right shade of brown, the board was the right shade of green, her skin was the right shade of white people-beige, and the angle of her arm, the pattern of dots, and the chalk in her hand were all precisely as I had seen them in a dream when I was six years old.

I sat there for a few seconds, sort of stunned, wondering at the utter strangeness of the fact—for it seemed like a fact —that I had dreamed the future. But "Study Skills" was one of those hellish classes where the teacher won't leave you the fuck alone, so I didn't have too much time to think about what the dream, or the fact that I had dreamed the future, might mean. Almost as soon as the rest of the kids in my row got back to their seats we had to move on to some other pointless nonsense, and my attention was diverted.

But that moment never left me. What had happened was incredible, and the feeling it gave me has never gone away. I wanted to tell someone then, and I have wanted to ever since, but who? And who would care? Even if I found someone who would believe me, it wasn't like I had dreamed 9/11. I dreamed that a girl was at the board drawing a line. Who would care about that? So I just tucked it away. It's just one of those weird things that has no particular significance but you still never forget, like the first time I saw a hawk getting mobbed by sparrows, or the time I saw a drunk driver sideswipe a telephone pole and then swerve across the highway and crash into a storefront. It's interesting, but that's it. Because of its narrow scope, this unbelievable, tantalizing psychic moment had to be relegated to the junk-drawer category of "memorable things." It was like having just the corner of a picture.

Eventually, the other thing I dreamed caught up with me too. By the time I was in ninth grade it was clear that my parents would only be together for a short time longer. For reasons that are not relevant to this story, I wanted them divorced as soon as possible and was looking forward to the day when I could move out of my father's house. I remember specifically having that thought while sitting in Mr. DeCaria's French class and staring out the window at the construction going on across the highway. I always made a point of looking out the windows in Mr. DeCaria's class because he had one of the very few classrooms in that school that actually had a decent bank of them.

Edinburgh High School was built in the early seventies and had been designed as a sort of experiment. The idea was to design a school in such a way that the building itself facilitated learning, but it seemed like a failure. Everyone found it unpleasant to be in, and it wasn't much to look at either. From the outside, it was essentially a rectangular prism with a few irregularities like loading docks and some odd corners I couldn't explain, one of which made a great niche for smoking. And it was made out of a strange material I have never seen anywhere else. From a distance it was just gray, but up close—like when you were smoking in the niche—you could see that the outer walls were made of large square sheets of white epoxy that had small black stones set in them at regular intervals. I have no idea whether that was part of the design plan or whether it was a cheap material being marketed in the seventies that never caught on or what. If part of the design plan, its purpose was not clear. The purpose we gave it was to act as a test of strength. While we were smoking, we would try to kick some of the stones out of the epoxy—it gave us something to do at school.

There were some strange things inside as well. Instead of regular cinder block walls there were thick sheet metal partitions between the classrooms, the idea being, I guess, that if they wanted a larger space than a single classroom, they could move the partitions to the side (they parted in the middle, sort of like a curtain, and folded up against either wall) and, you know . . . have more space. Apparently, they thought that would facilitate learning. The logic is not clear to me.

Another peculiarity was that there were very few windows, and most of them were narrow and deep-set, making them difficult to see anything out of. I suppose the point was to make use of natural light while also preventing distracted students like me from staring outside all day. But Mr. DeCaria's classroom, like the five others on the ground floor in the front of the building, had a normal set of windows like you imagine in a traditional classroom—six or eight of them running the whole length of the wall. So, if I had to be in a classroom, Mr. DeCaria's was one of the best ones to be in. Being able to look outside and see the sunlight made me feel connected to the world, like a part of humanity, whereas the rest of the building felt isolating and punitive, like juvenile hall or a huge Skinner box. During the forty-five minutes I was supposed to be learning French, I always looked outside as much as I could get away with, even though all I could see was grass and the highway and the blonde particleboard A-frames workers were erecting on the other side of it. I could tell they were building apartments even though only their skeletons had been erected, but I never dreamed I would live there. I mean, I *had* dreamed that I lived there, but I didn't realize that yet.

At the end of that school year my mother finally got the courage to leave my father. Things were complicated, and I stayed with my grandmother in my old neighborhood until everyone figured out what they were going to do, and where they were going to be. The dust had settled by the end of August, and the new order was that I was going to live with my mother in the brand-new apartment complex that I had watched being built from Mr. DeCaria's window. When I moved in there were only two or three days before school started. I don't remember anything strange about that time —no strange feelings, no wonders in the sky, no signs or portents. Just uneventful days in an unfamiliar neighborhood. I don't remember anything about going to sleep the night before school started, either, and if I had any dreams that night, they are gone now, too.

But the second I woke up the next morning, I knew that something very strange was happening. I got up and squinted my way down the hall to the living room, where I looked out the window, expecting to see something. For a second, I thought that I had been disappointed. All I saw was fog so thick that I could barely make out the windowless gray rectangle that was our failed social experiment of a school across the highway. I didn't say anything. I couldn't, really. I didn't have time to explain to my mother that I had dreamed this exact thing, that I had seen this smoky-looking fog surrounding this school from exactly this angle in a dream I had seven or eight years earlier, and that I was shocked at what was happening. And I didn't even try. Obviously, she wouldn't have believed a word of it—nor would any reasonable person—but in fact I had dreamed this future when I was six years old. I had seen a school I had never been to, from the window of an apartment building that did not yet exist, seven years before it was built.

Of course, it's not like the dream was prophetic in a significant way. To me, it was amazingly important, but just like seeing the girl at the chalk board, I couldn't see any reason for anyone else to care about it. I wasn't being guided to some kind of transcendental goal or realization. Nothing of consequence had been revealed to me, nor did anything special happen on either of those days. Or maybe it did, but at this remove of time I recall nothing about either day except the specific moments when I realized that I had previously dreamed what I was seeing. Frustratingly, even though it hints at some kind of unseen power or process, what I was seeing was totally ordinary and meaningless except for the fact that I had seen it before. I waited for something else to happen, for some bigger revelation to follow this small one, but it never did. There was nothing else. It was a failure of a premonition. Imagine it had been delivered in words as a prophecy—that the Sybil was standing over the volcanic vent, breathing in toxic fumes rising from deep in the earth, and saying, "In five years, a girl will be called to the chalkboard to connect some dots. Then, three years later, it will be foggy one morning. Not foggy enough to disrupt the flow of traffic, but still... pretty foggy."

More than twenty years have passed since that day, and in all that time there have been no other moments when I realized that I had dreamed something that was now happening in front of me. And there have been no paranormal events of any other kind in my life—no weird noises, voices, specters, UFOs, sasquatches, nothing—except the ghost story I'm about to tell. Point being, it's not really fair or accurate to say that I'm prone to experiencing the paranormal because the only experiences I've had have been sort of pointless, and weak. I suppose there is an argument to be made that two pointless, weak paranormal experiences—three, counting the ghost story—are more than the average person is likely to have had. Maybe that's true. But it's also true that my claim to paranormal sensitivity or whatever it's called is very weak because these two little pissant experiences barely count. The only one that really counts is the ghost story, which I guess I should tell now.

When I was twenty-eight my wife and I moved to Columbus, Ohio, where I found a teaching job. We had been warned in advance to live at least so many blocks away from the university if we wanted any peace. Since going south put us right in the heart of the city, going west put us across the river, and going east put us in run-down neighborhoods, we looked mainly to the north. We found several decent apartments, but they were more than we could afford because my wife wasn't working yet. We despaired a little until we followed High Street far enough north and found a place that suited our budget. Right across from a big, wooded park in the middle of a really nice neighborhood there are three crumbling beige-brick buildings full of shut-ins, weed dealers, unwanted elderly, kids who just started at *The* Ohio State University, slightly older kids who just got jobs, underachieving middle-aged couples, and for some reason a lot of blind people who live there by themselves in studio apartments—I don't know what the story is with that.

We signed a year lease and left when it expired, but we left because there were roaches and the air-conditioner barely worked and the lady with weird scabs in her hair who lived at the end of the second-floor hallway refused to throw her garbage away, not because of anything eerie. Sometimes there were noises, but at least eighty people lived in that building, so it was normal for there to be noises—no reasonable person would expect anything else. None of the other ostensible signs of a haunting happened. We never felt weird or cold (except in winter) or thought we were being watched or touched. Nothing ever went missing and then reappeared somewhere else. The neighbors told no stories. No pictures ever fell off the walls for no reason. Electrical appliances never malfunctioned (except the air-conditioner). Everything was perfectly normal. We just wanted to get out of there because of the roaches and the heat and the trash smell.

My wife was working by that time so we were able to look at better places, and though the next building we moved into was only a little newer it was in much better shape. It was part of a large complex owned by a real estate company that had all the buildings remodeled every so many years and kept them well-maintained. We told the property manager why we were so eager to get out of our old building, so she let us move in on the fifteenth and gave us a prorated first month, but our old lease didn't end until the thirtieth, which gave us fifteen days to move. Having so much time made us lazy. We began by just moving a couple boxes per day. After work, we would load up her car—the only car we had—with as many boxes as it would hold, drive to the new place, unload everything, and then go back home. One day when I wasn't teaching, I rented a truck and moved all the furniture. After that, we lived in the new place, and when my wife would come home we'd drive back to High Street and grab this and that to bring back.

After six or eight days, I got sick of moving in this piecemeal way, so I decided that in the morning I would drop her off at work, take the car, and get the move over with. I spent that morning making trips back and forth until there was barely anything left in the old place—a small coil of coaxial cable, a lamp that didn't work but that she wanted to keep because it was in her house growing up, one coat in the hall closet, multiple coat hangers in all the closets, a cordless drill in a plastic case, a screwdriver, a loose AA battery, four paperclips that somehow ended up on a windowsill, a folding chair, twenty-three cents, a picture left leaning against the wall—the kind of nonsense that might as well have been thrown away. Not caring much about these items, I fucked around and ran errands until two-thirty in the afternoon, when I went back to the old place to get them out of there, lock up, and drop off the keys. I mention the time because so many ghost stories take place at night, when people have just been woken up by what they think or claim is a ghost. They always say that they know they were awake, but that evokes a lot of justified grumbling because they can't really *know* that. But I can. It was 2:30 p.m., and I had been up and doing physical labor since probably 7:30 a.m. *Plus*, I had just driven to the old place, walked up three flights of stairs, and then down the hallway half the length of the building. Whatever else might be true, there is zero chance that I was sleeping.

In any case, when I got back to the old apartment and

opened the door, there was a guy standing there, and it looked like he was talking to someone. There was nothing about him that said *ghost*. He wasn't transparent, or shadowy, or filmy white, he didn't look dead—there was nothing unusual about his appearance except that he was making it in my apartment, where I didn't think he belonged. But he looked so normal and so at home that it never once occurred to me that he might be even a burglar let alone a ghost. I thought maybe he was with the landlord, or showing the place to a prospective renter. He was just a guy—an older guy—standing there talking. He was short. Maybe 5′5″ or 5′6″. He was dark skinned, possibly Hispanic, but seemed more like he was Greek or Italian. Maybe Jewish. He was wearing a beige or light gray suit and a skinny tie that was maybe brown or faded black, which was on the strange side because this was more of a jeans and T-shirt kind of place. In fact, he may have been the only man in that building (myself included) who even *owned* a proper suit. But it should be noted that it was not very nice. Like, even though he was wearing a suit, nobody would have said he was well dressed. It was kind of rumpled and worn-looking, and his shirt collar was messed up—the points were a little bent, curled up just the slightest bit, and a little yellow. And his tie didn't lie exactly where a tie should, and the knot was a little askew. He looked kind of beat up or like he had been awake for several days.

I mentioned that he was talking, but I need to explain that. The layout of the apartment was that immediately on entering, you are in the living room, but the kitchen is just to the right. It's all one big room, but the right half has a linoleum floor and the left half has carpet. This man was standing where the carpet stops and the linoleum starts, and he was talking in a calm but animated way to someone in the kitchen, or so it seemed. But it wasn't that simple. First, there was no sound. It wasn't low or quiet or whispery—there was no sound at all. That was peculiar. When you see a guy talking, gesturing with his hands, and moving around you expect to hear something—at least the rustling of his clothes—but there was nothing. Had he been an actor on a muted TV, if you turned the sound back on you would have expected that he would have been very easy to hear. Even somewhat loud. But, again, there was no sound at all. Second, though he was facing the kitchen and talking as though to someone there, there *was* no one there. The kitchen was empty. There was just this old Italian or Jewish guy standing there at the edge of my living room, wearing a rumpled suit, talking silently to someone who was not in my kitchen. I wasn't expecting that.

After I opened the door, he kept talking for a second before he turned and looked directly at me, right in the eye. At that point, I expected that he was going to explain what he was doing there—again, maybe that he was with the landlord, or showing the place. But he didn't explain. He just did that thing you do when you want to acknowledge that you're in the wrong—that *my mistake* gesture, both hands open, palms flat and facing the person you wronged. And he wore the embarrassed grin that most people wear when they make that gesture. Even without words, it was a very clear statement: *my fault, man. Sorry.* Then he disappeared pretty much instantly. And that's it. That's the ghost story.

I stood there for a few seconds, astonished that a man had disappeared right in front of me, and—strange as it sounds—that was a definite thing. He had to have disappeared because there was no other way he could have gotten out of my sight. There wasn't even a closet he could have gone into or any furniture he could have hidden behind—he was in the middle of an empty room in an empty apartment. The only way he could have gotten out of my sight would have been to turn around, take three or four steps *toward* the hallway, then go two or three more steps *down* the hallway, and then go into one of the bedrooms or the bathroom. If that had happened, I could not have failed to see it. But even if for some unlikely reason I blacked out or something and *did* fail to see it, he would have been trapped in the apartment because there was only one exit and I was standing in it. The only other way he could have gotten out would have been through the windows, which were three floors up. Three floors might not sound like much, but go up to the third floor of a building and look out the window. How would you get down if you had to? Once you figure that out, then add the complication that you're sixty-five and wearing a suit. Three floors will seem pretty high, then. So, whether or not there's such a thing as a ghost or spirit or whatever you want to call it, as a point of fact I *did* see a guy disappear in my apartment. Or, failing that, I for no clear reason hallucinated that a guy was there, that he was like *my fault*, and then disappeared. One or the other of those things is a fact. I'm not tied to the first thing, but the second seems almost as unlikely.

After he disappeared, I took a cursory look around the apartment, knowing there was no one to find. I checked the bathroom, the bedrooms, and their empty closets, but there were no old guys in beige suits. After that, I made two or three trips out to the car with armloads of the irritating little things that didn't seem important enough to pack, and left.

The apartment was now completely empty, and there was nothing else to do.

At this point in most ghost stories, you get to the *then I found out* part. As in, for example, *several years later, I ran into the landlord at the grocery store and told her what I saw. She reluctantly told me that sordid tale #74812 occurred in that apartment, and it turns out that the dead guy in this particular iteration of sordid tale #74812 looked exactly like the ghost I saw, and he wore a cheap, rumpled suit when he went to work*—the mystery is explained, big rush of satisfaction. But I don't have that. I never saw the landlord again. When I stopped by the rental office to drop off the keys no one was there. I slipped them under the door in an envelope. But even if the landlord had been there, it's unlikely that I would have made a fool of myself by telling her this story if for no other reason than that she was pretty, and no guy wants to look like a delusional imbecile in front of a pretty woman. (Actually, I'm sure there's a guy out there somewhere who has that exact fetish, but I'm not him.) I don't have any of the other resolutions ghost stories sometimes feature, either. I never heard anything about the building afterward, or went down to the hall of records to find out more about it, or went to the city library to check newspapers on microfiche for a headline about sordid tale #74812 occurring on the north side—I had a job and a wife and serious things to do. Nothing else ever happened with this story until I wrote it down just now—and it ends just as pointlessly as my psychic experiences did. It goes like this: some dude was there for a second, and then he wasn't.

I'm not sure I have anything intelligent to say about this. I have things to say, but maybe they're silly. For instance, since I saw that guy disappear, I have read several books that are purportedly about real ghosts. I have to admit that I have questions about the authors' credentials and the evidence on which they base their conclusions, but I wasn't able to find any books on this topic by anyone I didn't have the same questions about. Some of these authors agree that there are two kinds of hauntings—one is called a *residual haunting*, and the other is called an *intelligent haunting*. Residual hauntings are where something awful happens and, the authors speculate, the physical material of the place absorbs the psychic energy (a thing that no one has attempted to demonstrate exists) of that event, and every so often the drywall and floorboards and so on sort of *replay* the event, so to speak. So, for instance, let's say a guy kills himself in a room. These people claim that sometimes, under unspecified circumstances, the room can by some unspecified process record that event. Then, if afterward the room sort of plays it back from time to time—playback is caused by an unspecified mechanism—in such a way that it is visible and/or audible to people, that is called a residual haunting. The important thing to know about this kind of haunting is that the ghost isn't actively making decisions and cannot interact with you. It's just an image doing the same thing over and over like a video. An intelligent haunting is a haunting in which the ghost is mentally and temporally present in that it is able to perceive and interact with you, and you are able to perceive and interact with it.

If, in the interest of gaining some intellectual ground, we grant that there really are hauntings, and that they really do take these two forms, that enables me to classify the haunting of apartment forty-three as an "intelligent haunting" insofar as the guy was thinking, making decisions, and acting in the present—he saw me, thought about what that meant, decided to leave, and did so, not as an image recorded to video reenacts what its original did in the past, but as an act of its own free will at the point of time's arrow. But I don't know that it adds anything to the discussion to call it an intelligent haunting, and in granting that these two forms of haunting exist without any evidence whatsoever we gave away so much ground on the back end that any ground gained on the front end is ill-gotten. And I don't know what else to say. The books don't offer much else. It belongs to no science. Scripture is dogmatic and obtuse. It seems like the most reliable source of information on this topic is folklore. All I can do is sort of glance at the event, compare it to "what they say" about ghosts, and wonder.

I feel a frustrating pressure to change my entire belief structure because of this one event, but I can't bring myself to do it. Maybe because of the feeling that it is impossible to make any progress or arrive at any conclusion on the basis of an image of a man that blipped in and out of my perception in just a few seconds. The implications of the image are massive *if* we make certain assumptions about what the image is, and that justifies changing my belief structure. But because his appearance was so brief, and the information he gave us infinitesimal, we don't have any good reason to make those assumptions. And there is no new information coming in that might tip the balance one way or the other. The man I saw is not likely to come back to me or to make himself available if I seek him out—to the best of my knowledge, he only appeared in that apartment *once* in the year that I lived there, and he only did that after he apparently thought that I had vacated permanently. Even if I found him and was able to discuss with him what he was, *what if he lied?* Or what if he didn't know the truth? It is not difficult to imagine a man who does not know the truth about himself. I could try to get new information by continuing to read these questionable books but that information is tainted. I strongly suspect that *they* lie or do not know the truth. So, I'm stuck. There's nothing else I can do here. My ghost story is that I saw a thing. And life goes on.

4

THE MAN IN THE MIRROR

Alice Binderman was a thin, mousy, unpleasant-looking woman who wore thick glasses, was timid and fearful, and had created a cavernous void of a life for herself. After college, she was not prepared for how quickly her college friends and acquaintances disappeared, and she was alarmed at how few new acquaintances she was making out in the world. She was afraid to track the actual numbers, but even several years out she was sure there was a net loss. Despite her alarm, she could not reverse the trend, and after a decade or so there was no one in her life but her mother, who she didn't *want* there, and her beagle, Rodney, who wasn't particularly affectionate or obedient or easy to deal with. Rodney was twelve years old and consequently spent most of his time asleep in the corner of the living room, dreaming and farting and half-barking. When he woke he wanted out, and then he wanted food, and then he wanted to lie down again. At some point, Alice found that she and Rodney were in an emotional war of attrition and were doing things to spite each other almost daily. He ripped her socks to pieces, so she "accidentally" bought the kind of dry food that he wouldn't eat, and so on. Her relationship with her mother was similar.

After Facebook became popular enough for her to hear about, she tracked down her college friends, but that forced her to realize that she was never as close to them as she thought she had been, and she found that they were not enthusiastic about getting back in touch. She had pictured long phone calls detailing their lives from the point of leaving school all the way to the present. But they all had jobs and husbands and children and were not interested in interacting with her beyond occasionally liking the photos of Rodney that she posted with ironic-affectionate captions.

She had her share of sexual relationships, but only angry failures were interested in her. They were usually some combination of short, scrawny, fat, pushy, bald, broke, and old. They were largely apartment dwellers. They were largely bitter about their divorces. Most of them talked loudly when they were alone with Alice but quietly in other circumstances. Most of them thought that pretty much everything would be better if people would just listen to them. Some had pencil-thin mustaches they were vain about. Most had low-level jobs that they took very seriously and exaggerated the importance of. It seemed to her that she attracted these men because she was timid, and they knew they could push her around. And they did. She was thirty-six when the last of them was done with her, and she felt a profound and ugly sadness. Though she was desperately lonely, she stopped dating altogether and made a conscious decision to simply run out the clock on her unwanted life. Then Rodney died, and there wasn't even anyone to fight with anymore.

She found him frozen and stuck to the grass out back one morning. Even though she had resented him for years by this point, she found peeling him off the lawn remarkably difficult. This was somewhat mitigated by the thought of the flood of sympathy comments she would get on Facebook when she tearfully (in writing) announced the death of her beloved dog. She actually drafted the post in Word prior to logging in. She wrote and rewrote carefully and finally posted the most sentimental-looking photo she could find—Rodney licking her face as she knelt beside him in a park, some ten years ago, before the war had begun—with the text that she had labored over like a poem. She considered the number of notes, likes, and sympathy comments that she got a triumph, the pinnacle of her year—she had even gotten the offer of a phone call from one of her college friends, though ultimately that call was never made. But then she realized how sad this all was, and not because of Rodney. After that she spent an hour and forty-five minutes Googling over-the-counter sleeping pills and their drug interactions. The only reason she proceeded no further in that business was that she didn't want people to think she did it because of the dog.

In the months that followed, she spent a lot of time lying on her couch in near silence, just listening to the refrigerator running, thinking it was stunning how empty a life could be. When she was young, it had occurred to her that her life might turn out to be a boring one, but she had assumed it would be easier than this, that it would be filled mostly by mundane things that would make the time pass, and that it would be over before she knew it. She never realized how small was the space mundane things actually occupied in a life like hers, how little time they took, and how little they would distract her. Grocery shopping. Clothes shopping. Laundry once a week. Paying bills on payday. Sometimes getting the car serviced. This was all she did after work. It left her with huge tracts of unused time. The emptiness of her life was vast, and it terrified her that if she were unlucky she might spend five more decades in it. For a while she cried every day, but that stopped for no clear reason. She couldn't understand why she didn't cry anymore even though she was desperately sad. It was so incongruous that she thought maybe something was wrong with her physically. It was as if she no longer felt her feelings so much as she just recognized them, categorized them, and put them to one side like boring mail.

Things were so bad that she stopped thinking logically. Even though she was desperate for things to do, she decided that she wanted to stay home from work. She would think up plausible reasons to call out, but when morning came she would chicken out at the last minute and go anyway. She always felt uneasy when she stayed home from work, and when December came, the upsetting shortness of the days amplified the effect. Depriving herself of the human interaction she got at work did not sound like a good idea anymore.

She considered seeing a shrink but had no trauma to report, had suffered no beatings (not even from the angry, bald, short, failures), and had experienced no neglect, so she really didn't know what she would talk about. Everyone, her whole life long, had been mildly pleasant most of the time, and mildly unpleasant for the rest of the time, but that wasn't upsetting, even to her. The idea of seeing a shrink simply because she was lonely was humiliating, but as the days continued to go by and nothing improved, she decided she might do it anyway. She looked into it, but finding out that the co-pay was fifty dollars, and that her insurance would only pay for five visits, instantly put it out of the question.

Her life was ugly, she decided. She hated it. She longed for death, but death fled from her, and she felt like it would never come. She thought about suicide again, but that was dramatic. It was in her personality to quietly submit to the way things were rather than to act dramatically, so she bowed her head to the ugliness and loneliness, and life went on interpreting her silence as consent.

Around the middle of December, something odd started happening. Alice found that while lying on the couch, listening to the refrigerator run and contemplating why she didn't cry anymore, she could hear a muffled sound that seemed to be coming from the bathroom. It took her a long time, maybe six days or so, to realize that the bathroom wall faced the backyard and the sound was actually coming in from outside. The sound was more or less intermittent white noise. When she concentrated on it, it never became much more distinct, and she decided that it could be the wind blowing or leaves rustling. That kind of sound coming from a backyard might not seem like cause for alarm. The reason it alarmed her anyway was that she was pretty sure there was no wind, and there was nothing out there that should be moving. She had no trees or bushes, and the neighbor who lived behind her had a wooden privacy fence. After having lived there for so long, she felt like she could mostly distinguish between sounds that came from her side of the fence and sounds that came from the other side. This one seemed distinctly on her side, and what concerned her most about that was that she had a blind spot.

Whoever had lived there before her had put a tool shed in the backyard—the kind that looks like a scaled-down barn—and it was both longer and taller than normal. Because it would be awkward if it were arranged in the normal way, it was placed sideways along the back fence in the left-hand corner. This created a long, narrow strip of waste space between the shed and the fence, maybe eight feet wide by twenty feet long, and it was the waste space that concerned her. Someone could creep in there and stay out of sight if they had a mind to.

That space was already a source of anxiety for her. All summer long yellow jackets and other wasps seemed to go into and out of it with such frequency that she was sure there were multiple nests. Plus, poison ivy grew out of control there, and it was so thick she didn't think she could get rid of it. And even if she could, she didn't think anything good could be done with that space. The previous owner had used it to dump what looked like years of ashes from charcoal grilling, so the soil wasn't fertile. It was whitish, lumpy, uneven, and it looked *off* somehow. A few thin, sickly shoots of weeds emerged around the edges, and some haggard, misshapen crab grass, but even in the lushest, wettest summers, when the rest of the lawn thrived, no proper grass would grow there. Even now, in December, when everything else was as austere and colorless as the ash, that space looked strange. The leaves were gone, but over the years the poison ivy had claimed the sides of the waste space to a height of at least six feet, forming a living trellis of spidery roots that clung menacingly to the fence and the wall of the shed. She knew they weren't dead. They were just dreaming, and in a few months the spring sun would fill them with new poison. She hated looking at them.

Finally, Alice's curious alarm got the better of her. She walked silently into the bathroom, opened the window, and listened intently. She didn't hear anything for a few minutes, but then it started again, even though there was no wind. She believed this was the case before, but with the window open she could tell for certain. No wind. And yet there was that sound. Alice quietly closed the window and called the police. In about twenty-five minutes, a Crown Victoria pulled up, and the officer verified for her that no one was back there, and if someone had been there they left nothing behind—no cigarette butts, no footprints, no trash, or evidence of any description. She felt foolish but not wrong, and she was still afraid. Something was making that sound, even if it wasn't a person.

She listened carefully for the next four nights but heard nothing. On the fifth night, when she thought she had finally calmed down, the noise returned. But now she didn't trust herself. The fifth night was not still like the night she had called the police. There was a mild wind, and though she *felt* like she could hear the muffled sound underneath of it, she had to admit that it could have been in her mind, so she did nothing.

She doubted herself for three more nights before the stillness returned and the muffled sound was again clearly distinguishable. She slipped into the bathroom without turning on the light, slid the window up as softly as she could, and listened. It was so quiet that she could hear the occasional car or truck passing on the freeway more than two miles north. The only other disturbance was the muffled sound in her back yard. She listened very carefully for what seemed like fifteen or twenty minutes before she decided it was not made by a person. No one could be doing something back there for so long without accomplishing it, or getting tired and resting, or making some kind of noise—sighing, exhaling loudly, coughing. It was more like some mindless, automated thing, acting without purpose, without result, without tiring. Maybe it was an animal, but it couldn't be a person. She was relieved at this, but now she was overcome with the need to know what it was. Operating under the assumption that it was some small suburban animal—a possum, a skunk, a raccoon—she put her clothes on, found a flashlight and, to avoid making too much noise, went out the front door.

She slipped around the side of the house and quietly opened the back gate. The latch made a little ringing sound, but it wasn't too different from the sound it made in the wind sometimes, and she hoped it wouldn't scare the animal off. She made her way slowly and carefully toward the shed, but as she drew within fifteen feet she heard something different from before, what she was sure was a long, slow exhalation of breath. Her confidence that the thing was not human evaporated instantly, and she found that she was trying hard not to piss herself. A person—almost any person—could easily subdue her, do anything he wanted to her, and here she was alone with him, barely dressed in the dark. Her impulse was to turn and run, or even to scream. But if she ran she wouldn't find out, and might never know, whether it was a person. And if she screamed and it was a person, the person would probably run. She wouldn't have a description or any information at all to give the police, so how could they find him? They might not even believe her since they had already been out there on a false alarm. She decided that she needed to know for certain what was making the sound, and now was the time to find out. She kept going. When she reached the shed, she heard it more clearly, the sound of something breathing, struggling. She took a final, long step, and turned the corner, and switched on the flashlight.

The thing she saw was not unlike the possum she had expected. It was light in color, but not any particular color. There were varying shades of gray, from steel to almost white, and in some places there were hints and patches of tan and brown and even black. The thing was of roughly human shape, but looked like it was made from a mass of waste material that had partially melted and then congealed. And its predicament was strange. It was half in the ground, as though it were trying to climb out of an old, filled-in grave, but it was so much a part of that grave that separating one from the other was hopeless. That was the sound that Alice had heard all these nights—the sound of the thing trying desperately to pull itself up out of the earth.

She looked carefully at the thing, and could tell that it was not a human being even though she could only see its arms, head, and torso. The arms were inarticulate, handless, fingerless, blunt, but they appeared so powerful that she was sure it would free itself any second. The head was bulky, rudimentary, like something a child would make from a mass of clay. The features were faint, but they sagged dramatically, and the expression on its face was not one of hate or rage, but of misery, a stark, frightening sadness intermingled with pain of the same sort that babies evince —mindless, primal sorrow that does not know its cause, or that there could be a remedy. It was otherwise blank. There were no clothes, there was no hair, it did not speak or give any sign of recognition, and did not seem to even be looking back at her, or cognizant of where it was.

As she studied it, something in her brain assumed that there was a mistake, a misunderstanding. The thing just *had* to be something recognizable coated in mud, that had a strange but ultimately sensible reason for being in her backyard, and she spent some time actively trying to force her vision to change, to resolve the thing into a person, to see the substance as something that coated a real, living man and distorted his appearance. But there was nothing coating him. The substance and the thing were one. And it was not flesh. As far as she could tell it was a being made from the mud and ashes dumped in the waste space year after year and somehow animated like a golem. Alice tried to scream, but only a little moan came out with her breath. She evacuated into her pants, but she still couldn't move; she could only gape.

She began to shake so violently that she dropped the flashlight. It rotated in the air as it fell, and when it hit the ground it was pointed in the opposite direction. The waste space behind the shed was utterly black. Alice gasped and stopped breathing, not quite knowing why, and briefly considered whether the thing she had seen was real. But in the silence of her halted breath, she could hear it, the *thing*, breathing and struggling—the same noises she had heard through the bathroom wall. She let out a little yelp and tried to move, but feeling the wet cold that had crept into her pants, she stripped herself naked in two compact movements, ran around to the front door, entered, and locked herself in.

Alice had always pictured dramatic episodes in other

people's lives as being caused by actions performed by some outside force, as though those people were possessed by a demon or a certainty that their strategic plan was the *right* thing to do, the *smart* thing. But now that she found herself in a dramatic episode of her own, she realized that she had an array of choices before her, that she might pick any of them, and the resulting consequences would not necessarily be the ones she wanted. She froze. And nothing happened.

The minute hand on the clock moved almost imperceptibly. The refrigerator fan switched on. And there was nothing else. She had to decide. She shut all the lights off and walked as quietly as she could to the bathroom, where she pressed her ear to the screen of the still-open window and listened. For a moment she almost felt relief, but then she heard it again. A calm came over her, because she knew where the thing was, and because for all the time she had watched it, the thing had failed to make any progress. It was still back there, still struggling, presumably still stuck. She just had to figure out what to do now. She couldn't call the police. She couldn't have them find her clothes in the yard that way—she would rather die. And anyway, she had called the police before and they found nothing. She didn't want to look desperate and out of her senses again. She considered getting into her car and leaving, but she had no place to go and didn't have the money to stay at a hotel. And what if she spent money anyway and it turned out that the thing wasn't real? How would she get by for the next month? She decided to shower.

She could smell herself and was deeply ashamed, so she showered without the lights on. Through the window she could still see the burning flashlight she had dropped on the ground and formulated a plan around it. Anything that wanted to get from the waste space to the house would have to pass in front of the light, so she would watch it intently as she showered. If she saw anything that seemed to move past it or distort the light in any way, she would dry off quickly, dress, and get ready to take some kind of action. Though she thought of herself as a meek person and knew that she was not physically strong, she was able to do this with a relative calm, mostly because she was not convinced that the thing would be able to get out of the ground any time soon or, once having gotten out, be able to move particularly well. The thing looked like it would be lumbering and clumsy and more likely to fall over than anything else. By the end of her shower, she hadn't seen anything move past the light, so she dressed herself quietly and prepared to pass the night in the only safe place she could think of. She went around the house, locking all the doors and windows and double checking the ones she already knew were locked. Then she took her cell phone, pillow, and blanket up to the attic, pulled up the steps, and slept on the plywood floor in all of her clothes, wrapped in a blanket and a comforter.

The next morning she woke to her alarm clock going off at the normal time in the room directly below her. She tried to listen under the sound of the alarm, but no matter how hard she tried, she heard nothing but the incessant digital screech. After what she later found out was twenty-two minutes, she lowered the attic stairs and crept down. Everything was just how she had left it. She was starting to question her sanity and whether anything had really happened, but when she looked out the bathroom window she spotted her clothes on the lawn next to the burned out flashlight. She still might be insane, and it was possible that she had hallucinated the entire thing, but at least she knew that she had been in the backyard. She wanted to run out and put the clothes into a trash bag before the neighbors woke up and saw them, but then she considered the *thing*. She hesitated at the door but decided she had no choice. She had to move those clothes.

She went outside with a black drawstring trash bag and picked the clothes up—all of them, not just the pants and underwear—with the bag the way people pick up dog shit, tied the drawstrings, and then tied several knots in the bag itself before she went back to the fence to put the bag in the trash can. She hoped to God that her neighborhood's legion of raccoons wouldn't tip the trash can over while that was in there.

Alice looked toward the shed. It was day now, and there was too much background noise to hear the thing if it was still there, but she had to know. She picked up the flashlight as she walked back through the yard—it was made of anodized aluminum, and had several D batteries in it, so it could serve as a weapon if she could get the courage to use it. But when she reached the waste space, there was nothing to see. There was no disturbance in the whitish soil—it wasn't raised or moved or broken. There was even frost on it.

Without showering or eating, Alice managed to make it to the office on time. Once there and settled, she did quite a lot of work, which surprised her and made her as pleased with herself as she could be under the circumstances. At the very least she felt that the situation had been well managed. Last night she hallucinated a monster, shit her pants, ran into the house naked, and slept in the attic—all of which was troubling. But she still made it to work and was productive while there. That was something.

As the day went on, she found herself immersed in what she was doing and oblivious to last night. Like all people at work, she had a prioritized list of pending items, and the ash monster in her backyard was at the bottom of it. At one point, she was even calm enough to ask her cubicle mate for one of the chocolate mints she kept in a little blue and white Chinese dish. It was like a normal work day. But in the moments between tasks, or in those off times—walking to and from the bathroom, waiting for the Task Manager to End Process—the thing came back into her thoughts. And once the sun started to go down and she started printing the delinquent tax checks—the beginning of her last task of the day—she got a sick feeling in her stomach. It was a powerless feeling, like something bad was going to happen. And then it did—she clocked out.

She made the drive home as long as she could make it. She stopped at the bank to withdraw twenty dollars she didn't need right now, stopped to eat at a restaurant that served wine, and stopped at the grocery. The pretention she labored under was that she had imagined or dreamed the thing in her backyard, that this was a regular day, that she was going about her regular business. But she knew this was not a regular day. The grocery was the last place she could think of to stop, and as she calmly panicked in the aisles, looking for things she would gladly pretend to need, fear of the thing welled up in her and pooled like tears under her eyes. She stood very still, started breathing through her mouth, and gripped the handles of her basket so hard that her already pale hands became almost paper white. She would have to face it.

Or not.

Alice could not bring herself to abandon the role of a sane person whose life was undisturbed. In a small way, she became indignant, and *refused* to. Rather than running around all night, dodging the issue, she would have to show herself *again* that the thing had only been her imagination. It was already dark by the time she left work—the shortest day of the year was only two days away—so she picked up new batteries for the flashlight. When she arrived home, she installed the batteries, walked straight through the backyard, directly to the waste space, turned on the flashlight, and saw the same undisturbed light-colored dirt that she had seen that morning. The frost had melted in the sun during the day and had not yet reformed, but everything else was the same. She even walked back into the waste space and looked all around. Everything was just as it had always been. She pretended to laugh out loud at the idea that there had been a *thing* here and lingered longer than she wanted to, looking carefully at the brown poison ivy roots, pretending to think about how to kill them in winter (maybe they'd come off with a paint scraper?) so the leaves wouldn't come back in the spring. Then she walked more slowly than normal back to her car, where she gathered her groceries and took them inside.

That night she decided to do something new. She would drink wine and listen to talk radio while cleaning her kitchen. Normally she didn't like talk radio. She hated people who sounded authoritative, who pretended to know things that were really only their opinions. But suddenly she didn't feel threatened by that anymore and decided to see who she could find. Unfortunately, there was nothing on—FM was mostly rock or rap or top 40 stations, and AM was mostly news or religious talk, which didn't count. She supposed that morning and later at night were really the peak times for the sort of thing she was looking for. But she did leave a rock station on for a little while as she cleaned and recalled something her high school boyfriend had variously called the Pink Floyd rule or the Led Zeppelin rule. The rule was that if you tuned up and down the FM band, at any time of the day or night, there was at least one Pink Floyd or one Led Zeppelin song playing.

She vividly remembered a time they had tested it, and it was true. They were at the corner of Route 40 and 896, which at that time was a pretty desolate area. His car idled a deep rhythm. He put it in neutral and hit the gas a couple times because he had done something to it, and he liked the way it sounded. Something was said. They checked the rule. "Black Dog" was on WMMR.

She had her first orgasm in that car. He drove fast and talked loudly. He smoked Marlboro Reds, which he pronounced *Mallbro*. He hadn't bothered to break up with her. He had just stopped calling.

Alice smiled to herself, pretending to sing a little of it as she cleaned her counter, though she only knew the first eight words. She preferred Floyd to Zeppelin anyway.

Once the kitchen was clean and she was drunk, she decided to try to sleep on the couch with the TV on. This was not likely to happen. She was a fitful sleeper and needed darkness and silence, but she hoped that since she was drunk she would just pass out. There were complications. She couldn't find anything on TV just like she couldn't find anything on the radio. She had pictured a simple operation: putting something on, lying down, and listening until her consciousness faded away. Instead she found herself switching channels and scrolling through Netflix for something with many, many episodes. Eventually she just lay there listening to CNN, but rather than her consciousness fading, she found herself actually watching, periodically tilting her head so the images would be right side up. Then she started to sober up, and could feel her heart pounding. There was nothing for it but to go to bed. She dragged herself there, leaving the TV on and turned way up, but obviously this kept her awake. At last she had to turn it off and risk having something other than the TV interrupt the silence. In bed she purposely elected to breathe through her mouth, which was louder than through her nose, so that there was some kind of white noise to keep any outside sounds from intruding. That was the correct formula, and she fell asleep.

Maddeningly, she woke up seven minutes before her alarm went off. Though she would normally lie in bed for long as possible, there was no use today. When her eyes opened, instantaneously she was wide awake. She tried not to mourn the lost minutes and headed for the shower.

When she backed out of the driveway that morning, she made a show of not looking in the backyard even though it was right in front of her, right where she would naturally look. She looked in the rearview, at the dash, at the transmission indicator, at the radio, but not straight forward. She checked to see whether the raccoons had tipped the trashcan over, which thankfully they hadn't, but she refused to let her eyes focus on anything else in that direction. The yard was just a blur of green as she turned her head, and she was not interested in whatever nonsense might be happening back there.

But when she got to work, things were less than normal.

Whereas yesterday she had been able to prioritize and get things done, today she couldn't focus or do anything physical with any grace at all. She dropped two different stacks of checks. She knocked her empty coffee mug onto the floor. She got her purse strap caught in the caster of her chair and wound up having to upend the chair and pull the caster out to get the strap free. In the process, she got grease and dust on her hands, purse strap, and shirt, and then she almost fell over trying to right the chair. She wasn't thinking of the *thing* all that time, but she was aware that she was doing everything wrong because she was putting all her energy into avoiding thinking of the thing. She was in a kind of silent panic, feeling that at any second it might all come back, and she didn't know what she would do if that happened.

The December darkness also upset and disoriented her. The clouds were so thick that day that the sun never seemed fully present. If she stood up at her desk and looked over the cubicle divider, she could see a window and a piece of sky, but it wasn't worth the trouble because it was brighter inside the office. It even seemed more colorful in the office, even though the office furniture was black and the cubicle walls and work surfaces were a noncommittal color that was either light gray that had yellowed with age or light beige that had faded with age. She expected that the sky would brighten up at least a little bit as the day went on, but noon came and it was the same dark gray it had been at eight thirty. It was as if the sun hadn't actually risen but only skimmed along the horizon, like winter in Scandinavia.

And then so, *so* early, the sun started to go down. Alice couldn't stand the darkness, the colorlessness, the way the fluorescent lights made everything hideous. She considered going into the ladies' room to cry for a while but was too busy and just never got around to it. Then it was five o'clock. Her cubicle mate had a blurry black-and-white photocopy of Fred Flintstone sliding down the brontosaurus's neck push-pinned to the cubicle wall above the blue and white Chinese dish. Alice guessed it was supposed to be funny, but it just reminded her of traffic. "See you tomorrow!" her cube mate chirped, impossibly excited about life, and just about skipped toward the door. Alice sat down and cried a tiny bit before she clocked out, but then straightened herself up and walked very normally to her car in the dark, wet parking lot.

Though she loathed that office, the car was even worse. Her car was old and seemed to have invisible holes that other cars didn't have, holes that let in air and noise and moisture that better, newer cars sealed out. The sky, while churning its dreadful gray clouds, had also drizzled rain all day, and the cold, wet air had insinuated itself into those invisible holes, like tiny hands searching for something hidden. Now the cold and wet were everywhere, had contaminated every surface. When Alice got inside, the interior was as humid and cold as the open air, as if the car had been no shelter at all, and both her eyeglasses and the windshield fogged up immediately. And the fog was not the thin fog that appeared on windshields when it was freezing cold and disappeared after the defroster had blown on it for a few seconds. It was the thick condensation that came with rain and lingered long after the defroster started blowing hot. Alice knew she would have to wait a while for the windshield to clear, so she started wiping off her glasses with a tissue. But the tissue just smeared the moisture around. Eventually it started to come apart and leave tissue dust in the condensation, and when she put her glasses back on everything was in a haze and every light source had a halo that she knew would not go away until her commute was almost over.

Finally two sharp little peaks of clear glass appeared, right where the air first hit the windshield, so she prepared to pull out of her parking space. She wished she could sit quietly, wait for the air to heat up, and drive only once the windshield was perfectly clear, but she urgently wanted to join the line to get out of the bottleneck in the parking lot.

She was frightened as she backed out, and frightened as she semi-blindly joined the queue, and only felt the tiniest bit of comfort knowing that the windshield would be slightly clearer by the time she had sat through the two cycles of the red light it would take to get on the road. She turned on the radio and began tuning up the FM band as she waited. "The UCLA defense can't get off the field." Country music she didn't recognize. A breathy woman's voice singing something sentimental over synthesized music that sounded like 1986. Country. Country. The opening of "Stairway." Michael Jackson's "Man in the Mirror." Commercial—"brought to you by. . ." Someone talking about the Eagles. Something that sounded like techno but may have been a commercial. "The Humpty Dance." Talking that she didn't know what it was about. Some horrible sounding heavy metal thing with synthesizers. Something that was definitely from the 80s, with a high-pitched man's voice, but that she could not identify. Rolling Stones' "Shattered." A boring-sounding song she didn't recognize. "December 31st, Philly night life will change forever. For more information call. . ." "Cum on Feel the Noize."

The light changed. A group of cars escaped. A group of cars that included Alice's took its place. The light changed a second time, and she was on the road fighting blur, haze, oncoming headlights, intermittent wipers that left streaks and made ugly stuttering noises, bottlenecks, turn lanes that people were trying to get into or out of, two different freeways at a standstill, people getting into the lane that was moving only to have it stop. When she was two more lights and a right on red away from home, she was delayed by the *fucking asshole* who pulled out of the gas station in front of her and then went twenty miles an hour. But eventually she arrived.

She entered the house cautiously, afraid that something might have happened in her absence, but everything was silent and just how she left it. After she took her coat and boots off, she sat down and cried strenuously for two minutes. She still wouldn't let herself think of the thing, but she listened carefully for it between recovery sobs and heard nothing. This, however, did not put her at ease. Though it was pitch dark outside, it was still only five forty-five, so daytime activity was ongoing. The white noise it created acted as a sort of background radiation that filled in all the spaces where the sound she was so afraid of might actually be. She knew that she wouldn't really be able to hear the thing until the din of traffic died down and the night was quiet.

After she washed and dried her face, she ate a sad little sandwich with a tall glass of water and the TV on, and then all at once felt that she was too emotionally exhausted to do anything but rest. If the thing was out there, it was going to have to break down the back door and come inside before she was going to do anything about it. By 9:00 p.m., she was asleep.

Alice likely would have slept the whole night through, but the goddamn raccoons tipped the trash can, and that had her up and out of bed, moving timorously but purposefully. Fear and a diluted kind of desperation compelled her to address these situations immediately. She wasn't afraid of the raccoons—she had heard about raccoons that were aggressive, or would stand their ground, but the ones in her neighborhood politely ran away as soon as she opened the door. Instead she feared rabies, fleas, mites, and whatever other parasites and pathogens she might be exposed to while cleaning up after trash-eating outdoor animals. Sometimes she found it upsetting enough to cry over, depending on how messy things were in the driveway, and if she wanted to feel all right again, she needed a decent amount of time to clean herself up afterwards—she could practically feel the giant garbage can bacteria crawling around on her hands. She would feel rushed if she waited until morning, and the sleep she would get would be bitter and disturbed, so no matter how late it was, or how tired she was, she always opted to clean up right away and then try to salvage what remained of a night's sleep.

She was already in the driveway before she remembered what else she might find outside her house. The raccoons had scattered like a flock of big gray roaches, except for a little one that started to limp away but then climbed up a pathetic stick of a tree the neighbors had planted between the driveways. It wobbled back and forth in the crook of a branch that was roughly eye level to Alice, waiting to see what she might do. She looked it right in the eye for an uncomfortable amount of time. After a few seconds it seemed clear to her that they were each waiting for the other to make the next move, so Alice started cleaning up. She was in a full squat, pushing trash back into the can, when her head popped up as if she had heard something, though there had been no sound. It was as if she had received a signal through some kind of antenna that could sense change. She looked at the tree. The limping little raccoon had climbed down and gone off somewhere when she wasn't looking. Everything was silent and still except the wind. She turned around in a circle, pointing the flashlight everywhere that seemed relevant. There was nothing. Then she thought of the waste space in the backyard.

She cautiously approached the fence, shining the light over the grass, and saw several thick clumps of light-colored mud where there had only been grass before. She cautiously opened the gate and went into the yard. When she shone the light into the waste space, she saw what looked like the aftermath of an eruption. There was a cavernous void in the shape of a grave, but much larger. Modern graves in commercial cemeteries, she knew, were not actually six feet deep. They were only deep enough to cover the coffin. But this hole may have been as deep, and was definitely as wide as six feet, and it was much longer. The thing that had come out of it must have been immense. She could hear her heart beating and could feel it in the palms of her hands and the balls of her feet. Then she turned around. The clumps she had spotted from the driveway no longer appeared to be randomly distributed. From this angle they clearly formed a trail to the back of her house, to the bathroom window, which was *open*. The screen hadn't been raised or removed. It had simply been pushed in. There was mud all over what remained of the frame. She must have left the window unlocked the last time she opened it to listen to the noise in the backyard. And now the *thing* was in there.

Alice raced back through the gate and stumbled through the trash in the driveway. For a second she thought that something had caught her by the ankle but then she realized that her ankle had gotten wrapped up in the leg of her pants, the pants that she had shit in, bagged and tied up, and stuffed to the bottom of the can. The raccoons had torn the bag open, and now her pants were dragging behind her, following her down the driveway toward the street. Fear overcame disgust and shame, and she ripped them off her ankle, smearing a glob of cold shit on the back of her forearm as she ran. She tried to scream, but only a high little moan escaped from deep in her throat, and she very abruptly found herself at the bottom of the driveway, standing in the gutter. She turned and looked at the house. From the front, everything seemed perfectly normal. But the flashlight in her hand was suddenly very heavy, and she felt weak. She meant to sort of bend at the waist and catch her breath, but that led to half kneeling, which was very uncomfortable on the concrete, and soon she found herself sitting on the curb, waiting for she didn't know what.

Her options were limited. She couldn't go to a neighbor, half-dressed with shit on her arm, and ask them to call the police because there was a monster in her house. She also couldn't sit on the curb until the sun came up, hoping that the thing in her house would disappear at sunrise. Essentially all she could do was go inside and see what was there —*whether anything was there*, she tried to tell herself. But she knew very well that it was.

She may have sat there until morning, but soon she saw

a car's headlights coming down her street. It hadn't gotten any lighter outside, and there was no change in the quality of the darkness, but somehow, having seen headlights, she got the sense that despite the blackness it was actually morning rather than night. She started to feel the pressure of her job—of showering, of getting dressed, commuting, and earning her living. She couldn't go to work without sleep. She couldn't go to work without showering—most certainly not now—and she couldn't stay home without a good excuse. If she was going to be murdered by the thing, or gravely injured and sent to the hospital, she needed that to happen as soon as possible. She also didn't want to be seen by the driver, who was rapidly approaching, so she quickly went inside.

When she got inside she closed the door behind her and listened. She could hear nothing but her breathing. She was desperate for the ordeal to be over, so she pretended to herself that this was confirmation that there was nothing in the house, and pretended to be relieved. She attempted to go about her business under the auspices of this false confirmation, but soon found that she just couldn't pretend well enough. Her body was stiff. She was scared to get too far away from the front door or even turn toward the bathroom where she knew, deep inside, the thing was. She was all but paralyzed. She knew the sound of her breathing was masking the other sounds in the house. It took her almost thirty seconds to bring herself to stop breathing like that, but once she had, she knew immediately that the thing was in there. It almost seemed like it only started breathing when she stopped. And she could hear its mere existence. The thing had turned from dirt to mud in the daylong rain, and though it didn't actually drip audibly, it seemed to her that the wetness itself had a sound that she could hear under its muffled panting.

She couldn't stand here forever—this was the same stalemate as standing outside. She had to go in there and make something happen. She had the flashlight but didn't believe it would do her much good as a weapon, so she abandoned the idea of fighting in a real way. Instead she formulated a plan. She would find the thing and hit it with the flashlight, just to see if it was physically real. If it was, she would run outside screaming. People would hear her and call 911, the cops would come, and whatever was happening would get resolved. If it *wasn't* real, she wouldn't feel anything when she hit it, and could go to bed. In the morning she could find a shrink on her insurance provider's website, and whatever was happening would get resolved. She turned back for a second, opened the front door, and left the storm door slightly ajar. Feeling safer now that she had primed the exit behind her, she crept forward, toward the bathroom, where she knew it was waiting for her. She held the flashlight out in front of her, in her right hand, and advanced while turned sideways so that when it was time to run, she would only have to turn halfway around before she could sprint for the door.

She peered around the door jamb, and where she expected to see a threatening, monstrous thing, she instead saw what at first seemed like a mass of mud, a whole grave's worth, in a mound on her floor. She crept closer, still turned sideways, ready to bolt should it move, but it just lay there breathing and making wet sounds. She studied it for a while and soon could make out its thick, rough, human shape that had somehow been crudely cut out of the strange soil in the waste space. It had was leaking dark, transparent fluid that formed little pools in the patterns in the linoleum, and eddies where the water was still running. Of course, her bathroom rug was ruined.

Though she was terrified, Alice needed something to happen, so she started making noises to test how alert it was. "Hey," she whispered, but it did not respond. She thought for a bit, and whispered, "What are you?" but apparently not loudly enough to be heard. Eventually she tired from standing so still, and from fatigue she accidentally tapped the wall with the flashlight. The thing's head moved in the unmistakable way that a living thing's head moves when it hears a sound it wants to identify. This sent her running to the front door, where she held her breath for a long while, half indoors and half out, waiting for it to follow her, but it did not come.

She thought of her plan but could not bring herself to run outside screaming. It just wasn't in her to make a scene, or disturb people. She almost thought it would be arrogant —pompous—for her to expect other people to wake up, get out of their beds, and run to her aid or call the police and entangle themselves in an hours-long event that profited them nothing. Why should they involve themselves in her drama? What right did she have to expect anything from strangers?

Finally she called, "I know you're there." Nothing. "*I know you're there*," she said somewhat louder. This time the thing responded physically to her voice. It sounded like it was moving. She thought it may have been trying to stand, because now she could hear water dripping off it, like a wet towel had been hung up. She backed a little farther out the door and involuntarily took deep breaths, terrified that it would come charging after her any second. But still it did not come. There was only the sound of wet mud, of water streaming down through the loose material.

When Alice made her way back to the bathroom, the thing was standing upright, as she thought it might be. What she did not anticipate was that it was facing the mirror with its back to her. She could discern no facial expression from this angle in the dark, and could infer nothing about its attitude from its posture. It simply stood there, a massive hulking golem that barely fit in her bathroom, expressing nothing, betraying nothing, only looking neutrally into the mirror, like an object that had been placed there by an outside force.

It had been standing quite still, but it awkwardly turned toward her at the same time that she heard a loud sound, which she realized a second later was her own scream. Alice backed up against the wall and took the thing in fully. It was a foot and a half taller than her and more massive than any man. Its body was mud and rocks and thin, sickly, dead roots, but mostly the strange, light-colored soil that reminded her so much of charcoal ashes. It was a thing beyond death, that wore an expression of deep and horrifying sorrow, a thing devolved, corroded, discarded and left to rot in the mud of the past, forgotten by everything now living.

The thing started moving toward her, and she found that she could not carry out her plan. Instead of running outside, instead of screaming and praying the neighbors would wake up and take the trouble to help or call the police, she just stood there watching it advance. She couldn't even turn away. She just closed her eyes and flattened herself against the wall, as if moving back that extra centimeter would put her out of its reach. The thing put its hands on her. It was as shockingly cold as the winter rain that had fallen all day. Murky water so cold that she couldn't believe wasn't frozen dripped down her shirt. Her body contorted before she consciously registered how cold it was, but she did not try to twist out of the thing's grasp. Instead she accepted her fate and mildly lamented the fact that not only was she going to be murdered, she was also going to be horribly uncomfortable while it happened. *Some girls get murdered in bed.* But the thing stopped. It loomed over her like a storm cloud, emanating moist, frigid air. It was silent at first, but then it began to make a noise. The noise was indecipherable, jagged and raspy, like something just starting to fry in grease, but soon Alice could tell the thing was repeating itself. She was able to distinguish each iteration of the only syllable it seemed able to say—*why?*

Alice heard it again and something in her changed. Before she realized what she was doing, she tore at it. She tore at its arms and they fell apart, slipped through her fingers, just handfuls of mud that fell in formless chunks to the floor. She ripped at its shoulders, raking her fingers down through them, and it bled rivulets of hideous brown water and shed massive gobs of itself – it seemed to be dissolving almost on its own. She was elbow-deep in its chest when she undermined its structure and the upright bulk of the thing came down on her. A grave-sized mass of mud that had risen and come looking for her now knocked her to the floor and covered her entirely. She struggled with the remains of the thing—clots of mud, stones, roots, ancient skeletal leaves, unidentifiable organic material. She pushed it off her body and finally raised herself and stood unsteadily against the wall. The thing had lost whatever spirit had animated it. It lay still, inert and depersonalized, no longer anything but mud.

Alice had no idea what to do. She couldn't shower. The mud on her was so thick it would clog the drain. It was in her hair, all over the lenses and frame of her glasses. She couldn't imagine how to get mud out of the hinges or even where to start wiping off the lenses without scratching them. The mud was so thick that she couldn't wash these clothes. They would have to go into the trash with her other clothes that, she realized just now, were still in the driveway. She couldn't leave the bathroom hall because she would track mud all through the house. She was stuck and so frustrated she couldn't even cry. She just stood there in the watery mud that was seeping into her carpet and shivered convulsively in the numbing cold.

Finally, Alice took her dripping clothes off and made her way to the kitchen, retrieved the key for the lock on the shed, and went out to it just as she was. In the darkness she could make out almost nothing but knew approximately where the shovels—all left behind by the previous owner—might be, so she stumbled in that direction, taking comfort only in that it was far too cold for spiders. She selected the one with the squared-off head, made her way back inside, and began shoveling the mud out through the bathroom window, shivering, completely naked, on a December night. This she did in silence but for her sniffing and heavy breathing until it was legitimately morning, signaled only by the increasing number of cars hissing by on the freeway two miles off.

By that point the bulk of the dirt was gone, but the shovel had gouged and scratched the linoleum beyond repair, and there was still a layer of mud left. She would have to get down on her hands and knees and scrape it up with a butter knife or some smaller instrument. Even in the cleanest spots there was a thick, shovel-resistant film of brown that looked like it could never be removed, only smeared around into different concentrations. She felt certain that she could go through an entire twelve-roll package of paper towels trying to get the film off and there would still be residue in the cracks and around the baseboards. The hall carpet was ruined, too, and she couldn't possibly afford to have it replaced, so she would just have to live the rest of her life with a huge shit-brown stain outside her bathroom door. She comforted herself with the thought that once it completely dried out, she could potentially make some progress vacuuming it up over a series of weeks or months, but deep down she didn't really think that would work. She believed her house was ruined.

Her alarm went off at 6:00 a.m. because it had been set to go off at that time every day, but she wasn't going in to work. She called her supervisor's number without even having a lie ready to tell, but because she had had very little sleep and had been naked and cold and laboring like a ditch digger for over three hours, she sounded bad enough that very few questions were asked and genuine concern was shown. When the sun started to come up, she again remembered that the pants she had shit in, and the trash the raccoons had spread all over her driveway, were still in plain sight. That became her top priority. Carpet be damned, she got some dirty clothes out of the hamper to put on her filthy and now sweaty and cold body for long enough to step outside and pick everything up. She would have to do this very quickly as there was still mud all over her face and hair, arms, everywhere. *What would people think?* She managed to stuff everything back in the can with no bags and no care—she would have to live with the garbage men seeing her shitty pants—and got back inside just before her neighbor came outside to walk her golden retriever.

At this point she took stock. There was no way she could shower like this. There were still hours of cleaning ahead before she would be able to get into her bed without completely ruining the sheets. She would have to keep cleaning the bathroom, and then do a cursory cleaning of her own body, like rinsing dishes before putting them into a dishwasher, before she could shower. But she was utterly exhausted. She tried to cry for a little while but was unable. Instead she closed the bathroom window, lay down on the brown stain on the carpet, and shivered in her third set of ruined clothes, hoping to sleep even for just a few minutes. But there was no sleep for Alice Binderman.

By that afternoon, she had gotten things clean enough that she could move around the house without spreading the mud any farther and had managed to shower, but there was still so much to do. First order of business was to get some new glasses. She was careful enough with glasses that she never needed a spare pair, and though she had kept her old ones like she was supposed to, she couldn't find them. She had run her glasses under the faucet for she didn't know how long, and luckily they had cleaned up some, but the arms could no longer bend without grinding due to the grit in the hinges, and the lenses were more scratched than was acceptable. She also had a serious concern about the shower drain. Toward the end of her shower, the water started circling the drain slowly in a way that she felt was a warning that it wouldn't take much more mud or even water. But the glasses had to be first. As long as she had to use these glasses, she would be in trouble.

The goddamned optometrist refused to make new glasses for her without a visit and eye exam, but luckily he was able to squeeze her in for an appointment that same day at three thirty. The waiting room at his office was also a showroom for frames, so she felt uncomfortable and like she was in the way as more affluent people tried on frames they were clearly choosing because of how they looked rather than because they would be fully covered by insurance. She wound up having to wait until long after three thirty to be seen but didn't feel entitled to complain because she was being squeezed in as a favor. As she waited she couldn't help but dwell on how expensive it would be to get a plumber to fix her drain, but then it occurred to her that she was going to have to select new frames just like the affluent people. She got up and started to look so she could have something cheap picked out by the time her exam was finished, but the very moment she stood up, the nurse called her name and she had to go back into the exam room.

When she finally got out of the doctor's office, it was four fifty-five. Alice was about to enter into the deepest segment of rush hour traffic on a day that was threatening snow, when it was already virtually dark. She had dilated eyes, and glasses that were so finely and thoroughly scratched that everything was already blurry. She wanted very badly to cry but could not. She wanted very badly to scream, but the best she could do was to breathe heavily. She wanted very badly to call a cab and leave her car in the optometrist's parking lot, but that would only create additional complications. She wanted very badly to call out of work again tomorrow, but without a doctor's note her company's sick-day policy would not accommodate that. As much as she hated the idea, the only thing she could do was to drive home. If there was an accident and she survived, then she could get a doctor's note that no one could argue with. She felt a bit of relief knowing she would solve this either way until she remembered that she would still have to call a plumber. That made her nervous, and she kept checking her pulse—she considered a heart attack an acceptable solution too.

Alice was only partially relieved to get home, knowing that more problems awaited her, the most pressing and expensive of which was getting a plumber. She did not feel capable of inventing a lie to explain to the plumber the huge stain on the carpet, the ruined window screen, or the dirt everywhere. But Alice was a morning shower person. She had to shower in the morning or she felt impossibly dirty and greasy and gross for the whole day, and that was more discomfort than she could accept after what she had just been through. If she had to go to work, she had to shower in the morning. And *full shower*. She could not abide a whore bath, no matter how thorough. So she called.

To Alice's great surprise, the plumber's answering service picked up and did not act as though this were an unheard-of request. As if it were routine they said they would send someone, and not at some remote future date but within a couple hours. When she hung up she briefly grinned and shook her little fists with a tightly contained glee. She could not believe this was happening. She had done things. She had fought off and seemingly killed the *thing* from the waste space, she had shoveled its remains out the window and cleaned up the majority of the residue, she had gotten new glasses (not *gotten* them, but had them coming), she had driven home under appalling conditions, and now a plumber was coming. It was as if things were going right—or had gone horribly wrong but *she had the power to right them*. When the plumber came, he didn't comment at all about the stain, her appearance, the size of her pupils, the screen, the house, or anything else. He quoted her a price, snaked the drain, ran her credit card, and was gone, leaving her completely alone.

It was 9:00 p.m. Now that she knew she could stop working for the first time in eighteen hours, a profound exhaustion came over her, and the only thing more powerful than that exhaustion was hunger. She noticed just now that she hadn't eaten or drank anything at all in that eighteen hours. Nothing. She immediately had two glasses of water, which in a few minutes time cleared up a headache she hadn't realize that she had, and then set about making herself dinner. This being done, she ate quickly, steadily, and when her dinner itself was gone she found herself staring into the cabinet looking for something salty and filled with carbs. After eating the remainder of a box of Wheat Thins so quickly that she was out of breath by the end, she made her way to the couch where she lay down and, after some brief adjustments, knew that she would not get up again until morning, even with all the lights still on. There was nothing important enough to move her out of this perfect position, that could rouse her from the depths of the warm couch cushions. And then she was out.

Alice woke about six hours later and was not sure why. Had something fallen? She was still exhausted and found it difficult to even raise her head. At first she thought it was due to the lights being on but found that she could nod off for a few minutes before being startled awake again. Something was happening. When she was finally awake for real rather than just drifting in and out, she realized that there was a sound. It was a hushed sound, something between the wind blowing and leaves rustling. She listened carefully for a long while, trying to decide whether it was wind or something else, and it struck her that she had heard that sound before. That exact strange, quiet, but very persistent, unchanging sound, like a branch in the wind. Alice stood up and held her breath, but it sounded like she was still breathing. She felt a chill all over that she could not suppress, and as it moved through her body, she executed a little involuntary contortion so violent that it hurt her back. It couldn't be. The thing had dissolved into nothing and had to be shoveled out through the window. *The window*—she had unlocked it days ago to listen to the sound in the yard, and she had closed it again after she had stopped shoveling, but she never locked it again.

Alice ran into the bathroom, but it was too late. The thing was forcing its upper body through the window, which it had crookedly pushed up, and it was looking her right in the eye. The thing was different now. It no longer seemed bewildered like a newborn creature. It was not looking around confoundedly or hypnotized by its reflection in the mirror. It seemed to see Alice in a tight focus, certain that she was the one it was coming for. And it was more agile than it had been, and more potent. Even perched on the window frame, pulling its massive bulk forward, it seemed poised and strong, more like a big cat in a tight spot than a toddler about to fall. It was bigger, and its face had changed. There was anger in its expression, and determination. Just looking at it was a revelation—she knew for certain that no matter how she tried to stop the thing, it would prevail. It would not be stopped.

Alice took a few steps toward the window—a token effort to fight—but when she saw how its eyes followed her, her body failed like a defective part, and she crumpled to the floor. She was so frightened of the thing that she did not dare rise to her feet to run but crawled on her hands and knees toward the door. She let out a brief scream, but it did not leave. It *would* not leave. She wept openly as she crawled into her bedroom, where she locked the door and pushed her nightstand across the doorway. But she could hear that the thing was still coming and knew that it would come in here too. She sat in a corner of the room, drew her knees up to her chest, wrapped her arms around them, and tried to compose herself, to bravely face the thing that was coming, to accept with equanimity that it was here now, and that she would have to live with it. Or if it ultimately killed her, to accept that, too.

5

DISAPPEARING

The Pennsylvania Turnpike seems interminable, and other than the familiar blue-and-yellow Sunoco stations every fifty miles or so, there is little that hints of civilization or safety. Starting from the Pittsburgh side isn't as bad because the Turnpike cuts through or skirts several towns, which gives you the security of knowing you are reasonably proximate to other living humans. Sometimes you can even see them. But starting from the Philadelphia side is stomach-churningly inhospitable. Once you're out of King of Prussia and you get past the boxy, barn-like Lockheed-Martin buildings, you're effectively nowhere for the better part of two hours before you get to Harrisburg, which disappears behind you surprisingly quickly. Then you start passing places like Valley Forge National Park, State Game Lands Number 52, State Game Lands Number 46, State Game Lands Number 156, State Game Lands Number 145, State Game Lands Number 246, and State Game Lands Number 169. Then you go through a series of tunnels that go underneath or through Blue Mountain, Allegheny Mountain, Tuscarora Mountain, and Kittatinny Mountain, after which you're just north of Cowans Gap State Park and State Game Lands Number 53 —and then you start getting into some fairly rural areas.

But even though you're passing these places, mostly what you're looking at are trees and rocks in different configurations. Sometimes just trees. Sometimes trees with some gray-blue rocks sticking out of the ground. Sometimes trees and blue-gray rocks on a hill. Sometimes just rocks on a hill, or just trees on a hill. Sometimes giant Himalayan-style mountains with a few trees. Sometimes you're driving along the edge of a cliff, and you mainly see trees and gray-blue rocks that are far away, where the land seems to begin again after an impossible gap. Often there are hills on both sides, so you seem to be driving longways through a tiny valley, or along a weird U-shaped channel. It's surreal and claustrophobic and irritating because you eventually start to feel that there's no end. But in certain circumstances you still have to take the Pennsylvania Turnpike. There's no getting around it, for instance, when you're moving from Philadelphia to Columbus, Ohio, so obviously that was the way they came. Kylie and Jack.

They started at five in the morning, when it was still nighttime dark, and were nowhere by daybreak. But they were not uncomfortable. They had a lot to say to each other in the way new couples had a lot to report about the past and discuss at length even though they were not a new couple—they had been together for three years already.

Kylie had taken many road trips with a woman she used to work for, had been everywhere in the tri-state area, and liked to tell stories about that. Once they went to New Jersey to repair costumes for a local production of *My Fair Lady*, and they saw a giant rat in the parking lot outside their motel eating something that hadn't quite made it into the dumpster. Her boss acted like nothing was going on, but Kylie screamed her head off, and she couldn't eat for the rest of the trip. The next day she passed out from low blood sugar and fell onto a stitch ripper, cut herself, and bled all over one of the costumes. The actors and even the wardrobe people were really cool about it, but the director fired them and claimed he was going to sue them, and they never got paid.

Jack's stories were mainly about the progression of his delinquency through various age brackets, which he marked in academic terms. In middle school, he would sneak out at night to shoot car windows with a BB gun. He said there was something satisfying about the crash of the glass, hitting his mark from cover, then sneaking away unseen, unheard. Eventually he had shot out so many windows that there was a brief report about it on the local news, and even though he was just a stupid middle school kid, they never caught him. In high school, he was a pot dealer and once got pulled over with three ounces in the center console, which made the whole interior smell like fresh, unburned weed. The cop signaled to Jack that he could smell it but only wrote him a speeding ticket and let him go, which he explained was the first time he was really cognizant of white privilege. In college, he enacted all the college drinking clichés with only a few individualizing flourishes, and he told Kylie about them. This basic kind of storytelling went on for hours, and they were content with it. It wasn't so much that the stories made them content— the stories weren't that good—they just enjoyed each other, loved each other in the way that couples love each other in the beginning, before bitterness overwhelms them.

The problem for Kylie and Jack was that when they mapped their trip from Philly to Columbus, the Turnpike itself appeared to be the bulk of it. It just looked that way on the monitor because Pennsylvania was one long, approximately rectangular block, and that weird horn of West Virginia stuck up between Pennsylvania and Ohio and broke things up visually. Plus the more symmetrical squarish or pentagonal shape of Ohio masked how wide it was and made the second leg of the trip seem shorter. But in fact the second leg, starting from New Stanton, where they would get off 76 and get on 70 to continue west, was almost the same distance as the first leg. And in actual experience the landscape seemed to confirm the deceptive impression one got from the map. Whereas the Pennsylvania Turnpike was mountainous, forested, and claustrophobic, Ohio was only briefly hilly before flattening out for a time and making the horizon almost visible. Once literally out of the woods, it was lighter, sunnier. It seemed that, having arrived somewhere visibly and objectively different, your destination must be close. The hours that followed were frustratingly long and inexplicable.

Jack had made the trip once before and knew that it was deceptive. He had endured all of Pennsylvania before he stopped for the first time at the West Virginia "Welcome Area," which was really just a parking lot and a bathroom, and he felt as though he had effectively arrived, that he had only the rest of that weird West Virginia spike and then half of Ohio to go. And then he drove four more hours, thinking every time he saw an exit or a sign of civilization that he must be almost to Columbus. But he was still nowhere.

Eventually, this cycle of anticipation and disappointment built up a kind of frustrated exhaustion, which made him feel like he was never going to get anywhere. Kylie was not prepared for this, and though she listened to Jack when he told her and understood in the abstract, it hadn't sunken in.

Kylie got jittery right around the time they reached New Stanton, and when they finally did get off 76 and onto 70 she was slightly giddy. "We're almost there!"

"We're really not."

She frowned playfully at him.

"Seriously. It's going to be four or five hours."

"No, it's not," she said and smirked. Kylie was so tiny that she could comfortably sit cross-legged in the bucket seat. She folded her hands over her crossed legs and turned to look out the window. She had a way of simply denying facts she didn't like or that didn't fit her plans and proceeding as if her denial unraveled them. She was trying to do this now. But she only gave the appearance of smug calm. Inside she was troubled. When, after an hour, they were still in Pennsylvania, not even to West Virginia yet, she found that she needed to be out of the car.

"I want to be somewhere that's not a gas station. I've seen enough potato chip bags and three-year-old trail mix in those weird plastic tubes. They look like giant fucking condoms. My grandma would slap me if she saw me pouring nuts into my mouth out of a dick-shaped bag. If she were alive. It's not ladylike. We should get off at an exit, find an actual restaurant, and sit down for a while."

"OK. We can do that."

"You don't want to."

Jack said nothing.

"Why not?"

"Look." Long pause. "We don't really know where we are. If we just get off somewhere, there may not be a restaurant there. We may just wind up in the fucking hills or something."

"They're not going to build an off-ramp into the hills."

"You're right. That's sensible. OK." Another long pause. "But you realize that the longer we linger, the longer it'll be before we get there. We still have like four hours to go. If we stop for an hour or so, it'll then be five hours before we get there. And of course that means that we'll miss our first appointment. I mean . . . are you OK with that?" They had appointments with property managers all lined up so they could look at apartments after they checked into their hotel. They were both anxious to keep them.

She wasn't OK with missing them but said "Can we please stop?" anyway.

They had just passed through the town of Claysville, but they didn't know that. It was the middle of summer, all the trees were thick with bright green leaves, and they couldn't see through the greenbelt. Or in the few places where they could, what they saw looked less like a town and more like a suburban neighborhood that had installed itself into a hillside. But soon after Kylie asked to stop, they saw a sign that said EXIT 6, 231, CLAYSVILLE. When they got off, it was pretty desolate. There was an Exxon station and a long two-lane road with nothing but trees in one direction and a Cycle and ATV Super Store in the other direction.

They pulled into the gas station. "I'm going to fill this thing up," he said. "Which way do you think is our best bet to find someplace to eat?" He pointed both ways down the road. Jack was trying to be compassionate, but the circumstances made the question sarcastic anyway.

Kylie covered her face with her hands for a two-second beat. "Let's just get something here and then keep going."

Jack got out and started filling the tank. "I'm going to see if they have a bathroom at this place."

"When you get back please tell me the bathroom's not disgusting so I can go too."

She watched him for a couple seconds as he walked inside and then turned her head. It was Tuesday, July 31, 2007 at 10:17 a.m., and it was the last time Kylie ever saw Jack.

She opened her door and put the seat back all the way down to try to get as comfortable as possible while the leftover cold air mingled with the outdoor heat. She was trying not to cry. After a while the gas pump stopped. She got up, put the nozzle back, got the receipt, screwed the gas cap on until she heard three clicks, closed the weird little gas tank door, and lay down again. It was getting so hot that she wanted to turn the car back on, but Jack had taken the keys so she had to suffer, sticking to the cloth seat, periodically licking the salty sweat off her upper lip. She lay there long enough that her comfortable position became uncomfortable, but she didn't move. She wanted Jack to come back and find her the way she was. She wanted to express that she was suffering by the position of her body, because that way she wouldn't have to take responsibility for saying it, which would make her feel like a child. For his part, Jack had known that she was suffering but couldn't do anything about it. They were on the road. And he certainly couldn't do anything about it now that he was gone.

For a while, Kylie thought that Jack must have been having stomach trouble, but all at once it occurred to her that too much time had passed even for that. Something was definitely wrong. She was halfway to the door of the gas station when the attendant—a tall, thick, African-American man with a gray baseball cap with a capital G on the front—came outside. "Did that guy come here with you?" They understood who they were talking about.

"Yeah. Where is he?"

"He went into the bathroom."

"But that was like fifteen minutes ago."

"It was nearly thirty minutes ago," he said.

They knocked on the bathroom door, tried to talk through it, but there was no answer at all. The door was made of several plies of thick sheet metal and had a big satin-textured stainless steel door knob on it, so there was no breaking in, and the attendant, Alan Turner, didn't have the key. After forty minutes had passed, Alan called the manager, Harrison Payne, but it turned out that he didn't have the key either. He told Alan to call the police and that he would be right down.

The Donegal Township Police department was just on the other side of the turnpike, so they were on scene in a few minutes, and just a few minutes after that the fire department was there to open the door. But Jack was not inside. The police, led by sergeant Thomas Moore, did a cursory search of the area and found nothing except the Honda CRF450X that police suspected had been stolen from the Cycle and ATV Super Store down the road two months prior by a Claysville teenager named Ethan Coe . It looked like he, or someone, had crashed it behind the gas station, not a quarter mile away from the store, and had left it hidden in the tall grass. But there was no Jack.

Alan Turner was interrogated aggressively and threatened off the record until the police had time to go through the security footage, which cleared Alan completely and provided zero clues as to Jack's whereabouts. It showed that Alan was the only other person who had used that bathroom that day and had not been in there for two hours before Jack's arrival. It showed Jack enter the store, speak to Alan briefly, then go into the bathroom. After a while Alan knocked on the door and spoke. After that, he went outside and returned with Kylie. All his movements were accounted for. There were some subtle and very brief variations in the light levels on the tape, and they looked a little strange, but there were no missing frames—the perfect continuity of the time stamp proved that. Alan was not involved, and Jack had not left the room.

The bathroom itself was investigated closely. There were no windows. There was only one door. There were no hidden entrances. The air-conditioning vent was too narrow for Jack to fit through, but they unscrewed the vent and checked inside anyway. The dust showed that no one had been through it, but they followed it to its source. They found nothing. The exhaust fan in the ceiling pushed air through a pipe that was no bigger around than Kylie's forearm and led to an exhaust vent on the roof that was screened in, and the screens were intact. By all appearances Jack had simply disappeared.

Washington County police were called in. They brought their K-9 units with both German shepherds and bloodhounds. They could only track Jack to the bathroom. One of the hounds sat right down on the tile floor and didn't want to go any further, or even get up. Beyond that the hounds found no scent trail. They took the dogs through the woods behind the Exxon, eventually emerging in people's backyards or on cleared property owned by businesses. They searched houses and yards. Advanced Oilfield Services, which was just Northwest of the Exxon, had a stabilization pond. The police dragged it and searched all the buildings on the property, but found nothing.

Kylie didn't hold up well through this. She spent a lot of time crying at the police station, and when the sun went down she got a room at the Montgomery Mansion Bed and Breakfast, the only hotel anywhere near the Exxon, and spent the rest of the night crying there. Jack had taken the car keys with him, so the police had to drive her, and they came back the next morning to bring her back to the police station to wait for the outcome of the search, but there was no outcome. She waited there all day and was told periodically that they still hadn't found him but to hold on because they would and that he had to be somewhere.

On day three the FBI, Jack's parents, and Kylie's mother all showed up within an hour of each other. The FBI asked her all the same questions the police had asked, but didn't appear to do anything else. Jack's parents, who had never much liked her, questioned her as often as the police did and looked at her resentfully, as though it was her fault, even though they were moving to Ohio because of *his* job. Her mother was very quiet and just tried to keep Kylie calm.

For a while there was a lot of noise about this in Claysville. Jack's disappearance was not explainable. There were discussions about UFOs and meth dealers in the woods—neither of which had been spotted—but there was no satisfying explanation of where he went or how. The bathroom had been locked from the inside, and the videotape showed him going in there. He had to have disappeared *in there somewhere*. That wasn't possible, but no one had any good ideas. They only had goofy ones, like there was a secret door in there somewhere and that Jack had stumbled into it. What happened from there varied from person to person and telling to telling. The door led to a tunnel that had been created by meth dealers or junk dealers, like those tunnels from Mexico to California, and Jack had been killed by dealers who were less than happy to find him in there. Or the tunnel actually led below ground and Jack had lost his way or fell into a nineteenth-century mine shaft. Or the tunnel had been used by human traffickers, and Jack had walked into slavery. But there was no evidence for any of this. The police had searched every square millimeter of that bathroom, and then the FBI did the same thing. Some kid wasn't likely to find a secret door that they couldn't. And yet the explanation that he *had disappeared*, not in the sense of just going missing but in the literal sense, obviously didn't stick either. Claysville was willing to consider many different things, but literal disappearance wasn't one of them.

Soon the commotion faded away. Kylie and her mother stayed in town, but no new information came to light. The police told them they would be notified if they found anything, but there were no notifications, and the police checked in less and less frequently. At the end of two weeks, there was still no sign of Jack, so Kylie and her mother quietly packed up and went home to Philly. They did not return.

Jack's parents stayed in town twice that long. His mother, Dolores, was tireless and searched everything again —the whole area behind the gas station, the woods, and all the property up to Advanced Oilfield Services. She lobbied to have the stabilization pond dragged again—and it was— but Jack was not there. She was reduced to wandering through nearby neighborhoods, knocking on doors, asking whoever answered if they had heard or seen anything. The people of Claysville looked at her sadly and said no, they had seen nothing, heard nothing. It had been Dolores' plan to put together all the events of the day and come up with a narrative that would at least lead to an idea of what might have happened, but to her great frustration there were no events. Or there was only one—Jack went into the bathroom. Eventually, even Dolores gave up. She had met dead ends everywhere, and she couldn't stand to wander around Claysville anymore, looking broken, begging people to tell her anything about that night, her husband following her solemnly, looking at the ground. So they packed up and went home, too.

The FBI was keeping tabs on the police case, but the police had nothing, so they stopped looking and waited for information to come in. None did. No witnesses came forward, and there were no anonymous tips. It was just quiet. People remembered what happened, but no one in town knew him—no one had even seen him except Alan Turner—so Jack was just a name on a roster of missing persons. After a while he wasn't even a reason to stay away from the gas station anymore. People were still a little nervous going there, but it was the most convenient place to get gas on the way to work in the morning, and they figured as long as they stayed out of the bathroom there was no danger. And it turned out that was true. No one else went missing, and after ten years no one even talked about the disappearance anymore.

But there were strange things that went on. Alan Turner kept his job, as it was clear that he had nothing to do with Jack's disappearance, but he didn't keep it for long. He told his sister, Rose, that he sometimes heard things. A couple times when it was quiet and he was alone in the store, he heard a faint voice, "The way you can just barely hear a voice through a wall sometimes," he told her. He had gotten into the habit of turning the radio off and listening carefully all day, *trying* to hear that voice, though, he told Rose, it almost never worked that way. The voice came when it wanted to and not when it didn't. He even tried yelling to it, the way you would yell to a person trapped in rubble, but he never heard anything back. When Rose suggested that he was just hearing things and scaring himself because it was dark outside, he dismissed that. "It's not always dark. Sometimes it is. Maybe it's more noticeable then—late— because it's quieter and there's less background noise to drown it out. But sometimes it's in the middle of the day. And I'm not scared. I *want* to hear the voice. I want to know what it's saying. What he has to say about where he is, wherever that may be."

Alan began petitioning Harrison Payne to keep the station open overnight, arguing that they could potentially do some business late. He volunteered to work the 10:00 p.m.–6:00 a.m. shift he was proposing, but Harrison was not open to it. When Alan closed up at night, he turned the radio off and took his time, but there was only so much to do and so much time he could stand around listening, mopping the floor, washing out coffee pots and so on, and he never left later than ten thirty. Soon, Alan's brother-in-law offered him a job that paid so much more that he couldn't turn it down, so he quit the Exxon, and that was the end of it for him. But it continued for others.

Eight months after Alan quit, a new employee, Theresa Mitchell, started work and immediately had experiences that she couldn't explain. When she was left alone there for the first time, she felt sure that Harrison had driven away and then somehow came back to watch her, to see how she would do by herself or whether she would steal. She felt this so strongly that she didn't bother trying to confirm it. She just somehow knew that another person was in the building with her. Just where this person was she didn't know, but she thought that maybe there was an office she hadn't seen yet, a small room in the back or something, where he was hiding. Eventually she found this exhausting because she felt like she had to pretend to be working every single moment. A big part of working at a gas station is standing around, waiting for people to come in, and when they don't, there's only so much work to do before you read or talk on the phone or stare out the window. Theresa, afraid to lose her job and certain she was being watched, kept making up work to do—counting the cigarettes over and over, and so on. The next day she asked another employee, Jessica Patterson, how long Harrison was going to keep watching her. Jess was confused, so Theresa explained. Jess told her there was no office except the one behind the register, and there were no rooms other than what she could see. She didn't think Jess had lied to her, but that night Theresa felt the same way, and just as strongly. She looked everywhere but found no one and no hidden offices. The gas station really was as plain and boring as it looked.

After a week of feeling like this, Theresa was convinced that if it wasn't Harrison, someone else must be watching her, that some stalker had found out that a woman was working there alone at night and was planning to rob or rape her or both, so she asked her boyfriend, Troy, to sit with her. But Troy quickly became restless, and she didn't feel any safer with him there, so he was dismissed.

After that, she noticed some other strange things happening. She started seeing flashes of light the way she did once when she had cyclitis and had to go on prednisone. They couldn't give her antibiotics because the infection that caused it was viral, so she just had to suffer until it went away, and she had all types of strange problems with her vision. When she moved her head too fast, or just before or after she blinked, she saw flashes of light, like someone took a picture, only not as bright and of shorter duration. She was afraid that the cyclitis might have come back because, of course, she had the virus forever. But being bored to death in a Claysville gas station, she had a lot of time to pay attention to what was actually happening, and she noticed that sometimes there would be a flash when she hadn't blinked or moved at all. There was just a flash for no discernable reason.

She thought maybe the fluorescent lights were flickering until just by chance there was a flash when she was looking right at them. She saw clearly that they didn't change in intensity. The light was coming from elsewhere, but it didn't seem to be coming from anywhere in particular. It was as if the air itself sort of lit up. She remembered hearing on TV that you couldn't actually *see* lightning, or electricity of any kind, that when enough energy was applied to a gas, the gas itself would emit photons, or light. That was what you saw when lightning flashed, rather than electricity itself. She wondered now if there was some kind of high voltage situation, but Harrison assured her that wasn't possible.

Like everyone from Claysville, Theresa knew about Jack, so she developed a cautious little suspicion and would sometimes test it. She had never played with a Ouija board, but she knew from TV how it was done, and though she never actually went so far as to buy or make one herself, she started to ask questions out loud, to see whether anything would happen. And sometimes things did happen. It started when she was closing on a Wednesday night. She had seen an inordinate number of flashes on that shift, and as soon as the clock struck ten and she locked the door, she said, "I'm getting the fuck out of here. Fuck this place. You going to miss me?" And the light flashed. Theresa had a lot to do and was in a hurry—she had to count the drawer and the cigarettes, run the reports, and drop the money in the safe—so she didn't stop to consider the flash. But it briefly registered with her that it had happened. She felt like it was probably a coincidence that it flashed at that exact moment, but she remembered it the next night, and started asking questions.

"Are you that guy?"

Flash.

"Why are you here?"

Nothing.

"Are you dead?"

Flash.

"Where are you? Where's your body?"

Nothing.

"Did someone kill you?"

Nothing.

"How did you die?"

Nothing.

"Is your name Jack?"

Flash.

"Holy shit." She had scared herself and spent the rest of the shift pretending that she wasn't seeing the subtle flashing and trying not to ask it questions even in her mind. She was convinced, though, that if she had made herself a Ouija board that she could have talked to him. She didn't work there much longer.

A few years later, a teenager named Charles Boyd said he was quitting because "Shit moves around in there, dude. For real." The incidents he was referring to were not of the floating refrigerator type, but regardless of how small the movements were, and the insignificance of the objects, things did move. Charles was sure.

Though he wasn't much of a talker, or a very good one, Charles had an excellent memory. He wasn't eidetic or a savant, but he had a greater than average talent for recalling exact details, which meant that he could also recall, among other things, exact arrangements and spatial relations of things on a shelf or a countertop. Whereas Alan Turner and Theresa Mitchell might not have noticed if things moved a very short distance, or may have noticed but thought nothing of it or assumed that their eyes or memories were playing tricks, Charles knew when something moved a few centimeters or even when its orientation changed just a bit —if it turned just a centimeter clockwise, for instance. And he was sure that this happened frequently and that it happened *"exspecially"* to items near the bathroom.

There was one incident in which he left a soda on the counter next to the register, and when he came back it was, he estimated, almost three inches closer to the edge of the counter. But other than that, almost everything that moved was on the shelves back near the bathroom. The store was rectangular. The cash register and checkout counter were on the west side of the rectangle where there were wire racks stocked with gum and candy, and the entrance was in approximately the southwest corner. On the north wall, in order from west to east, was another counter with coffee pots, a microwave, a small freezer section, and a series of shelves containing, from bottom to top, antifreeze, windshield washer fluid, transmission fluid, motor oil, a display of windshield wipers, Rain-X, ice-scrapers, and gloves. This was the critical shelf—east of it, with the door facing south, was the infamous bathroom. The central floor space was occupied by three aisles of junk food and one aisle of rudimentary auto maintenance and repair stuff—fuel injector cleaner, power steering fluid, Fix-A-Flat, and so on. The eastern wall was all refrigerated soft drinks, and the southern wall was glass that faced the pumps and the road.

It was accepted at the Claysville Exxon that the windshield wiper display was going to fall down from time to time, and the countenanced explanation was that whatever dumbass installed the housing had installed it crooked. Rather than trying to fix it, they propped a jug of antifreeze under it, which kept it up most of the time. When it did fall, though there was usually no one near it, employees assumed that someone had moved things around or done something that destabilized it, and that it fell later on due to vibrations or whatever. But Charles Boyd never saw anyone moving anything near that display. Even so, he could tell that the quarts of oil immediately underneath the windshield wipers moved, too. The way they moved varied. Depending on what, Charles didn't know. What he knew was that they would either slide just a bit toward the bathroom, or they would sort of twist on their axes, as if someone had grabbed a quart by the cap and turned it maybe a sixteenth or a thirty-second of an inch counter-clockwise, so that the left-hand (western) corner kicked out toward the aisle just the tiniest bit.

When he first noticed this, he thought it was due to customers. Customers seemed to touch everything, even if they didn't mean to. But, again, he didn't see people messing around over there. People in Claysville knew what weight of oil their cars needed, and they knew before they bought it whether they were going to buy Exxon or Pennzoil, so they didn't tend to fool around—they took what they needed and paid for it. So, then Charles attributed it to clumsiness—when they picked up the quart they wanted it moved the others. They were packed tight, so it was like taking one billiard ball out of a rack—they would all clack together and shift a little. But then he realized that they didn't sell oil every day, or at least not every shift. And yet sometimes, during shifts where he was watching, none were sold but the quarts still moved.

For a while, he didn't think too much of it. He just noticed these patterns, always assuming there was some explanation. People were brushing up against them, hitting them unconsciously with the hems of their coats, or there was some vibration—maybe trucks on the turnpike made that shelf vibrate, or when either the freezer or the refrigerators kicked on, somehow a vibration made its way over there and slowly moved them. But then he decided that during the boring hours when there were no customers, he would check. He waited for the freezers to kick on, and went over and felt the shelf. Nothing. Waited for the refrigerators to kick on, and went over and felt the shelf. Nothing. He even stood there with one finger just barely touching it, waiting for trucks to go by, but when they did he still felt nothing. There was no reason they should move. And then he saw it.

One night he sat his soda down, went away for a minute or so, and came back to find it had moved. He knew that though his memory and spatial awareness didn't fail him *often,* they still could and did fail from time to time. But he felt so sure that he knew exactly where he had put the soda down and had what he considered the extra confirmation of a ring of condensation that seemed to show it had slid over. When he saw it, he said out loud, "What the fuck? What the . . . fucking fuck, dude?" At that moment something made him turn toward the oil, and he saw the biggest disturbance he ever would see—six different quarts of oil moved the tiniest bit south, and twisted the tiniest bit counter-clockwise, *while he watched.*

They didn't move all at once, or in tandem. They moved separately, slightly differently, at slightly different times, but all in roughly the same direction, the way you might expect a school of fish or flock of starlings to move. And they didn't move like they were alive—they moved like inanimate things that were being acted upon by a force, and as soon as the energy of that force dispersed, the movement stopped and they went limp, like iron filings when you remove the magnet. After this, Charles Boyd started to doubt himself. He was so sure he *couldn't* have seen it that he convinced himself that he *hadn't,* that they had already been moved, and that when he had turned to look his eyes had deceived him somehow. And he was going to prove it to himself.

There were twelve quarts of Exxon 10W-40 Superflo on the shelf that had been the most active. He packed them tightly together so that movement of any kind would be easy to discern and returned to his post at the register, where he would stand a vigilant watch. About three hours later, the quart that was easternmost moved, slid as if pushed, about a quarter of a centimeter further east. This time there was no mistaking it. He wasn't blinking or looking away or just turning toward it or doing something else. He was looking right at it—had been for some time—and it moved. He went back to that shelf, and stood there for a long time waiting for it to move again or to hear or feel some kind of vibration, but there was nothing. After a few minutes, he began to walk back to the register. As he did so he was sure that he heard a faint voice. The next morning, August 1, 2010, he called Harrison at home and told him he quit. When asked why, his famous reply: "Shit moves around in there, dude. For real." He left it at that. And Harrison understood.

By that time the place already had a reputation for being haunted. People other than Alan, Theresa, and Charles had experienced things, though none quite so dramatic as these stories. And it seemed to be different for everyone. Supposedly Roger Carson saw something—saw Jack, he said—standing outside the building, but there were questions about that story, about Roger Carson being a known pothead, and about how Roger Carson would even know what Jack looked like. After Cam Connolly started working there, he got to where he couldn't dream about anything else at night but Jack, so he had to quit. Dave Watt said that one time when he was paying for gas someone touched him on the shoulder, but when he turned to look there was no one there. The windshield wiper display kept falling, and when people looked closely, the housing *was* crooked, but not *that* crooked—it was being pulled down.

They were small things, but the people who experienced them swore they were true.

In June of 2016, during an evening thunderstorm, the roof over the east half of the store caved in, presumably from the weight of some water pooling there. The cave-in ruined the bathroom and a good portion of the stock. The concrete under the bathroom floor had buckled a little too. All this would have cost a good bit to fix, so everyone lost their jobs, including Harrison, and the owner sold the property to a development company. There were plans to knock the whole thing down, build a big Wawa there, buy roadside advertising on the freeway, and really make some money. In September they brought in earth movers and an excavator to remove the debris and dig up the tanks, and when they started knocking down the old building and cracking up the concrete pad underneath, they found Jack right where the floor had buckled.

Alan Turner was questioned again, but they still had nothing on him. Video is video. The former owner of the site was questioned as well, but they had nothing on him either. The working theory was that Jack had seen something he wasn't supposed to see, and some people killed him and stole off with the body. Then after the police and the FBI searched and pretty much gave up, the perpetrators came back, dug up the concrete, put the body down, and then poured new concrete right on top of him. But that was problematic. It was never explained who did the killing, what Jack had witnessed, how they could have gotten in and out without being seen—the place had been literally demolished and no secret door or room or passage was found—and there was no evidence that new concrete had been poured. It was just speculation to try to explain facts that couldn't be explained.

The strangest part was that Jack was *inside* the concrete, as if it had in fact been poured over him, even though that concrete pad was put there fifteen years before his birth. It turned out that once his flesh had dehydrated and rotted away, and only bones were left, hollow spaces were left in the concrete. When the roof caved, and all that weight came down, those hollows broke right open, and a little extra force from the construction crew exposed the bones. Everyone in Claysville knew who it was, but obviously it was confirmed through official channels. Jack's wallet was in the pants, and DNA confirmed it.

Construction was halted indefinitely.

6

THE DEATH AND SECOND LIFE OF THE CROW HERO

*Life is easy to live for a man who is without shame,
a crow hero, a mischief-maker, an insulting, bold,
and wretched fellow. But life is hard to live for a
modest man, who always looks for what is pure, who
is disinterested, quiet, spotless, and intelligent.*
—The Dhammapada, verses 244-245

James Alison was fat and not physically small but small in some nonphysical ways. He spoke with his chin tucked into his chest like a boxer but without resembling a boxer in any other way. He spoke softly and hesitantly, like a child who was afraid of being hit. He hunched over and looked at the ground when he walked, kept his hands shoved deep in his pockets, and only made sporadic eye contact. People avoided him because he wasn't good at small talk. He felt unwanted and ran under the assumption that other people didn't like him, so he often said nothing, thinking he was doing others a favor. It didn't occur to him that he was just making things awkward. Because he had nothing else to do, he read a lot, so people were a little frustrated or annoyed when they did manage to get him talking. He seemed to have a lot of detailed information about strange topics, and people didn't know how to respond, which left everyone embarrassed and quiet. People always thought he was a little off, even if some of them thought he was kind of smart. Unfortunately, he was not able to use his intelligence for any good purpose.

He graduated from college in 2009, which by itself was inauspicious. Having made the mistake of studying literature, and having no welcoming home to move back into, he had no option but to take the very first job he was offered. Given the number of people who were out of work at that time, he felt fortunate to have a job at all even though his was low-paying, physically taxing, parasitic, and boring. And because he felt fortunate to have that job, he found it difficult to look in earnest for a better one. Though this may have made a measure of sense for the first year or two, he never seemed to come out of it. It was like he carried the feeling of the recession with him years after its alleged end, and this withered both his will and his ability to escape the bunker he had dug for himself.

At work, James Alison was paired with James Tadeusz Waclaw Silwon, so they were referred to by their last names, which was embarrassing for Alison mainly because Silwon made it so by the way he called him Ali. Silwon had some uncanny abilities. For instance, the ability to make two different people interpret the same thing differently, simultaneously, with the very same action. When he called Alison *Ali*, it was not in the way that you might call Muhammad Ali *Ali*, it was in the way that you might call a girl named Alison *Ali*—with the emphasis on the A rather than on the I. But Silwon used a little trick of pronunciation that made him appear to be straddling the line between Muhammad Ali and Ali pronounced *alley*. So Silwon went around work calling Alison *Ali* and no one took any particular notice of it except Alison, who knew what he meant and who it shamed and humiliated time after time.

Alison wasn't just being sensitive or paranoid. Alison and Silwon worked alone together and almost exclusively out in the field—they arrived at work, loaded up a van, and went out to a job site, where just the two of them would work all day. Another of Silwon's uncanny abilities was the ability to maintain two completely separate personae. When they were at work together—actually together in the building—Silwon never said anything inappropriate except the weird little way he pronounced *Ali*. He seemed like a good guy. But once they were alone, Silwon's personality changed, and he amused himself by being openly and cartoonishly antagonistic toward Alison. The *Ali* thing was the smallest detail in the litany of insults.

On one occasion, in July of 2014, they were together in the van, headed out to a new address in Salem Woods, and Silwon started in on Alison as soon as they pulled out of the parking lot. "Dude . . . you're such a bitch. Such a cunt, dude. That's why the universe conspired to give you that last name and then to have people call you by it in your professional life. Because you're actually an Alison in a James' body. It's sad. Or it would have been sad in times before now, but they have that surgery now, gender . . . reassignation? Reassignment? Some kind of thing—you know what I'm talking about. You could be fine if you would just save the money and gather the courage." Alison did not respond.

Silwon made comments like this more than once a day, and not responding was often Alison's strategy. Sometimes he responded with a half-smile, as if it were a joke, and a softly-spoken, not-very-confrontational "Fuck you." He sometimes responded by pretending it didn't bother him and muttering something like "Whatever" or "Shut the fuck up." Less often he made gestures toward ribbing Silwon back, but these gestures were never taken seriously, and often Silwon continued making degrading remarks as though Alison hadn't said anything at all. This kind of torment went on all day in the field, but as soon as they were back at the office, around people who might recognize it as harassment, Silwon resumed his friendly and seemingly-respectful demeanor, calling him Ali with that little smirk that made other people think Silwon liked him but let Alison know that Silwon despised him, knew him for the worm he was—that he felt sure, deep down, that he was.

Alison despised Silwon back, not because of the way Silwon treated him—that, he could have endured—but because of the kind of person Silwon was. Despite having the same terrible job as Alison, Silwon was effectively rich, or middle class, due to his wife. His wife was a fat, loud, unattractive, unpleasant, but very successful attorney whom he placated however he needed to in order to keep driving her Audi and living in her beautiful fieldstone house just over the state line in PA. She was a partner at her firm, and she made so much money that working was more or less a gesture on his part. The little bit of money Silwon made wasn't terribly useful to him or his wife, so he mostly drank his wages or spent them on his latest girlfriend, silly after-market products for a pickup truck he sometimes drove, "tribal" tattoos, or ridiculous-looking clothes that were meant for younger people. When she wasn't around, he openly demeaned his wife, referred to her as "tubby" or "the ATM," and flaunted the fact that his girlfriends—"side pieces," he called them—were more or less physically perfect.

Alison tried his best not to be disgusted by this, but it was very difficult. He had met Silwon's wife, Ashley, and though she was in fact fat, loud, unattractive, and unpleasant, she was also ethical, honest, and decent. If you could deal with the way she expressed herself, you could see that she was kind underneath her attorney's exterior, which made her almost likeable. Several times at company functions, Alison had seen alcohol transform her into something entirely different. Once she had three or four drinks, her vulnerability, which Silwon would have you believe was mythical, would surface like the Loch Ness monster. No one could believe it, but there it was. In that state she seemed like a person who had been deeply hurt and who would do anything to have someone defend her, take her side. She would downplay her undeniable accomplishments, effectively begging, Alison thought, for her audience to validate them. The fact that Silwon could see such a damaged and deeply sad person as prey, and have the gall to despise her behind her back while living on her dime, enraged Alison. It would have been better if he hit her. He was sure that Ashley would have preferred it.

There was also a point of contention between them that Alison tried to ignore and that Silwon continued to press. Silwon believed that Alison was a twenty-eight-year-old virgin—his running joke on the topic was that Alison was a virgin because men didn't count. In fact, Alison had had sex with a handful of different women, but he seemed so embarrassed about saying it, and defending the truth of it, that Silwon honestly did not believe him and tortured him worse when he defended it than when he didn't. Silwon frequently mentioned this in contrast with the fact that his rich wife effectively did his bidding (which she did), that his girlfriends were model-hot (which they almost were), that his wife knew about them (which she did) but didn't dare do anything about it (also true), and that he was able to get away with it because he was simply superior to "Ali the virgin"—because women saw him as desirable and Alison as disgusting.

The way Alison saw it, Silwon wasn't a very attractive guy. He had a triangular face with creepy hollow eyes, big brow ridges, a pointed chin, and a flat head. Alison once saw a picture of the fossilized skull of a hominin called *Homo heidelbergensis*, and he felt sure that if you stretched some tanned leather over that skull it would look exactly like Silwon. But Silwon also had traits that he imagined women could appreciate. He was tall and lean and had those almost incidental muscles that were defined and hard-looking without being superhero-fake or PED-giant. He was tan winter and summer, supremely confident, and when he wanted to he could convincingly pretend to be benevolent with a touch of friendly irony. But Alison had to admit that whatever was or wasn't wrong with Silwon, Alison himself wasn't very attractive. He was a little balding fat guy who stammered in front of pretty women. But still. He wasn't a virgin. And in his view, the fact that Silwon's wife put up with him because she didn't think she could do better didn't make Silwon universally desirable. It made him an immoral leech. Silwon scoffed at that notion whenever Alison brought it up. Saw it as a sign of Alison's weakness and effeminacy. Somehow just his scoffing defused it, made it useless in argument. But argument wasn't everything.

When he wasn't amusing himself by commenting on the virginity myth, Silwon dwelled on Alison's weight. He said things like, "How do you expect a woman to get close to you, anyway? Just, like, physically proximate? Any human woman who found herself in the gravitational field that an object as dense as you creates would instantly be crushed like a beer can." Alison was not actually *terribly* fat. He was about 5′8″ and wore a 38 waist.

But Silwon would not stop. Not about his weight, not about his supposed virginity, not about his timidity, not about his sexuality, not about his difficulty talking to women, not about his financial difficulties, and not about his name. Silwon truly believed that there was something deeply wrong with Alison, and he was so completely without empathy and conscience that he found it too amusing, too deeply hilarious, to keep quiet about it. Rather than listening to the radio or a podcast to occupy his mind at work, he tormented Alison.

James Alison, however, was not quite what James Silwon thought he was. Alison was not quite the weakling or wimp, was not quite the coward. He was more like a person with a traffic jam of feelings and thoughts, who didn't know which ones were appropriate to talk about. The fear of looking stupid if he said inappropriate things kept him quiet and made him hesitant. But inside, he was confident. He knew what he thought and what he felt, and one of the things he thought was that it was smart for someone like him to keep to himself because experience had taught him that other people didn't feel the same or think the same. If he told the truth about himself, people would look at him strangely. Inside him there were boiling volcanoes of hate and cool fountains of love, even for James Silwon. There was a thing deep inside him that said that even people who went out of their way to make themselves appear to be our enemies weren't our enemies. They were lost souls trapped in their own problems, which caused them a kind of distress that made them think that acting like enemies would relieve them of it. When they behaved horribly, rather than hating them, it was more humane to consider how horrible the distress that made them act that way must be and to have compassion for them. Even during their most hateful moments, the times when they attacked most viciously, they still were not enemies; they just had not yet developed the ability to calm themselves and live quietly through the distress. Therefore, at all times and with all people, even with James Silwon, the appropriate attitude was one of kindness and compassion. A part of Alison truly believed this, and when he could bring himself to be conscious of it, he actively tried to behave in accordance with this idea, which he considered his guiding principle.

But there was another thing in him, a competing principle, that was dark, cunning, and capable of behaviors as complex as a spider's. A thing that was always present but not always apparent, a thing that thought and planned, that was busy at its own kind of work, though it was as still and silent as a stone. This spider recognized excellence in Alison and saw a foolish pomposity in Silwon. It said that Silwon could not understand stillness or silence, so he misinterpreted it. It said that Silwon's pomposity led him to believe that he could get the best of Alison, but that with just a little effort he could devastate Silwon. When Silwon was berating him, Alison sometimes smiled to himself, savoring this secret and the knowledge that with just a push off the bottom, he could rise to the top—all he had to do was try. And when Silwon really got to him, he liked, actually enjoyed, thinking about the things he might do if properly provoked.

These opposite impulses often played with each other in Alison's mind. There was always the potential, he knew, for them to become warring factions, but he felt certain that if it came to that, compassion would win. He was not even concerned. There were nights, though, when he longed to battle openly with Silwon. It took a lot to overcome Alison's guiding principle, but in the case of Silwon there was a lot of material to work with, and Alison had never learned to forget. There were certain things that haunted him, that would never go away. Sometimes they were things he had said or done that he was embarrassed about and that he thought must have made other people think badly of him, but more often they were things that people had said or done to him that he found infuriating or humiliating. And there was no expiration date on them. He couldn't forget about some of them, no matter how long ago they had happened. He remembered when he was in the seventh grade and he got beaten up by a much younger kid, and his friends just stood there gaping at him because they couldn't believe he was letting it happen, and they never let him live it down. Eventually he couldn't face them anymore and he quit coming around. After that they smirked at him when they walked by at school. In the ninth grade a girl named Audrey Fields had gotten indignant and loud with him for asking her out and said, "You think I would go out with *you*? Have you *seen* yourself?" All of her friends laughed. These incidents were decades old, but they still had the power to keep him up at night. And Silwon's comments were more and more frequently on the list of incidents that stuck in his mind and would not leave him alone.

Not all of the things Silwon said bothered Alison in this way, but over the years a couple of them had. And then a couple more. They would have been easier to dismiss if Silwon had been just another meathead saying meathead things—he could have ignored that altogether—but Silwon wasn't a meathead. He looked like a meathead and acted like a meathead and wore his baseball hat backwards, but he was a very quick wit and had a facility with words that made his comments seem clever—and to give him credit, they were slightly clever—but they were ultimately superficial. It was like they were written out beforehand by some mediocre talent, alone in his apartment, trying to show off. But Alison remembered some of them word for word and, maddeningly, the more complex they were, the more often and the more vividly he recalled them. Sometimes he felt like they would always be with him.

IN EARLY NOVEMBER OF 2014, word came that Silwon had put in his notice. He had gotten a better job, an office job, at American Alliance, where wage slaves all over the tri-state area dreamed of working. It was effectively the best company—the highest paying with the best benefits and the most security—that a college educated knowledge worker without a degree-specific vocation could hope to work for. People retired from there. They were known to head hunt. People who had worked there for a long time sometimes paid off their student loans. Sometimes drove new cars and bought houses rather than renting apartments. A job there was really the best that people like them could hope for. When Alison next saw Silwon he said, "Congratulations, man."

They were in the office, so Silwon replied, "Thanks, Ali," in the way that he did and gave that smirk. The people standing around them thought they would miss each other. Alison thought he was happy for Silwon. But later, when they were alone in the van, Silwon started again.

"Now that I'm gone, who is going to properly fuck with you? Point out the things that need to be pointed out? You know, virgin, there really is something wrong with you. No doubt. Jokes aside, I know you like girls. I see the way you look at Linda Casey, even as fat as she is. Checking out her ass. I mean, it's round, it has the correct shape for a woman's ass even though it's like super-hefty size-wise. I understand what you're looking at. But you say nothing. Not even to fat girls. It's really odd. You know how many women I've been with?"

"How many?" Alison asked, smiling to himself. He was genuinely curious.

"I don't know. You see? That's how many. By the time I got out of college, the number had hit seventeen, and I lost track after that. In the ten years since that time, quite a lot, though. Maybe three times that number. Definitely twice that number. And that's the point. A normal, heterosexual man ought to have had sex by your age, but you're so weirdly autistic, with your muttering and your gut, it's never going to happen for you."

"I'm not a virgin, I've told you."

"You realize that you're only going to get weirder and weirder as you age, right? You're twenty-eight. By the time you're thirty-eight you're going to be quieter, older, poorer, fatter, and just more bizarre. It's like you're slowly drifting away from the earth into space and all you can do is watch it get smaller. I'm not going to tell you who said this because you'd refuse to acknowledge the wisdom in it because of who he is, but I once heard a very famous, rich, successful person say on TV that when his mother died, he felt like an astronaut on a spacewalk if that cord, that tether, had broken. He felt like he was no longer connected to the space shuttle, like he was just out in space alone, drifting slowly away." Silwon paused for a good seven or eight seconds. "That's you, virgin. It's like you're getting further and further away from the whole . . . *good* part of humanity and life and just drifting out into nothingness. By the time you're sixty-eight, assuming you make it that long without, like, a myocardial infarction—which would actually be the best thing for you—if you make it to sixty-eight, you won't have had any human contact for twenty years, and you'll be some weird old man who goes walking around the neighborhood all day, talking to himself, gesturing, no longer even embarrassed that other people see him gesturing because he so direly needs the relief of talking out loud to this imaginary person that that takes precedence over all considerations of . . . dignity. I'm actually sad for you, virgin. Seriously. You're a sad man."

Alison's smile diminished, just slightly.

They were driving to a job site. Another house that had been abandoned and then sold in a foreclosure sale. They were tasked with assessing the property for their employer, Diamond State Investment Group, LLC, deciding what work needed to be done, writing an honest estimate, and actually doing it if the partners decided to move forward at that time. When they arrived at the house, they both saw that they would be working here for a while. It would certainly be Silwon's last project. It was the kind of house that Diamond State knew they could turn over quickly. It was in a good neighborhood, Charlan, and it was a big two-story with a basement and a two-car garage. It had light-purple siding and a black roof, so the house looked like a giant bruise, but otherwise it was fine. It was probably only vacant and in this condition due to an adjustable rate rider. Three pages tacked onto the end of the mortgage had ruined this family's lives, the parents' credit, and probably the marriage—these houses that were bought at foreclosure sales were never taken from intact couples. They always split. Every time.

When they got inside the house, they parted ways. Silwon assessed the second floor, and got into the crawlspace to check the roof, while Alison assessed the ground floor and basement. The property had a lot of issues due to neglect. It needed some roofing work, some carpeting, some of the drywall needed to be repaired, and almost the whole place needed to be painted, but there was no water damage and no mold, which meant that Diamond State would want everything done quickly so they could start marketing right away. A part of the basement floor was also damaged, and new concrete would have to be poured. Alison recognized this as soon as he got down there—he had done this part of his job fifteen times since 2009—but for whatever reason he didn't write it down, or photograph it, so it was not on the report. And for whatever reason, he didn't mention it to Silwon either. It went unrecorded. He did not think about why he failed to record it or formulate a reason to tell himself. He just let it go, acted as if he didn't know.

Within days Diamond State issued them instructions to proceed with property preservation, and right around that time, Silwon announced to "Ali the virgin" that because he was getting ready to start with American Alliance, he was also leaving his fat, loud, unpleasant wife. "She's an attorney, but there's still nothing she can do to me," he said. "We have no children, so she can't keep them away from me. And there's nothing material for her to take from me, or try to. I owned nothing when I came to the marriage, and I will leave it with nothing. But that's fine. I had shelter from the recession, and she had me, and now we're parting ways."

"So, this is mutual?"

"Ha! No. She's crying and yelling at the same time. But I'm done, which means that she has no choice but to be done. I had to give the car back, though. That's the rub. Peace to the A4. But I still have my truck. I guess it's an everyday driver now." It turned out that Silwon had already moved out of his wife's place and was renting a tiny one-story house closer to American Alliance.

He was excited to be rid of Ashley. "It's hard enough to get a regular woman to shut up, but a woman attorney? It's impossible. Especially a fat one who hasn't had much affection from men? In her whole life? Impossible. Just constant noise, and *loud*. Now that I'm rid of her, I'm going to start enjoying music again as my hearing returns to normal." In addition to music, he was planning to enjoy drinking a lot and seeing as many women as he could, which he said was likely to be more women than Alison would ever even meet, including women he stood next to in line at the grocery store. Silwon seemed energized at the thought of his new life. He was louder, more animated, and more aggressive than normal.

After work that day, Alison went to the bank and withdrew three hundred dollars in cash. He took the money to a home improvement store and bought six eighty-pound bags of concrete which he loaded into the back of his 1985 Chevy Astro. He then returned to the house in Charlan and unloaded them into the basement. Despite the cold, he was covered in sweat, and despite being strong from doing physical work for a living, he felt weak and was shaking.

On Silwon's last day, the Friday before he started his new job at American Alliance, he remained as loud, animated, and aggressive as he had been since he left his wife. Conveniently for him, it was the very last day of work on this house. The last day was always easy because all they really had to do was paint—a quiet activity that gave Silwon plenty of time to talk at Alison with no power tools or loud noises to interrupt or drown him out. You're fat, you're gross, women are disgusted by you, you're strange, you're mentally ill, no one will ever like you, your life will only get worse, death is the best outcome for you—it went on all day. Alison said almost nothing. Silwon even thought for a while that Alison was purposely stepping back to give him more space than usual to rant on his last day. He accepted this gesture and increased his efforts. Even when they were in different parts of the house, Silwon periodically shouted in his stentorian baritone, knowing Alison couldn't help but hear. As they finished and began rolling up the drop cloths and putting them into the van, Silwon started again. "You look fat as shit today, bro," he said. "Seriously. Have you been eating more or working out less? Oh, wait, you don't work out. That's how so much blubber congealed into that mess of a body to begin with. Right. Gotcha." Alison smiled to himself.

"That's not a joke, Ali, that's some serious shit. It's really disgusting the way you look. Have you ever considered that if you're not going to work out you should eat less food? That way the fat doesn't just keep building up and building up. I mean, you should see yourself from the side, bro. I mean, actually, you should *not* see yourself from the side because that would depress you, which doesn't help with motivation. But you should know that from the side you look wide as shit. Like two fat bitches stuck together. You know, like there's a front fat bitch, and your gut is her FUPA, and then the rest of your hideous girth is like the back fat bitch who is stuck behind her. You should, like . . . eat fewer carbs. That's really the issue. Bread. No bread, no pasta, nothing with wheat, really. No potatoes. Zero, and I mean absolutely *zero* sugar. You should stick with lean proteins like fish and chicken and then just vegetables. Broccoli and spinach and that type of thing. Because . . . I guess I'm wasting my time. Even if you lost weight, you'd still be an unfuckable weirdo. You'd just be a thin one. That's not really an improvement so much as just a difference. At least you can get some kind of enjoyment out of food, right? Food and beer? Just keep at them. Think of food and beer as like you're chopping down a tree. Every bag of Goldfish crackers you eat, every big, fat, slovenly beer you suck down, is just another chop at that tree, another chip that flies off the trunk, and sooner than you think you'll get all the way through, the tree will fall, and then your soul will ascend—you will have earned the sweet release of death. We all have to have goals. Even unfuckable fat weirdos."

"Suck my dick," Alison said quietly, his smile diminishing.

"That's a problematic request. It presumes that your

dick could be located with just human eyes, which . . . clearly it cannot. It only exists on a quantum level, like a quark or the Higgs Boson. Like, it only exists theoretically. Like, we've made certain observations about you, and based on those observations—such as your beard, your ever-increasing baldness, and the fact that you store your fat in your gut rather than your hips and thighs—we must conclude that theoretically you are male and therefore have a dick that exists somewhere in the space below the area we estimate to be the former site of your waist. But no one has ever seen it, and as yet even the strongest electron microscope is not able to actually *show* it to us. We have to wait for the development of better equipment that is not likely to come into existence during my lifetime or yours. Until then, we just have to take on faith that it exists because it sort of *must* exist in order to explain the other observations we've made about you. Point being, I *can*not suck your dick because it cannot be located with current technology. Probably with shrinkage over the years, and your generally low testosterone level, it has gotten smaller and smaller through exit and now it orbits some cluster of neutrons at light speed."

Alison's smile diminished further but then grew again. Silwon closed the back doors of the van and turned around with a broad smile. Alison then turned as if to go back in the house. "Where are you going, Ali? We're done."

"I actually left some stuff in the basement. Come on and help me."

Silwon started walking, but with an irritated, confused look on his face. "This doesn't make any sense. We didn't *do* anything in the basement. Why did you put stuff down there?"

Alison made no answer. He just kept walking. He opened the basement door and started clomping down the bare wooden steps with Silwon behind him, complaining. "What *is* this? What did you leave down here? There had better not be much to carry, because I'm out of here. I'll take the van and leave you here. Do *not* doubt it."

When they reached the bottom of the stairs, Alison bent down and picked up a five-pound drilling hammer that had been left on the third step and absent mindedly brushed some concrete dust from its face. Noticing that the hammer didn't look like anything the company owned, Silwon pushed past him, and finally stopped talking as he looked around. There were neatly stacked bags of concrete, a small mixer, a wheel barrow, two five-gallon buckets brimming with water, a stack of two-by-fours, a garden hoe, and a long-handled trowel standing by a section of the concrete floor that had been broken out and piled up. On the other side was a mound of dirt, and a shovel against the wall. Silwon just stood there, quietly looking, with his hands on his hips, for about ten seconds. When he turned back around, Alison was standing between him and the stairs.

"I don't know what the fuck you were thinking, but this is the stupidest thing you've ever done. And that's not something I expected. You're a weirdo but not normally in a stupid way, just a fat mush-mouthed loser way, or like a shut-in with a cognitive deficiency way. But this is flat-out stupid. I'm leaving. Give me the keys to the van." He put out his hand. Alison did not respond in any way. "I'm not helping you with this," Silwon insisted. "Give me the keys." Alison calmly raised the hammer and smashed Silwon on his temple with the flat side of it. Silwon's legs collapsed under him, and he crumpled into an awkward mess of limbs and torso on the floor. He did not move again. Alison examined him carefully. The side of his head had sort of caved in, but there was very little blood, so Alison guessed that his heart had stopped. He was dead. The look of Silwon's head had changed dramatically, and not only because of the new concavity about his left temple. The pomposity, the aggression, the sarcasm had all evaporated, leaving behind a vacant, rubbery skin-and-bone mask that didn't look like part of a human anymore. Alison didn't have to turn away or vomit or gag. He could just stare at it, and he did so silently for several minutes before getting to work.

Alison dragged what had been Silwon over to the hole he had dug beneath where the damaged concrete had been, took its keys and cell and put them in his pocket, and pushed it into the hole. He tossed the chunks of the old concrete floor, which he had broken out with the drilling hammer, on top of Silwon, who was almost completely covered by them as Alison had predicted. Now he would have to fill in as much of the dirt as would fit, tamp it down, wet it down, tamp it down again, and then he could start pouring new concrete over it. He was pleased by this. Even if someone dug up the new floor in thirty years to replace it again, they wouldn't bother to dig down to where Silwon was. And even if they dug a little, they wouldn't bother to remove all these thick, heavy concrete chunks from on top of him. No one would ever find this body, Alison thought. Not ever.

By this time, it was close to 5:30 p.m., and the office had closed. In the hour it took him to get back to Diamond State through rush hour traffic, the office had emptied out completely, as he knew it would. He clocked himself out and, using a tissue, picked up Silwon's time card and clocked him out too. He sat his own cell phone down on the workbench and then drove through the black winter evening to the house Silwon was renting and let himself in with Silwon's keys. He used a T-shirt that was laying across the back of the couch to wipe all the fingerprints off the phone and put it on the charger. He wiped down the doorknob with the tail of his own shirt, stuck the key in the door, pulled it closed, locked it, and drove back to work, where he picked up his own cell phone and then dropped it off at his own house, being careful to put it on the charger as well. If the police tried to determine where Silwon's phone had been that night, triangulating its location through the towers it pinged, it would look very much like Silwon had returned to Diamond State at a normal time and then went home. If they tried to do the same thing with Alison's phone, it would look like he had done pretty much the same thing, only he went home later. But he wasn't overly concerned about this. He had already figured out that he could plausibly tell the police that it took him a little longer than normal to unload the truck because Silwon was in a hurry to leave on his last day, and he had told his work buddy to go ahead home, that he would unload the truck by himself.

He then drove back to the house in Charlan, pulled the van into the garage where it wouldn't be seen, and began the job of filling in the hole and pouring new concrete. By 9:30 p.m. the concrete had been poured, smoothed, and was setting nicely, level with the rest of the floor. He cleaned everything up and loaded the tools and equipment into the van when he realized that he was getting tired and weak, and that he needed food and water. He stopped at Denny's on his way home, and it turned out to be the perfect time—

late enough to miss the dinner rush but early enough to miss the drunk kids rush. He nearly had the place to himself. The first thing he asked the waitress for was a tall glass of orange juice, and when she came back with it, he ordered a full meal with coffee.

After he left, he drove behind a nearby shopping center and turned his lights off. He dumped all the leftover concrete, empty concrete bags, the displaced dirt that wouldn't fit in the hole, and the drilling hammer into a dumpster. He arranged some trash bags and all the cleaning rags over top of it all, and drove back to Diamond State, where he unloaded the van, carefully cleaned all the tools, and then locked up, taking some bolt cutters with him. He moved his Astro behind the building where it wouldn't be seen, took a black coat that he kept behind the seat, and drove off in Silwon's truck. He knew of an infrequently used boat ramp near Augustine Beach, which was about half an hour or forty minutes away, and he planned to ditch the truck there. He figured that this time of year it would be used infrequently, if at all, before spring. The way there was a narrow two-lane road with an unbroken double yellow line—not that there was anyone to pass tonight—which skirted impassable brackish marshes almost the whole way. The tall dead cattails were like a wall and briefly made Alison feel as though he were invisible. But only briefly. He knew that if he didn't continue to pay close attention to what he was doing, he would make a stupid mistake that would get him caught. He was beginning the riskiest part of his plan, so he tried to stay vigilant. Things were not going to get easier.

When he got to the beach, he sat for a minute in the truck and looked at the lights of the cooling tower across the river. He wanted so badly to sleep. The boat ramp was gated and secured with a chain and padlock, as he had expected. He cut the chain with the bolt cutters he had taken from Diamond State, opened the gate, and pulled the truck through it. He knew there was deep water right off the ramp, but he didn't have any idea how long the engine would keep running once it hit water or how long the truck would keep rolling once the engine died. This was one of the risks he knew from the beginning he would have to take, but now it looked profoundly large. Alison straightened out the steering wheel, opened the door, and got out of the truck with the engine still running, his foot on the brake and his hand on the wheel. After several seconds of hesitation, he let go. Silwon's truck slipped into the black water, slowed a bit, but kept rolling and completely disappeared below its surface. After a moment of transcendent joy, Alison's fear rose again. He worried that it might have stopped short, that it might be visible from the bank in the daylight, that it might be found sooner than was convenient. But he resigned himself to that possibility. It was another risk he would have to take—had already taken. Alison closed the gate and, figuring that a cut chain lying on the ground would be suspicious, threw it far out into the water. He zipped his coat all the way up to his neck and walked back toward the road to begin his long trek home.

Alison knew there were many problems with his long walk home, and they made his stomach turn. The road had no real shoulder, and it was Friday night, which meant that if or when drunks came past he might get hit or yelled at or physically fucked with or even just noticed. And he was completely exposed to police. No one had any business walking on this long, empty road that wound through the marsh in the middle of the night, *especially* not with a set of bolt cutters hidden under his coat. If a cop drove down this road, he would be caught on sight. He couldn't even run. *Where are you coming from? Where are you going? Why do you have bolt cutters?* There were no satisfactory answers to these questions. And he couldn't ditch the bolt cutters because he had to bring them back to work. Otherwise it'd be noted that they went missing, and that might lead to him. This was the biggest hole in his plan. The biggest risk.

His heart pounded as he walked, and every time he saw headlights he wished he could just throw the bolt cutters into the marsh. He was perpetually out of breath and desperate to get to a safe place. He knew from exploring as a kid that there was a point on Route 9 that was just fifty feet or so from a paved trail in the back of Battery Park. His plan was to find that spot, cut through the woods, and travel the rest of the way on the trail where he couldn't be seen. The trail was narrow and dark, and no one would be back there in winter at this time of night. To the west, the trail was concealed by trees and brush, and to the east was the river. Once he made it there, he would have perfect privacy. He just had to find a way through. The distance from the roadside to the trail was very short, but the area between was filled with water that was who knew how deep, cattails that were who knew how difficult to get through, and mud that was who knew how soft—Silwon might not be the only one who disappeared that night.

When he finally reached the area where Route 9 ran close by the trail, he started scouting for the easiest place to cross and found a spot where the gap was surprisingly narrow—narrow enough that he thought a younger, fitter man, not carrying bolt cutters and not wearing work boots, might actually be able to leap over the water, though there was no possibility that he himself could. He was trying to work out the best way to navigate that gap when he saw the glow of far-off headlights and forced himself into action. He held his breath and stepped into the water. He was desperately cold the second the water touched him and desperately frightened the second he started sinking in the mud. But he only sank so far—he was up to his waist in water and up to his shins in mud. He continued walking, angling his feet upward at the ankles to keep the mud from sucking his boots right off, and very soon he found himself climbing up the bank on the other side. When he reached the top, he was on the trail, in oppressive darkness, shivering uncontrollably, but he had made it all the way from St. Augustine beach to here without being seen.

He took off his boots and poured the water out of them. He took off his pants and socks and wrung them out as best he could, got as much mud off them as he could, but his hands were starting to get weak and numb, so he put his pants back on and his boots as well. He was in misery. Freezing cold, wet, exhausted misery. But he knew that he had to press on, so he started walking. The river was to his right, and he kept telling himself that the moon's reflection in its glassy surface was beautiful in order to distract himself from the fact that he was starting to go numb from cold. When he thought about what that numbness might mean, or might lead to if he didn't find a way to warm up, he considered the possibility that he might die from this ordeal, but it did not frighten him. Death seemed like it would be the best possible outcome, even a great relief. What he was afraid of was losing consciousness, being found, revived, questioned, and inevitably convicted of murder.

When he reached the entrance to the trail, he paused to make sure no one was in the parking lot, beyond which was a pitch-black field—again, perfect cover for another long distance. Once he had crossed the field he had to walk through New Castle proper, the little town that had been founded in 1651. But, as always, it was very quiet. The streets were narrow and poorly lit, packed with parked cars, and he easily made it through without being seen. When he emerged from New Castle, Route 9, which looped around the town, picked up again, now as a four-lane highway that he would have to follow for several miles before he'd be back at Diamond State. For the first mile or so there was no sidewalk, but on this side of town there was no marsh so he could walk in the woods that skirted it and be invisible. But after a while the woods ran out and there were neighborhoods and buildings on either side of the highway, which not only left him open but also left him with no place to throw the bolt cutters should the police drive by. He decided to stash them, wrapped in the coat, by the railroad tracks. He was then able to walk faster and with less fatigue in his arms. He tried to rest them by putting his hands in his pockets, but the pockets were so wet and uninviting that he had to let them hang, and he couldn't decide whether the freezing air or the freezing water was worse. At long last he was back at work. When he got into his Astro and turned the key, he saw that it was 5:23 a.m. It had taken him over six hours to walk home.

Alison—or just James now—drove back to the train tracks to pick up the bolt cutters, back to the river to throw his boots in, and then back to work in his still wet clothes—

freezing despite the heater—replaced the bolt cutters, and went home. When he got there he stripped naked right in the kitchen and threw all the dirty clothes in the whole house into the washing machine, dumped in too much detergent, and turned it on cold. He then took a hot shower and found that he was uncomfortable, and even in a little bit of pain, any time that his skin was not directly under the steaming water. He worried that he had gotten sick and about how that might look if he had to explain it to police if they came to talk to him. But he was too tired to worry right now. He stayed in the shower until the hot water ran out and the lukewarm water started to make his muscles hurt. He put on socks, underwear, sweatpants, a T-shirt, and a sweatshirt, and then turned up the heat. He took all the clothes out of the washer, put them in the dryer, and turned it on. Then he went to bed and slept deep into the next afternoon.

When James woke the next day he found that he was stiff and swollen but not sick as far as he could tell. He ate a big dinner-like meal, then lay down again for a long time, still wearing all the clothes he had put on the night before even though he was sweating. He stayed very still for a long time, consciously feeling his body, trying to gauge why each limb hurt. He tentatively concluded that it was due to standard muscle pain and stood up to test his theory. He was OK. He showered again to wash off the layer of sweat that had enveloped his body overnight, and dressed. He was a little shaky, and a little weak, but he was satisfied that he wasn't sick. He smiled to himself, got in his Astro, and went out. He paid cash for some work boots that were the same brand, style, size, and color that he had thrown into the river the night before. He also bought a pair of running shoes that were brightly colored and made him feel foolish, but he told himself that it didn't matter what they looked like, that it mattered only that he had something comfortable to wear. He went home, burned the receipt, put the stupid-looking but excellent-feeling running shoes on his sore, aching feet, and checked his phone for the first time since he had dropped it off the evening before. No calls, no texts, three junk emails, and one automated email from his bank. It was possible that no one knew that Silwon was even missing yet. He smiled to himself.

James spent the rest of his Saturday doing mundane things before having two bourbon-and-waters around nine and thirty, which was enough to make him feel dazed and eventually it put him to sleep.

On Sunday morning he decided to go for his first run since high school. It had snowed a week earlier. Since then, the remains of the storm had cycled between melting a little each day when the sun came up and refreezing when it went back down. A warm front had come through early that morning and attacked the errant drifts and leftover ice sheets, so the air was humid from melting snow, and there was a lingering coolness that came right up from the ground. There were rapidly hollowing convex plates of dying gray ice covering the sidewalks that had never been shoveled. Their jagged lips looked like they had been eaten by acid, and there was a deep hollow crunch with each step he took on them before making his way over the crusty snow that covered the grass strip between the sidewalk and the street.

As soon as he reached the asphalt, he automatically started running, relaxed his shoulders, dropped his elbows, and found that running more or less did itself. Although he was quickly winded, it felt familiar and comfortable, as if he had been missing it, and he was at a loss to explain why he hadn't been doing it for years. Within just a few minutes he had worked up a sweat. His battered feet were making him regret that he had done this at all, but he kept going as all the rest of him felt changed. He felt young and strong and as if he could take on any new task. After what he didn't realize was only twenty minutes, he had to stop running and walk back to his house due to sharp pains in his shins and the screaming blisters on the heels and balls of his feet that had formed during his Friday night trek, but he felt as if he had accomplished something, as if he had started something new, and it was going very well. He began to make exaggerated plans in his head, like quitting drinking altogether, buying some weights, and eventually becoming one of those men who manage to change their lives in the middle, defying the more obvious narrative of fat, fatter, fattest.

By the time James reached home, he could barely walk despite his new shoes, which cushioned everything to a degree that he couldn't believe after years of wearing nothing but work boots and old basketball shoes. As soon as he stepped in the door, he took off his shoes and socks and inspected his feet for blood. There was none, but the irritated pink patches under the popped blisters told him that work tomorrow was going to be hell. *I had better wear two pairs of socks*, he thought to himself. Catching a whiff of something, he said out loud, "Oh, God, I fucking stink." He was shocked at the power of it and wondered for a second if he was smelling something else. He left his socks off as he stood on the cold kitchen floor, drinking as much water as he could choke down between urgent breaths. The freezing concrete beneath the curled yellow linoleum gave it a numbing coolness that canceled out the pain from the blisters. Eventually, he moved to the living room with the intention of sitting down on the couch and not moving again until well past noon. But as he turned the corner, he found Silwon sitting upright, hands folded, back straight, in the middle of his couch. His complexion was now yellowish gray and he had a dent in the left side of his head, but he wore that same fucking smirk on his face. "Hi, Ali," he said and howled with laughter.

Alison did not move. He just stood there, gripping his big cup of water, hoping Silwon would disappear. But Silwon did not disappear. He smiled a broad and sinister smile and continued to look directly into Alison's eyes. "Holy shit," Silwon said, "this is so awesome. I wish you could see how absurd you are in other people's eyes. You ran for like twenty minutes, but you're acting like you just finished a marathon. If you weren't so disgusting you'd be hilarious." Silwon was a hideous sight. Alison could make out the purplish-brown spots all up and down Silwon's right side, where the blood must have settled and congealed after he fell to the floor and then was tossed down into the hole. When he smiled Alison could see that his gums were gray and white and that there was blood leaking from under the gum line, staining his teeth pink and brown. To the left of the hammer wound, a fleshy wing of skin with dried blood around its edges was now loose and flapped in a way that would have been comical if it wasn't so disturbing.

The smell of Silwon's body was overpowering this close up. It was like body odor amplified and mixed with vinegar, and when it entered Alison's nose it also produced a physical, tactile feeling, like a swarm of tiny bees was going mad and stinging the soft tissue of his sinuses. He tried to drink some water but felt as though the smell had somehow become a taste in the back of his throat, and drinking water made him feel like he was drinking liquid stench. Alison vomited up all the water that he had drank in his kitchen, fell to his knees, and was visibly shaking.

"Wow. So, you're a coward, and a weakling. See, that's one I wouldn't have guessed. The single positive trait you have—or that I thought you had—is that you're a working man, and I felt like at least you were physically strong. But here again you surprise me with the number of your shortcomings."

"Are you OK?" Alison asked, hoping desperately that somehow he might get out of this nightmare with only an assault charge or even an *attempted* murder charge. But that wasn't how things were.

"Really?" Silwon asked. "You hit me with a hammer, threw big chunks of concrete on me, buried me alive—I was alive, by the way—and paved over me, and you think that I could've survived it? You knew what this was, what I was, and what I was here for, the second you saw me. I *know* you did, so don't ask me any more stupid questions."

Alison stared at the floor as he stood up, never daring to raise his eyes, and walked off to his bedroom where he sat down to think, or try to, but nothing came to mind. He sat on the edge of his bed, hunched over, hands clasped, elbows on knees, and simply saw the carpet between his feet. When he heard Silwon move out in the living room, he cringed, his shoulders shrinking toward each other—but no thoughts came. He was stuck entirely in the present. This went on for maybe two minutes before he finally did have a thought—a completely involuntary thought. *What if Silwon comes in here?* The specter of Silwon's rotting flesh standing in his bedroom doorway, half in shadow, filled him with a more powerful fear than he had ever felt—it made his chest heave and his palms sweat and his eyes widen. He wasn't sure if it was the fear of being trapped with a living corpse and what it might do or the idea that he might not have a sanctuary, anywhere to get away from it and its overpowering, physically painful smell, but the terror he felt was immense. Almost as soon as Alison had that thought, Silwon appeared in his doorway with his yellow-gray lip curling above his hideous grin. "You don't want me in here, huh?"

Alison stood up and performed a series of completely involuntary actions. He felt like his body was under someone else's control as he covered his eyes with his hands, cringed, bent over at the waist, and said, "No no no no no. You cannot come in here, you are not allowed in here. You cannot come in here. You cannot come in here."

"But I'm already in here," Silwon said, still grinning, taking a step toward Alison. Alison cried out and fled to the corner of the room, where he stayed with his back to the wall and his hands over his eyes. He stood like that for some time, shaking, barely breathing, before he realized that he hadn't heard Silwon talk or move since he took that first step. He prayed to God that Silwon had been a hallucination and that now he was gone. He looked again. Silwon was closer still—right in front of his face, grinning. "Still here," he said and laughed sardonically.

Alison considered locking himself in the bathroom but decided that the prospect of sitting there for hours, waiting to see if Silwon would disappear, was worse than dealing with him. He reached out and touched Silwon and discovered that he was physical. He could plainly feel the slick synthetic fabric of the warm-up jacket he had been wearing when Alison buried him. It even felt as damp and gritty with dirt as he had expected.

"How did you get here? Did you walk? Did anyone see you?"

"Still trying to cover your ass, huh? Yes, I walked, just like you did, fat boy. And plenty of people saw me. *I'd like to report a walking corpse on Old Baltimore Pike. He was tall and dead and wearing a red jacket.* I told you, no more stupid questions, Ali."

"What do you mean, stupid? I'm supposed to be able to understand this?"

Silwon sighed with frustration, and his breath smelled of rotting meat. Alison did his best not to vomit. "Maybe I'm being unfair. Maybe you shouldn't be expected to know anything. OK. Fire away. What do you want to know?"

"What . . . *is* this?"

"Highly articulate question, Alison. Allow me to explain. I am the man you murdered forty-eight or so hours ago, and I'm back now to, uh . . . restore order."

"So you're going to kill me?"

"That's one possible outcome, sure. But my main objective is to remind you of who you are. You're the fat, mumbling, reject, shut-in, failure I've always said you are. You really think you're something since you killed me, and I can't abide that. You're not some conquering hero, you haven't won, you didn't prove you're better than me, you didn't win in the end, and you haven't gotten away with anything. The police already know your name and that you were the last person to see me. But you're so disconnected from reality that you think my death is some kind of windfall and that you can turn your life around now that I'm dead. But it's far too late for someone like you to turn your pathetic life around, and I'm not going to let you think you can. Good people like me won't let the sickening jokes of the world forget who they are. The cops are coming sooner or later. Until then, I'm going to torment you, and it's going to hurt, Alison. A lot. Whether you die from it depends on any number of factors. What's certain is that I'll make you remember your place."

Silwon advanced, and Alison, forgetting that he was standing in the corner, tried to back up, but found himself trapped. He wore an expression of abject terror.

"You look pretty scared," Silwon cackled. "That makes sense. That's appropriate. But I'll tell you what. If you're looking to mitigate some of the . . . unpleasantness and salvage what little dignity you have left, I'll make you a deal. You come quietly back to the house with me so *I* can kill *you* and bury *you* in that dank fucking basement, and I'll make it quick. You just die. No torment. And as a by-product you also don't have to rot in prison. It's cleaner this way. Easier for us both. What do you say?"

"I don't believe any of this."

"Let me ask you something. How many walking corpses do you know? And given that they've gone to all the trouble to come back from the dead, do you suspect that they waste their time lying to fat fucking losers?"

Alison wasn't sure how to answer. While he knew relatively few walking corpses, he was not clear on whether they would lie. "I don't know. But I'm not going anywhere with you," he said. He had arrived at a solid decision that he wasn't going to choose between any absurd options or agree to anything. He was going to ride it out and hope this thing that looked like Silwon would disappear.

"No such luck," Silwon said. "I'm not disappearing, and I'm not leaving you alone for another second. Not even to shit. You're going to have to deal with the corpse that you made, and I'm going to continue to rot." Silwon smiled and Alison shuddered. There was more brownish blood in his mouth, and a yellow film was starting to develop in a different shade than the normal yellow of Silwon's teeth. Alison buckled and gave in to his previous urge to lock himself in the bathroom. Once in, he opened the small window and began to breathe the cool-but-humid air through the screen. This seemed to revive him, and for a second he thought he could bring himself out of this trance or whatever it was and that the hallucination would stop—but it was only three or four seconds before powerful hands ripped him away from the window and threw him to the cold linoleum floor. Silwon stood over him menacingly. "I told you I wouldn't leave you alone for a second, and you made a liar out of me," he said, kicking Alison again and again wherever his defenses were open, each strike producing a deep, sickening thud.

Alison couldn't understand. Silwon had gotten through the door without even opening it, but his filthy work boots were as hard and heavy and real as they could be when they bounced off his ribs and deflated his lungs so fast he thought he would vomit. He could not tell what Silwon was.

"Look. It's all the same to me," Silwon said as Alison gasped pathetically on the floor. "In the end, you're going to hell whether I kill you or you go to prison. Right now it appears that you won't choose. Refusing to choose is its own kind of choice." He picked Alison up by his shirt and threw him against the hollow bathroom door, which buckled in the middle, collapsing the space within. Alison fell to the floor, a searing pain shooting through him. Writhing in response, he twisted onto his stomach. Deep bruises were forming on his chest and back, and he knew that he would not be able to move tomorrow if there was a tomorrow for him. Soon he was able to get to his knees, and he noticed Silwon seemed to be pausing or taking a break, which he had done before, and this made him further question whether Silwon was real.

"I'm *real*, fat boy. Get a good look!" Silwon said, pulling him up by his shirt, pulling his face very close. Silwon appeared to be deteriorating more and more each minute. His face was more ashen, and the skin on his face and hands was flaking off in patches, revealing putrefying flesh beneath. The smell of him was so strong that at this distance that Alison started to dry heave. Silwon ripped the bathroom door open, carried Alison out to the living room, and threw him down right in the middle of the floor. Alison was sure that his collision with the floor had broken his collarbone and found that he was involuntarily making some kind of long, continuous noise that was too urgent to be a moan but not loud enough for a scream. Silwon looked annoyed, like he was even tired of shaking his head at Alison's disappointing weakness, and sat down on the couch. It seemed like Silwon was bored with the tremendous beating and would rather watch TV.

"You *can't* be real," Alison gasped, but then Silwon walked over to him, knelt down, and began pummeling his face. The blows landed on his eyes, cheek bones, jaw, and directly on his mouth so Alison could taste the rotting flesh of Silwon's hands. Eventually he was so disoriented that he didn't realize what was happening anymore, and then the taste grew stronger. He was vaguely aware of something in his mouth, pieces of something mingling with the blood. He thought, *rotting flesh*, and began to vomit and then dry heave until he blacked out.

When Alison woke up, the sun was setting. His whole body felt damaged, and certain places on his face, back, and ribs throbbed with his heartbeat and were so swollen that he felt like they would split open if he moved. The rancid taste in his mouth had mellowed, and the sharpness was gone, but he still tried not to think about it because his chest was shot through with searing pain, and another dry heave would be excruciating. For a few seconds he thought he was safe, but then they came anyway—a series of five, six, seven dry heaves that he could not suppress. The pain was so vivid that he cried like a child, and even that hurt. He felt like his abdomen was being cut apart from the inside with razors. Eventually, he had to concentrate on breathing with his mouth wide open, as the sensation of the cool air seemed to block or at least inhibit his ability to taste anything. But soon Silwon was standing over him, looking down in anger at his murderer.

Silwon got on his knees next to Alison, who started to make a muted noise, but could manage no more. He only seemed to be inspecting Alison's face, but the fetid smell was too much, and Alison started to dry heave again. The razors in his chest sawed at him. At the cost of great pain, he twisted away from Silwon and, facing the other direction, tried to draw a clean breath of air, but he could not manage. He moaned in agony, tears running down his face in several streams. Silwon wrenched Alison back toward himself, and seemed to inspect his face carefully again. He paused for two seconds, and then landed a solid, overhand right directly on the most damaged part of Alison's swollen brow ridge, which exploded with pain. His body writhed so powerfully that Silwon was not able to stop him, so he stood again, spit on Alison, and went back to the couch, where he sat and turned the TV on.

"You get HD channels on this piece of shit TV?" he asked casually, "or do you have poor-people cable?" He looked at the guide, switched to ESPN HD, but only got a message that if he wanted this channel he should call an 800 number. "Fucking figures." Silwon found non-HD ESPN and seemed to settle on the couch. Alison pulled himself to his feet and staggered to the kitchen, where he tried to wash the taste of vomit and rotting flesh out of his mouth. He heard Silwon call out mockingly, "Don't go far." Although his success at getting rid of the taste was less than complete, the cool water, with its lead-pipe taste mixed with the coppery flavor of his own blood, was a bit of a relief. He let the water run for some time before pulling the dish towel off its hook and drying his face. Alison staggered back toward the living room where he found his phone, went to the mirror, took three pictures of his face from three different angles, and a fourth with his mouth open to show where three of his teeth had been broken off at the root. Then he walked right up to Silwon and took five pictures of him in a row. Silwon smiled for the first four, and then played air guitar with a scowl for the last one. He was more hideous, and more rotten, and Alison was afraid that he had seen some kind of larvae moving in Silwon's mouth.

"I know what you're doing, stupid ass. Trying to build up a defense. Like killing me was self-defense. But you'll have a metric fuck-ton of explaining to do because the time line doesn't work. I went missing two days ago, with my phone still at home today, pinging away every time some bitch texts or calls. And your pictures are time-stamped today."

Alison simply said, "It could work. It could work."

Silwon smiled and shook his head no. "It won't," he said and smirked.

"You're *in* these pictures," Alison said. "Here's you, right here at my apartment, on my couch, acting like an idiot. They may not get *exactly* what happened, but they will know you were here and playing air guitar to Buckcherry or Jackyl or whatever idiots like you listen to."

Silwon stood, grabbed Alison by the shoulders, and threw him into a tall bookcase. Alison bounced off it and fell to the floor before the bookcase bounced off the wall, fell on Alison, and then bounced off him. He groaned under it in desperate pain. Silwon sat back down to watch TV until Alison could drag himself out from under the bookcase, which took some time.

When he was finally out, Silwon stood up again, and things with him were worse. The quality of the smell had changed from incredibly intense body odor to body odor mixed with a stinging shit smell, and the shape of his abdomen was changing. "My organs are rotting and I'm filling with gas," Silwon said. "Because of you. You did this to me, you fat bastard." He kicked the still prone Alison in the side of his head, which put Alison out completely. "And I *do not* listen to Buckcherry."

When Alison regained consciousness, he could tell it was very late even though his eyes wouldn't focus. He was too foggy to realize it, but the reason he could tell was due to the profound quiet. The freeway was less than a mile away, and he could hear white noise from it as long as there was traffic. But now there was none, which only happened in the dead of night. The television was on next to his head, but somehow he couldn't quite tell what the voices on it were saying, and there were no lights on. The stench of death was immense. Alison thought *please let him be gone*, but there he was again, standing over Alison. "Not gone," he said, picking up the coffee table and slamming it down onto Alison.

"Please stop," Alison cried. He had raised his arms in defense, but they were no defense against the heavy wood of the table, and he felt the radius and ulna of his right arm snap in two, and the trauma to his left wrist was so severe that the feeling was an inarticulate flood of pain. He couldn't even scream.

"No, I don't think so. I told you, fat boy. You can come back to the house with me, or we can stay here and do this till the cops come. So far you have chosen to stay here with me. Are you changing your decision?"

"No. Please stop," he cried.

"I'm not sure that's the way I want to go with this, fat boy. Listen to you, still trying to assert yourself. *No, please stop.* Who the *fuck* do you think you are? *Somebody*, apparently. There's work to be done here, you fat, murdering, useless, awkward, dipshit failure," Silwon said, turning his attention to an array of kitchen knives he had arranged next to Alison's damaged body. "Now remember, this will hurt like all fuck, but I'm not going to kill you here. We'll have to go back to the house for that. Feel free to stay alive for as long as you want."

. . .

WHEN THE SUN CAME UP, James Alison had not yet come outside to go to work. He should have been in his Astro twenty minutes ago, but today there was no movement at all. There weren't even any lights. Inside, the alarm on Alison's phone had been going off for more than an hour, but nothing else stirred. An outside observer would not have heard this, though. All an outside observer would have seen was a normal one-story house that was in decent shape for this neighborhood and perfectly placid but for some big birds making raucous noise on the roof. It looked like no one was home.

Two men in a dark gray Crown Victoria pulled up and parked out front. They carefully observed the house for approximately three minutes before exiting the vehicle. They were both balding fat white men with pendulous guts, ill-fitting suits, gaudy tie tacks, and cheap patent leather shoes. One wore light gray, and the other wore dark blue with subtle pinstripes. As they walked up to the door, their hard soles clattered on the concrete drive, and it sounded like an overdubbed Foley track from a seventies movie. The man in gray knocked authoritatively on the door, but before he could say, "Mr. Alison," the door gave a few inches—it was open. They paused, listening intently. They heard nothing for a few seconds, but as their hearing adjusted, they could make out the muffled scream of Alison's phone in a far off room. The man in gray called out, "Mr. Alison!" Nothing stirred. He opened the door fully, and looked inside.

7
THE SMALLEST DEGREE OF HOLINESS

The masters of Hindu spirituality urge their disciples to pay no attention to the siddhis, *or psychic powers, which may come to them unsought, as a by-product of one-pointed contemplation. The cultivation of these powers, they warn, distracts the soul from reality . . . But unfortunately the knack of psychic healing seems in some persons to be inborn, while others can acquire it without acquiring the smallest degree of holiness.*
—Aldous Huxley, The Perennial Philosophy

George Corver didn't go around talking too much. He said what he had to in order to grease wheels or cultivate useful friendships or create positive impressions, but that was all, and he thought people who said more than they had to were irritating. He didn't like too many words fucking things up or distracting him and often watched TV with the sound muted even though he couldn't tell what was going on. He didn't even try to read lips or follow the story. He only looked. It was this tendency toward silence that had kept him from ever going to prison for more than a few years at a time, and this tendency toward obliviousness that got him through the sentences he had served. Most recently, he had done three years of a ten-year sentence for stealing a car—the last car he ever had—and it was his intention to keep from doing any more time. He was getting too old to be in Gander Hill. He wanted to rest in peace, in whatever sense.

The problem was that he had no skills and couldn't get a real job. At fifty-six, he was a dishwasher who lived in one room. It had a gas stove that he figured was nearly as old as he was. The oven didn't work, only the range did, so he was reduced to frying or boiling whatever he ate—mostly eggs. Seventy-seven cents a dozen, and they made him feel satisfied. And he usually had hotdogs on hand. Ninety-nine cents for eight of them, and they were nice and salty. But money was very tight, and every little thing was important, so during his time off he dug up bait. When he had enough for a day, or when what he did have started to look like death, he fished off the bridge on Wilmington Road, in Broad Dyke Canal, not far from the river. He knew he shouldn't eat those fish. There were signs all up and down the river warning people to "eat no more than one eight-ounce meal of fish per year" from this waterway. Which, of course, was stupid. If the fish were that poisonous, they clearly shouldn't be eaten at all. But he needed something to eat other than hotdogs and eggs, and if death was coming, he would patiently accept it whenever it arrived and in whatever form. He wasn't going to worry or lose his head over some imaginary future.

Corver didn't fish just anywhere off the bridge. He had a spot where he sat every time. And he had a spot within that spot. In the distance, toward the river, there were three trees clumped together, and their profile formed a little dip, a little U-shape—the left and right trees were of equal height, and the one in the middle was shorter. And these three trees cast an inverted reflection on the surface of the canal, so their reflected profile formed a little hill, almost like a triangle or an arrow, pointing away from the bridge and toward the river. The hollow part of the triangle was his spot within a spot. Every time he fished, he found that little triangle on the water and cast right there. If he missed, he would cast again and again until he got it in exactly the right place. It was worth his time. He knew things about that spot. He knew that he would mostly catch hybrid stripers and white perch there, which he liked well enough; and occasionally some yellow perch, which he liked better; the occasional channel cat; the occasional eel; and the occasional grass carp, which made good cut bait if nothing else —if he could land those fat carp without breaking his line. And as importantly, he knew there was nothing in that spot for him to snag, so it wouldn't cost him a hook and a sinker.

His rig was simple. A number twelve hook with a uni knot and the tag end pulled back through the eye so it would stick straight out when the line was taut, then about a foot or eighteen inches down from that hook a one-ounce sinker. A little piece of worm on that rig could catch any fish in that water. Anything more elaborate was a waste.

The casting situation was more complex. His little spot within a spot was maybe twenty yards from the bridge, which wouldn't have been a problem to reach but for the fact that there were sagging phone and power lines overhead, maybe ten feet high, and there was a four-foot stucco wall on the bridge to keep people from falling in. With this arrangement, he couldn't cast overhand or even three-quarters because he would get messed up with the wires, and he couldn't cast side-arm because the wall was too high. He had to cast somewhere between a Roy Halladay three-quarter and a Quisenberry-Eckersley side-arm, and then add an upward lilt just before drawing even with the wall to give it height enough to get to the triangle. He would perform this ritual as many times as it took. Once he saw the splash in the perfect place, he reeled the line almost taut, sat the butt of the pole on the sidewalk, rested the pole against the stucco wall, and then reeled it fully taut *but not tight*. Taut enough to keep the hook off the bottom, but not enough to pull that one-ounce sinker back toward him even an inch. Every time, he did it just this way. Then hoisted himself up and sat on the wall, dangling his feet over the canal like a kid, but he didn't kick—he kept still. He folded his soap-stripped hands in his lap and just watched the water. The patterns it made. He wasn't watching for fish or turtles, and he used no bobber. He just looked at the surface of the water. As the wind changed, the surface was busy like a thousand sharp peaks, and then dull peaks with contrasting colors that made it look like a checkerboard, and then flat like glass, and then with little undulations like the glass in a colonial-era building, then with ripples, like someone had thrown a stone. He watched without making any commentary. He didn't try to predict what was next.

At first, he knew everything that was going on around him, and he might be thinking about something and absent-mindedly rubbing his folded hands together. And then he started to concentrate on the delicious satisfying friction of the skin on his hands. The hands of a dishwasher who didn't use gloves were dry, the skin rough and peeling

—there was no oil left in such hands. And he could feel their texture. The jagged spikes of skin on one hand scraping at opposite angles the jagged spikes on the other, like Velcro, or burdock burrs, almost sharp, like horny scales. It reminded him of crocodiles, dinosaurs, or the monstrous snapping turtles that occasionally surfaced in the canal below him. But soon he would stop moving his hands and just sit. Just look. And feel the jagged skin.

Though he was still, he never slept. He couldn't get comfortable enough to sleep sitting bolt upright. Even if he could have, no one would ever have known about it because more than likely he would have fallen into that deceptively deep canal and been seen no more. He couldn't even close his eyes because while he was watching the water in a forward direction, in his peripheral vision he was watching the tip of the pole, always to his right. There was no trick to knowing whether he had a fish on. There was no leader on his rig, and there was no slack, so there was no doubt, and there were no subtle hits. Either the rod tip went crazy or it did not. If it just nodded a couple times, it was likely to be something drifting by in the water, a leaf or some loose duckweed that bumped his line—either that or something plucked his bait clean off the hook. His attention was focused simultaneously on these two things—the surface of the water in his forward vision and the rod tip, always to his right, in his peripheral. Once he got set up and focused, stopped rubbing his hands and thinking, he didn't like to move. He didn't want to miss the changes on the water by turning his head and looking around, and he didn't want to fool himself into thinking he saw the rod tip jump when it didn't or to miss it when it did. So he sat upright, as taut as the line, not moving, not thinking.

Corver did not wear a watch and didn't care very much about time anyway, so he didn't know how long he would sit there without moving. Some days the goddamn fish wouldn't leave him alone long enough to stop thinking or even feel his hands scrape against each other like the concrete hands of a statue. But sometimes they just weren't biting. He could fish all day and only catch one or two. Or when the tide was going out fast, there would be no fish at all. He would just sit and watch the river suck all the water out of that brackish channel, sending it out past the power plant to the bay and the Atlantic. But it wasn't really the river or even the ocean doing it—he had heard somewhere that the gravity of the moon pulled the water on the earth around, and that caused the waves and the tides. So he would sit there watching the moon drag that water by fast enough, muddy enough, strong enough, that the fish couldn't contend, and he wouldn't know how many hours had passed. But he didn't go home. He would sit and watch the smoky-brown lunatic water rush by, witnessing the force of that godlike satellite, feeling how small he was and how large was the power of the universe. And however long it stayed was however long he stayed. Sometimes he wouldn't go home until long after dark.

George might have done this—wash dishes, dig up bait, stare at the water, and catch and eat fish full of poison—until he died. But something strange happened one day. He had spent the morning cleaning the restaurant and washing dishes, but after the lunch rush it was so dead that they cut him loose. This almost never happened, so he didn't know what to do with himself. As he walked home in the stifling heat, squinting in the brilliant light—it was bright even when reflected off the sand-colored sidewalks—he decided to go fishing.

This was neither a smart nor a normal decision. Today just wasn't a good day for it. It was so hot outside that the fish weren't likely to be biting, and on the bridge there was no cover from the savage summer sun. His neck was already a dark brown from all the fishing he had done since May, and he was vaguely aware that he might get melanoma, though that didn't scare him any more than the chlordane in the fish. He didn't even have that much bait saved up from the rain two days ago. But he decided he was going—he felt compelled or like he needed to go—and he did.

The heat was an intense, stifling blanket. The air above the road didn't shimmer visibly because part of it was near-white concrete and the asphalt part was so old that it was now baby blue, but no sane person would lay their hand flat on it. Corver baited his hook with a wilted worm, casted, reeled in, casted again, reeled in again, casted again, and, finally hitting the right spot, reeled just a bit, set the rod against the wall, reached down, and with a half turn reeled the line taut, hoisted himself up onto the stucco wall, swung his legs around so they dangled over the water, folded his hands, slumped his shoulders, and watched the dead-still water. In twenty minutes, his hat and shirt were soaked, and sweat was pouring down his face, occasionally dripping and moistening his desiccated hands, but he paid no mind. He was busy watching. After another hour, though he had lost track of time altogether, he noticed a strange feeling. At first there was just a fuzzy euphoria and an unusual tightness in his right forearm. This feeling slowly intensified until it felt like there was a steel rod in the meat of his arm, trying to move it. At this point, it was not strong enough to move

George's limp arm without his assistance, but he found relief in slightly raising that arm, just half an inch or so off his leg, and then dropping it down. It seemed like this was what the will controlling the steel rod wanted him to do and was trying to do on its own.

George noticed this as if it were happening to some reed or plant in the water, to some fish, or to some other person, with perfect detachment and only slight interest. The thing most like a thought that he had about it was the vague notion that it was going to distract him. And it did. The feeling continued to intensify, and half an hour later the urge to move got so much stronger that he thought he had better investigate, so he calmly looked down. His arm was most certainly moving all by itself now. Though he was not alarmed, he picked the arm up and held it out to get a better look at its movement. There was a repeating flexion from the elbow down, with a duration of about half a second and a distance of about an inch now—twice what it had been. It was a massive tremor.

He put his arm back down, clasped his right wrist with his left hand, and concentrated for a few minutes. As he was watching the water in this pose, trying to stop the movement and everything else, he had a kind of dream. In the dream he was a presence who knew and saw almost everything and rose up into the sky. The presence had three-hundred-and-sixty-degree vision, like a spherical camera lens—he could see in all directions without turning and recognized no direction as primary or front. He could see the roiling clouds above him and the entire ground below him, littered with trash, in great detail, and he knew the history of it all—every plastic bag, paper cup, cigarette butt. There was a single red-and-white basketball shoe, part of a pair that had been purchased for $149.99 at Champs Sports in the Christiana Mall, lying on its side in the little grassy area between the bridge on Wilmington Road and the trees by the cemetery. Those shoes had been worn in a burglary by a man named David Vincent, who knew that he had tracked mud into the house he robbed, and had to ditch his shoes. He dropped them there the next day. The second shoe was nearby—a boy named Richard Brunelle had kicked it into the woods to clear the way for his father, who worked for the county and was cutting the grass one Saturday. Several feet to one side of the shoe was an empty bottle that had recently been smashed by a kid named Michael Emmanuel, who had driven by and thrown it from a white Olds Cutlass. He could see that the shards of the bottle were now held together only by the label. It said "Mr. Boston" above a crowned double eagle with a rectangle that said "Vodka." Under that it said "Screw-driver. Certified Color Added * Contains FD&C Yellow #5." And in bold: "Natural True Fruit Flavors." Under that in tiny caps: "11% Alc/VOL (22 Proof) Produced by Mr. Boston Distiller Owensboro, KY * Albany, GA * Los Angeles, CA." And there was a barcode with numbers that read 0 89000 01426 2, and in the bottom left-hand corner, in impossibly small type it read, "2520963." George Corver somehow could see this label in detail from what seemed like miles above. He could see a plane in the distance and the individual rivets that held it together, each fold and puff of mist of each cloud, and all the details of the horizon. He could hear, feel, taste, and smell everything, including weed smoke from somewhere—he could watch individual raindrops fall out of a cloud down past him and see exactly which blade of grass they hit or where on the ground they landed if they fell between. And he could see the cemetery.

It was late at night in this dream. There were two girls in the cemetery smoking Sinaloan weed grown outside Mazatlán. They were sitting in a silver 2001 Toyota Celica that had been assembled in the Tsutsumi plant in Toyota, Japan, Aichi Prefecture. The girls had parked in a back corner so as not to be seen from the road. They were very young—sixteen and fifteen—and very petite. They had a lot of product in their hair and too much makeup on, and they talked about nothing in trashy accents and in voices that were harsh for girls their age—all things that he hated. The driver, Katie Mitchell, wore a necklace with a Celtic cross pendant. Unlike anything else they had, it was beautiful and tasteful and just a bit heavy, almost like quality jewelry even though it was pewter and had been manufactured in northern Jaipur for eleven cents. The passenger, Jennifer Hill, had eight dollars—a five and three ones—wadded up in the back pocket of her jeans. And no one else was around. They wanted to get high in peace, and they had chosen this place because it was always empty. The road to the cemetery wasn't even a road—it had no name or official designation—it was just the back way into the industrial park on the other side of the woods. There was a caretaker's house directly across the unnamed road, but one of the infinite number of things George Corver knew in this dream was that no one occupied that house and no one would for a long time yet. Those beautiful young girls were alone, and there was no other living person within half a mile in any direction.

This dream seemed to him to have lasted perhaps ten seconds, but in reality he was unconscious for several hours.

When he woke, he was still sitting on the bridge, clasping his right wrist in his left hand, but the sun had long since gone down, and the tremor had stopped. He took stock of himself and calmly considered that he might die tonight. He had no water, and the heat and sun had leeched a great deal of moisture out of him, which he could feel in the weight of his misshapen clothes hanging off him. They were so thoroughly soaked in sweat that when he jumped down from the wall, he thought his jeans might fall down in spite of his belt. His hat was so soaked that he threw it in the water, knowing he would never be able to wear it again, and it sank immediately. All of his bait was dead, and the Styrofoam cup it was in was bone dry. Though the sun had gone down, it had somehow gotten even hotter outside, and he hated the prospect of walking home and hated even more the prospect of being there.

He started packing up his Spartan gear, and when he picked up his pole and started reeling, he found that there was a fish on it. He knew from its weight, its fight, and the fact that it was still on the line after however long, that it was a channel cat. Though he couldn't say why, he found this hilarious—the whole situation, everything about it—and laughed wildly as he reeled the fish in. A sweat-soaked, sun-battered man, laughing in the dark, fighting with an ugly, poisonous fish filled with chlorinated pesticides and industrial contaminants. He started looking around for police as he lifted the fish over the stucco wall.

Corver walked home carrying the slick gray catfish by its gill, and it wriggled powerfully every few minutes for a good part of the way. The humidity was overwhelming, and because he was so close to the woods, the marsh, and the river, he was besieged by insects—Japanese beetles flew in clumsy, lazy arcs and periodically thudded softly against him. Most of them bounced off, but he suspected that at least two or three were clinging to his shirt and jeans unseen in the dark. Mosquitoes and other flying insects equally difficult to see buzzed around his ears, nose, and mouth, and he inhaled more than one of them. Tiny swarms of black dots buzzed around each other, oblivious to him as he passed through their ranks with no other path to take, only half aware of their presence. In several spots on his back and arms he felt intense little stings like a hot needle that produced a sensation that was half pain, half itch, but when he swatted at these places, there was no insect there. He continued to sweat in streams and was very glad when he got far enough away from the river that there were fewer insects.

    The apartment he lived in was a single room above a garage that was accessed by a steel staircase that looked like a city fire escape. It was sweltering indoors as well as out. He went to the kitchen area, filled a pot with water, and dropped the fish, which had several insects clinging to its impossibly slick skin, inside. The pot was not big enough to hold the fish, so it slumped in a U-shape with each end bending upward against the sides. To his mild surprise, it still showed signs of life. He covered the pot and sloppily drank three glasses of water without stopping, with water spilling down his shirt, then set about closing all the windows so he could turn on the ancient air-conditioner. It was a rickety, rusty, post-war sheet metal cube that hung precariously out of one of his windows, supported by two thin struts that had been screwed into the chalky outer wall sometime in the early fifties. He fervently prayed that it would stay in place another year. But somehow it could still produce a powerful cold, and it took only twenty minutes or so to make the room uncomfortable for him in his wet clothes.

He inspected his clothes before stripping them off and discovered that he had been right—there was a Japanese beetle clinging to his jeans and another to the back of his shirt, which he flicked off, recovered, and flushed down the toilet. He adjusted the water in the shower so it was just that shade of warm that felt like it had a little undercurrent of cold swirling in it and tried to shower, but he felt shaky and weak, so eventually he just sat down and let the water pour onto him. The heat of the day was deep inside his flesh. Even after twenty minutes, the back of his neck and his arms, were much warmer than the water.

While he sat there he remembered his dream of delicious young girls getting high, alone in the cemetery, talking about stupid young girl things in stupid, trashy, young girl voices. He remembered what it had looked like inside the car. What the cemetery had looked like from above. What the inside of the caretaker's house had looked like, and how it had been empty. How far away the nearest living soul had been. It was the oddest dream he'd ever had. He was thinking about those girls and their skin and tits and thighs and hair when there was a loud metallic sound on the kitchen floor. He did not start at this sound but stood up. He assumed that the catfish had regained enough strength to try to flop out of the pot and had knocked it over in the process, and he was correct. He calmly toweled off and got dressed again, down to his boots, as he watched the fish's mouth open and close rhythmically. There was water everywhere, all over the peeling, yellowing linoleum, which he used dirty clothes to soak up before picking up the gaping fish. His boots made deep, sinister thuds on the floor as he approached it and picked it up with one wide hand stretched around its back, below the dorsal and pectoral spines, his fingers and thumb not able to come together under its distended belly.

He put the fish down on the counter with an angry bang, and it immediately vomited all the half-digested minnows and indistinguishable, rotting trash it had been eating off the bottom like a crab. He looked carefully at the fish and noticed that its bulging eyes didn't seem to be looking at anything. He imagined that if he had been captured by some monster and dragged off to its cave, and if knew he was at least to be killed if not eaten, that he would look at the monster, that he would not have been able to look elsewhere. But the fish's bulging, never-closing eyes were not trained on him. This irritated him. He wanted it to see him and to understand on some fish level what he was in relation to it, even if the fish understood nothing more primitive than *predator*. But it didn't seem aware of him at all. He felt insulted. He felt disregarded. So he did not kill the fish prior to cutting off the filets. He drew the fillet knife from his gear bag and made it feel his irritation.

Just before frying the fillets in butter and their own belly fat, he carried everything that was left of the fish down the rickety steel steps and out across the long backyard and threw it all into the woods, as was his habit, and stood there for a few minutes looking into the dark trees. He knew that the fish guts and bones he threw into the woods were usually eaten by possums and crows, or just rotted, and that if this were daytime he would be able to see remains here and there—spines, skulls, ribs, and tails, like in old cartoons. And there were still more of them hidden under leaves and brush. He had been out of jail for almost three years now and had lived here for all of that time, so the woods were littered with them.

He went to work the next day and the next and was largely able to get the food he needed from there for free—there was an order no one picked up in addition to some big portions that people left on plates. It was an Italian restaurant, and he desperately loved Italian food, like all right-minded people, but it seemed like no one else wanted to eat such heavy fare during the heat wave. It made him feel much better—stronger, in fact—to eat this much calorie-rich food. He felt like he had recovered from his strange night on the bridge.

On the third day there was a terrible rainstorm, and as he walked home from work in it, he knew that there would be a lot of bait crawling around that night. The garage he lived above was attached to a residential house that had been turned into a telemarketing office, and an asphalt pad had been poured over half the backyard to form a makeshift parking lot. For whatever reason, that parking lot was a good place to find worms after the rain, except that it was difficult to see them in the dark. At the far end, where the woods met the yard, there was a spot where the grass was covered with big piles of castings. He thought he might get some nightcrawlers from that area if he was quick enough.

But when he went out that night with a fountain drink cup from work, he found few that were usable. He cleaned up under the flagstones in the backyard and under the two old, fallen trees just inside the wood line, but when he went to the parking lot there were very few suitable specimens. Almost all the worms were too narrow to get a hook into and were so waterlogged that they were sort of transparent and probably dead already. Determined not to miss the opportunity this rain provided, he decided to go walking around the with his bait cup to see if there were better specimens elsewhere. He clipped his filet knife to his belt in case anyone came along bothering him, and set out. He went all around the schoolyard parking lot, behind River Plaza, over by the bank, by Churchmans Automotive, and all up and down the sidewalks in that area. After that, he was tempted to quit. He was far enough away that it would be a pain in the ass to get home, and going any farther would only make it worse. But he loved the feeling of the cool night air, knew it would be hotter in his apartment, and for some reason was drawn to his fishing spot, which was just down the way. It was risky because the air had that loose low-pressure feeling, which he knew meant that it might rain again at any second, but he decided to go anyway. He stood there leaning against the stucco wall, looking out on his spot within a spot —just looking—and almost thought, *I wish it was this cool when I fished here.* But before he could formulate those words, it started raining again. He was in the process of picking up his bait cup, turning around to head home, and saying *fuck* when, in mid-turn, he saw a silver Toyota turn onto the access road toward the cemetery. Then he just stood there in the rain, his hands by his sides, looking straight forward. A person in his head would have heard nothing. He himself heard nothing, thought nothing, said nothing. But somehow in the silence he was deciding.

He sat his bait cup down on the sidewalk and regretted not bringing the lid with him. He was afraid it would fill with rain water and drown the few miserable worms he'd managed to scrape up after all that walking. He looked around quickly, but being familiar with the litter on the roadside, he knew there was nothing he could cover it with, so he determinedly set off across the grass to see if what he believed was happening was actually happening. About halfway to the access road, he saw a single red-and-white shoe, and a few steps later he crunched something under his boot and stopped. He lifted up his boot, and under it was an orange label, on which he could just make out "Mr. BOSTON VODKA SCREW-DRIVER." He then looked straight up. *Am I up there?* He could make out nothing except the familiar clouds. The rain drops came down, and he followed one with his eyes, lost it in the grass—but he knew where it landed. And again he set out across the grass toward the cemetery.

When he entered the cemetery gates he knew where they were, what they were doing, and that they couldn't possibly have seen him, but he was cautious anyway. Instead of walking on the asphalt path, he went over to where the graveyard met the woods and skirted them, then came up behind the car, where he stood for a few minutes before creeping up to the driver's side window. They must have been high already because he stood next to the car for a little bit, totally in view, but they didn't notice him. He enjoyed standing there, just knowing that he was master of this situation. Enjoyed that he knew and they didn't. Until he started to make out what they were saying. The driver was talking rapidly.

"He was like, 'Hey,' and oh my god I was just like . . . 'Hey.' And then he just kept walking, and I was like, *seriously, did you just approach me like that after ignoring me for two days?* Like, oh my god, I can't. I just can't. Like, I *couldn't*. Just, like . . . *No*." That was enough for him. He walked right up to the window and knocked aggressively. Both girls screamed.

"Miss, open up."

There was frantic movement inside as the driver handed the joint to the passenger, who rolled her window down and expertly flicked it out into the rain. Then the driver rolled hers down, trying to appear innocent.

"What are you girls doing here?" The alarm on their faces told him everything he needed to know. He hadn't lied to them yet, but it was clear that when he did, he would have complete control of them. They were so young that they still automatically obeyed adults. They would believe whatever he told them, and they would do whatever he told them to do.

"Just talking," the driver, sixteen-year-old Katie Mitchell, said weakly. It was a child's terrified lie. Her friend, fifteen-year-old Jennifer Hill, literally shook in anticipation of his response. The reek of weed smoke hung robustly in the humid air, pierced with the cool mineral smell of the cemetery soil.

"I'm detective Riggs. That's my partner, detective Murtaugh." He gestured behind himself, toward the darkness of the woods. "If you were only talking, why do I detect the smell of marijuana smoke coming out of the vehicle? And why are your eyes glazed over like that? I can *see* that you're high." It was so dark that he could not see their eyes with any degree of detail, but he knew they believed him. He leaned down and looked across at Jennifer. "I saw you throw the marijuana out into the rain. Do you think I'm stupid? That I'm blind?" The fifteen-year-old began to openly weep. "You're both already facing trespassing and possession charges, and you've just added providing false information to a peace officer, but that's not even close to the end. You'll face additional charges, including destroying evidence, obstruction of justice, and littering. Littering is usually just a five-hundred-dollar fine, but given all the other charges, you're likely going to get a thousand dollars or more in fines. Do you have a thousand dollars, miss?"

"No," the passenger cried through her tears.

"What about your dad? Does he have a thousand dollars? Or even enough to get you out of jail tonight?"

"No," she cried again.

"I can tell by the way you're crying he's going to beat your ass, isn't he?"

"Please don't tell my dad!"

He turned back to the driver. "And of course, you'll be charged with possession with intent and driving while intoxicated."

Now she, too, was crying. They cried like children. They were children. "But I wasn't even driving." "You don't have to be driving. The keys are in it, and it's running. To a prosecutor, to a judge, that's the same thing. How were you planning to get home? Walk? No, you were going to drive. While intoxicated. Guilty. You won't be driving again for some time." He paused, mimicking exasperation, looking around, but really he was hiding a smile he could not suppress.

"Do you know what detective Murtaugh and I are doing out here, in the goddamn middle of the night, in the goddamn woods, in the goddamn rain? Waiting for a drug deal to happen here. Right here in this cemetery. Were you the buyers? Two little girls?"

"No, I swear," they both cried.

"Look. You're already here, already doing drugs, and you already lied to me, so I frankly don't believe you. In addition to the charges you are already facing, you are both now under investigation for conspiracy to purchase narcotics. I'm going to have to ask you girls to step out of the vehicle." They obeyed, and he led them down a path into the woods, where he claimed detective Murtaugh would meet them after he recovered the joint, which would be saved as evidence.

The cemetery was now empty and still. It continued to rain into the open windows of the Celica. The little, round, louvred air vents, the three gauges—tach, speed, fuel/temp/gear—stared blankly at nothing. Then there was some noise from the woods. Indistinct, but high pitched. The noise of movement. Then things fell silent but for the rain. After thirty-five minutes, Corver appeared again, alone. He climbed into the car, adjusted the seat, produced keys from his pocket, and drove out of the cemetery. He headed north on Route 9 and then spiraled around the 295 South ramp just past Collins Park, and was gone.

When Corver reappeared, it was very early the next morning. He was let out of a Cadillac Escalade at River Plaza, and he walked home with 708 dollars in his pocket, feeling loose and relaxed. Relieved. Not just physically but mentally. Michael was an old contact of his and very professional. By this time the Celica was already three-quarters of the way disassembled. They had started on it the second he brought it in, and he saw it again before he left—the body panels were already gone. Wouldn't be long before it had dissolved like sugar in coffee. There was no longer a car to be found.

When he reached his apartment, Corver opened a drawer and a box that he kept inside. He dropped a little Celtic cross into it, where it clinked against other little totems—single earrings; a dainty, narrow little watch; a little charm that was half moon and half sun with a face on it. Girls' things. He put the lid back on, dug the cash out of his pocket, hid it under a stack of shirts in the same drawer, then lay on his bed. Tomorrow he was going to buy some beer, he decided, and have a few drinks after fishing. But right now he needed to get some sleep so he could get up in time for work.

That evening it didn't occur to him until he was already on his way home that he had left his bait cup by the bridge the night before. This made him about as upset as he ever got. Fishing was important to him. His time there, with a calm mind, was without question the most important thing in his life. The closest bait shop was Master Baiter's, way down past the 13-40 split, and there was no way to catch a DART bus from where he was without it taking all day. It was a shame there was no way for him to keep that Celica.

When he reached his spot, the cup was still there, but the good worms had crawled out, and the weaker, smaller ones had drowned in the accumulated rain water and looked like they were dissolving. He had read somewhere that you could catch catfish using hotdogs, but he wasn't convinced a hot dog chunk would stay on a hook with the current in this water. At a certain point he gave up his anger and slumped against the stucco wall. After a few moments he hoisted himself onto it, swung around, and sat there just as he would have if he had been fishing. At first, something wasn't right, and it didn't occur to him for some time that his fishing rod wasn't in the right place. He tried just setting the rod up, but then it bothered him that there was no line, so eventually he got down and cast the sinker and bare hook out to their normal spot within a spot, setting up just as he would have if he had bait, and that did it. He was relieved. He hoisted himself back up onto the wall and sat calmly watching the rod tip out of the peripheral of his right eye, watching the water with all the rest. Everything was normal and right, and he could rest.

The surface of the water wore an interference pattern of evenly spaced points that looked like reptile skin when he noticed that there was an unusual abundance of crows and turkey vultures in the sky. He was puzzled for a few seconds before it occurred to him that they were probably in and out of the woods eating those girls. The vultures flew everywhere without a flap—east, west, north, south, and every direction in between—without ever seeming to go to the relevant spot. Even when one of them—and he had counted four so far—seemed to accidentally fly over it, it just kept going. The crows were harder to keep track of because they flew lower, faster, with more agility, and they could easily get in and out of the woods without his ever seeing them. But they were noisy. Like those girls, he snickered to himself, they would never shut the fuck up until someone shut them up. He had only seen four or five crows, and they weren't exactly on a beeline to the relevant spot, but he knew there were a lot of them nearby because he heard them cawing at each other in the distance—faint caws that he could only hear between the traffic sounds. His experience was that it was difficult to determine a wild animal's aim until it actually did the thing it intended to do. Wild animals went places circuitously, circled around, stood for a long time right next to the place they were going, then went away, came back, and stood next to it on the other side. Finally they would do the thing, whatever it was, and only then did you really know. So, seeing the vultures and crows flying everywhere except toward those girls didn't change his mind.

He was tempted to go into the woods to see what Katie and Jennifer looked like now and to satisfy his curiosity about whether the crows and vultures had started in on them yet, but he knew better. He didn't want to be seen on that access road, and certainly not going into or coming out of those woods in case they ever found those girls. Everyone knew that criminals returned to the scene of the crime. He wasn't going to do that. And he wasn't going to change his behavior one bit either. He was going to fish here as often as the opportunity presented itself, just like always. He was sure he was a familiar sight to the rich people who lived in those three-hundred-year-old brick houses in town, who drove past him day after day on Wilmington Road, and he wasn't going to suddenly drop out of sight after those girls disappeared. He was going to sit right here and not know anything.

But when he considered it, he felt sure that no one would ever find Katie and Jennifer. Or at least not for a long, long time. He knew that a lot of missing girls stayed missing. Their ghosts didn't walk in the night, and no crying witnesses came forward. They just laid where they were for years and years, and only the person who put them there had any inkling. That could easily happen in this case. Though the area was pretty well populated, it was mostly industrial. That access road only had three things on it— the cemetery, the caretaker's house, and the industrial park. It was too far away from any housing developments for kids to get to, but too close to people's property for it to be legal to hunt. It was just one of those waste areas, like the woods on a median strip or on the side of I-95 where no one ever had any call to go. Even if older kids went to the cemetery to get high, kids who drove and did drugs were not the types to go tromping around that far back in the woods. And even if they did, they probably wouldn't go running to the police to explain what they found while they were breaking the law. Or maybe they would. It was possible. But either way, there was no connection to him. No one had any reason to suspect. No one had ever had any reason to suspect him of anything except stealing cars. That and assault and driving while intoxicated and possession of a Schedule 1 narcotic and domestic violence were the only things he had ever gone away for.

Corver breathed in and out deeply. He felt the jagged spikes of skin on the fingers of his right hand interlock and pull against the jagged spikes of the left. He felt the broken skin between his knuckles, which hurt like sharp little paper cuts. He watched the water, the rod tip. The crows cawed somewhere and probably feasted on trashy dead girls. Cars drove by. He did nothing but breathe and look, with no interruptions from fish or anything else, for the next hour or more. After a while, he noticed an unusual tightness in his right forearm, and then there was movement. He was physically excited by this because of the dream he thought might come, but mentally he was calm. There were no thoughts. There was only awareness. Soon his arm was moving rapidly, and then it stopped. Corver's head slumped down slightly. When he woke up again it was dark, and there was a delicious new thing in his mind. He climbed down from the wall, gathered up his gear, and walked home in the darkness, glowing with savagery, brightly alive, like a thing on fire.

8
AN ACCOUNT OF SOME STRANGE DISTURBANCES ON OLD BALTIMORE PIKE

I don't know if this story will work in writing. I have probably told it more than ten times since it happened, and sometimes it comes off and sometimes it doesn't, but I feel like maybe it won't work right being written down. Like it will be easier to criticize or less believable or something. Still, though, I want to write it down so there will be a permanent record of it. The reason I tell it so much is that it seems like it's important, and like it shouldn't be forgotten, but no one knows it. That eats at me. It's a dark story. It's not going to make anyone happy. But it's like I have an *urge* to tell it. It also feels like if I tell it I'll get something out of it. Some kind of relief, or satisfaction, or something that'll make it a lighter burden. But that never happens. Every time I tell it I think I'm building toward something, but in the end, I'm still empty and unsatisfied. But maybe if I write it, I'll get the thing I'm looking for. But the writing is not going to be good. I'm more of a talker than a writer, and

I don't pretend that I can write a great story or anything. I just need to set down the facts as I know them, and then try to move on. And they *are* facts. I realize that it's going to look like a stupid bunch of lies after it's written down but this really happened whether you believe me or not.

It was October 4, 1994. I know it sounds cheesy to say that something like what I'm going to say happened in October, but it did. I know the exact date because my friends and I cut school that day to get the new Danzig tape, *Danzig IV*, and I just now looked it up on Wikipedia – that's the day it came out. Also, that date made me sixteen years old, so there's no mistaking it. That definitely *was* the date.

There were three of us. Me, Mike, and this chick named Lacey. Lacey was tall for a girl—taller than me by an inch or two—and thin and beautiful, with perfectly straight brown hair and braces that had rubber bands on them, so when she opened her mouth and you were looking at her from the side, you could see the rubber bands stretching from the top jaw to the bottom. But I still thought she was beautiful. The braces didn't affect my opinion at all. She was perfect. But that makes it sound wrong, because she wasn't my girlfriend and never became my girlfriend. Things just didn't go right, and later on there was an incident and we parted ways, but that isn't relevant to this story.

Mike was like Lacey. Tall and thin and good looking and with long hair, although his wasn't straight, and Mike had eyes so black you couldn't tell the iris from the pupil, so looking at him was weird and somehow confusing. Any sane person who saw the three of us would have thought that Lacey and Mike were together and that I was just this scrub driving around with them, but it wasn't like that. Mike knew Lacey first and was the one who introduced her to me, but they weren't interested in each other. He seemed to see her as just another random person, and she seemed to look at him the same way. And for some equally confusing reason she and I had instant rapport even though she was totally out of my league. She thought I was funny, and I thought she was what at the time I called "interesting." I suppose what I probably meant was that she had a different kind of life than I had, and as a result she said really mature, compassionate-type things I wasn't used to hearing. That contrast may have been what we liked about each other—she was mature and compassionate, and I was not mature and went around saying cartoonishly inappropriate things that shocked her in a way that she seemed to get a little thrill out of. So, we were fascinated by each other. Plus, we agreed about a lot of teenage things—music, who was an asshole, which teachers we hated—so we liked spending time together. So, she wasn't my girlfriend, but it was sort of like she was.

But I'm losing the thread. The situation was this: the new Danzig tape came out that day and I had a little money, so I asked Mike if he wanted to cut school with me while I went and got it, and then we could drive around all day and get stoned and listen to it. Of course he was on board, and he brought Lacey along because he knew I wanted him to. So after either homeroom or first period—I forget which—we snuck out the back of the school, got into my car, and went down to Main Street where there used to be this place called Rainbow Records, which later on was Rainbow Books, and now I think is a skate shop. We stood around out front until the place opened, then we went in and got the tape. That tape is long gone, but I remember everything about it. The cassette itself was clear, but it had red panels on it—like, the sides were red. And the album cover was black with an outline of what looked like the Danzig skull as a Rorschach test, and it had these weird symbols along one side, kind of like *Led Zeppelin IV*, but creepier. Everything about it was fucking cool, and to this day *IV* is my favorite Danzig album. Anyway, we got in my car, put it on, and drove around getting high as planned. I don't remember anything that was said, but I was sixteen and they were both seventeen, so there couldn't have been anything interesting. There must have been a lot of us going, "Dude, did you fucking hear *that*?" and so on. But even if it was profoundly stupid, it was also a really good time.

After a few hours, we ran out of places to go. Like I said, I had a little money, but I'd probably spent everything I had on gas and on that tape, so it's not like we could go out to eat or anything. We had gotten high, we had listened to the tape like three times, and driven all around Newark to the point where we had pretty much gone in circles. After a while there was an air of *what are we going to do now?* So we were headed south on 896, back toward school, but at the light right before the school, I said fuck it and made a left onto Old Baltimore Pike. Mike and Lacey were surprised, and there was some discussion like "I thought we were going back to school," and I must have said something like "I can't deal with that place today. Not like this." *Like this* meaning stoned out of my fucking head. None of us was going to learn anything that day anyway. We were essentially going back just to have a place to sit down.

While we were headed down Old Baltimore Pike blasting Danzig—and *IV* was the last record before he fired the whole band, so it was still John Christ and Chuck Biscuits and Eerie Von and that classic Danzig sound with all the pinch harmonics and vibrato and stuff—I remembered something that seemed relevant just then. There was an abandoned house at the bottom of the hill.

I knew, and still know, nothing about the house other than its location—it was at the intersection of Old Baltimore Pike and 273. If you were heading east, it was on the left side just before you got to the red light. The reason this was something that I had to remember, and the reason we didn't all know about it, was that the house was set back from the road and the trees and bushes and briars had grown up so thick and so high that you couldn't really see it unless you were looking for it.

The first time I had noticed it was about three years earlier. My mom and dad were taking me somewhere, and we were waiting in the left turn lane at that light. I was just staring out the window and noticed that there was a gap in the curb. All along that part of the road the curb was a certain height, maybe five or six inches, but at this one place there was a gap where the curb was less than an inch high. And it wasn't that the concrete had broken—the curb curved downward for a space of maybe six or eight feet, and then it curved back up and resumed down the road at the original five- or six-inch height. This was on purpose—it had been built that way.

It took a few seconds before it occurred to me that it was about the width of a driveway—probably because there was no driveway. Beyond the curb there was a gap in the weeds and bushes and brambles—vicious-looking thorns, growing in all directions—and what looked like gravel or rocks or something and trees drooping down over the area, but there was no driveway. The stuff that looked like gravel or rocks turned out to be the crumbling remains of the asphalt drive that had once been there. But I didn't know that at the time. It just looked like an overgrown vacant lot. But, having seen the curb, I figured no one would bother making it curve down like that if there was no reason to drive in there, so I started moving my head around trying to see through the trees, and sure enough, there was a house. The vegetation had grown so high and thick that, even though it was winter and there were no leaves, I could barely see it. As I moved my head, I caught a glimpse of the house here and there, but all I could tell was that it was in bad shape. There was no paint, and the wood looked rotted. I didn't think it was particularly important, but I never forgot about it, and whenever I passed by, I looked and tried to find it in the tangle of foliage. But for whatever reason this day, October 4, 1994, was the first time it ever occurred to me that I could actually *go* there.

Once I explained to Lacey and Mike where we were heading, there was universal agreement that, yes, we should definitely check out this abandoned house. To us, an abandoned house would be like teenage Disneyland. There would be license, space, and privacy to do all the stuff that people were always trying to stop teenagers from doing. Obviously, it would depend on the specific house, where it was situated and so on, but theoretically you could do anything you wanted there—break shit (preferably windows), get high, drink, smoke, fight, fuck, scream. This was twenty-five years ago, so I don't recall exactly what was said, but *Of course we're down with checking out this house, and why are we just hearing about it now?* was kind of the vibe from them.

I remember being a little concerned about someone seeing us pull in because obviously we had no business there, and I didn't want the cops being called, but when we reached that intersection, no one was around. In 1994, that part of Old Baltimore Pike was far less busy than it is now. During rush hour it could get crowded with people trying to get on 273, but really, unless you lived in one of those houses further east by the cemetery, that part of Old Baltimore Pike was just a back way to the mall—there was nothing there but woods.

I slowed way down and pulled in. The weeds were so high we could hear them brushing against the bottom of the car, and they were brushing against the doors and even the windows a little bit, but once the driveway started curving it cleared up a little, and it led around to the back of the house, where there was a badly cracked but still intact concrete pad where I parked. The fact that it led to the back of the house—the side facing away from the road—was perfect for our purposes. Even a curious person who had managed to spot the house from the road couldn't possibly see that my car was parked there. Three stoned teenagers with more weed to burn and a new Danzig tape had just found a structure that would give them complete privacy— you can imagine how we felt.

The house was awesome, and once we got inside I immediately started thinking about what Lacey might let me do to her if I could get her there alone, what I might need to stash in my trunk to make her comfortable enough, and so on. And of course I wouldn't bring this up to her, but it would be just like that part in *Texas Chainsaw Massacre*, right before they walk to the Sawyer property to try to buy some gas. I was stoked. The one negative was that the place seemed to have been empty for so long that there weren't any signs of humanity left. There were no tables or chairs or personal belongings of any kind. It would have been creepier if there were like a baby carriage with a weathered, fucked-up-looking doll in it or a closet full of old stuff. That would have given us something to think about, some way to visualize who might have lived there and when. But there was nothing like that. There were mainly just piles of broken wood and concrete, debris from walls that had fallen down or deteriorated, leaves, and a little bit of graffiti—and even the graffiti looked pretty old. It felt like no one, not even dumb kids like us, had been there for decades.

I don't know what Mike and Lacey thought, but I thought that was pretty weird. That and the fact that none of us had ever heard anything about this place. We were literally right down the street from the high school—five miles, tops—and at the age where just hanging out and smoking cigarettes is a cool thing to do, so it didn't make clear sense that there would be such an excellent place to do that that went totally unused. You would expect that lots of kids like us would go there and do crazy shit, and stories would circulate, and so on. But there was no talk about this place. Literally none. Maybe the fact that it was hidden meant that no one knew about it, but even that didn't wash. It wasn't *that* hard to see—I had seen it. Other people must have seen it too. It made me wonder whether there was some reason that kids our age didn't go to this house.

Anyway, we were there and we went inside and fucked around. We couldn't get in the front door, but the basement was open. It had had one of those sets of doors like in the storm scene in *The Wizard of Oz* that Dorothy's family uses to go down into the basement to hide from the tornado. The doors themselves were gone, and so was the steel housing, but the concrete part was still there, so we just walked down into the basement and checked it out—mostly empty—then walked up the staircase to what turned out to be the kitchen and explored the place.

Again, it was basically empty. Concrete, wood, debris, etc. There wasn't any wallpaper or paint or anything, and the walls were old crumbling plaster, so in a lot of places you could see the lath showing through, like the house's skeleton. The windows were virtually all broken out already, but there was this one room on the second floor that still had glass. *That* was the room we focused on. I guess you would call that the *master bedroom*, but in any case it was the biggest room on the second floor. That room was relatively clean, and the fact that the glass was still in the windows meant—or so we thought—that we would be able to go there at night and be relatively warm.

We were all walking around separately, but at some point we found ourselves in there together, and that was where we decided to get high. I remember taking a giant hit, holding it, and then blowing all the smoke into the attic through a hole in the ceiling, and Lacey saying something like, *It's like your soul is escaping.* While we were still smoking, Mike said it would be awesome to party in there, and Lacey lit up. She was like, *We should come back tonight!* and she started making all these plans. She said there was liquor that she could steal from her parents that they wouldn't miss for a while and that we would need stuff to sit on and something for light because obviously we couldn't start a fire in there. I forget who had the light, but I feel like it must have been Mike—either his dad or my dad had one of those Craftsman electric lanterns for working on cars—and suddenly those were our evening plans.

At that point, we had already explored almost the whole house and found that there was pretty much nothing in it. Mike wanted to go up into the attic, but there were no attic steps anymore, just a rectangular opening in the ceiling above the stairwell. He was going to jump up, grab the ledge, and pull himself up, but it turned out the attic was full of pigeons, and there was some discussion of whether he would fall through the floor, so we never went up there.

Not long after that, we went back outside. We couldn't go back to school at that point because we were so high that we were pretty heavily impaired—the kind of high where all you can do is sit down and feel it—so we just sat in my car listening to Danzig. As much as I love that record, it's really dark. I mean, the darkness is what you like about Danzig if you like Danzig at all—he's not likely to flip on you like Grievo at the Suicide Club—but it just seemed like something happened, which at that time I attributed to the music, where the mood changed. And I might be making this up, but if so it's not intentional: if I remember correctly, the song that was playing when we all sort of woke up was "Until You Call on the Dark." It's been twenty-plus years, but I really am pretty sure that was the one.

But anyway, we're all just sitting there, too high to go back to school or do anything else, and we've got no more weed, no more money, nowhere to go, just waiting for the time to pass, and all of a sudden something changed. Nothing *happened*, or nothing detectable, but something was different. So, picture this: I'm at the wheel, Mike's sitting shotgun, and Lacey is in the back, leaning forward, resting her chin on the back of my seat so her head's right next to mine, and we're all just slumped over, being stoned. It's like that for a while, a couple of songs at least, and then, all at once, Lacey sits back and buttons up her jacket and starts putting her shoes back on—she was one of those girls who always takes her shoes off—Mike rolls his window up, and I start the car. Like, all at the exact same time. And there was no talking. It seemed like we all felt the change and just knew we had to leave. I pull out onto Old Baltimore Pike and head west, back toward school, very slowly.

Apparently, we had been there for some time. When we arrived at that house it was like ten after eleven in the morning or near noon or something like that. School didn't end until two fifteen, but by the time we got back, it was very close to the end of the day—the buses had started parking in front, and the kids who had cars were already sneaking out to the parking lot. So, we parked there for a few minutes. And if I didn't say so before, the reason we had to go back at all was because Lacey was one of those girls whose parents, like, *kept track* of her, so I couldn't drop her off at home. She had to be seen getting off the bus with her sister or she would get into trouble. I know that sounds contradictory because there she was skipping school and getting high with us and making plans to come back and get drunk, but that's how things were with her. Her parents thought she was under their control, but she snuck around and essentially did whatever she felt like she could get away with.

We waited there until it was late enough that she could walk in the back door of the school and straight out the front and get on the bus. Once she was gone, I drove Mike home and then went home myself, and that was pretty much the end of the abandoned house business for a couple days.

I know that sounds contradictory, too, because we had made plans to go back that same night, but we didn't. For whatever reason—probably Lacey couldn't get away, but I honestly don't remember—we didn't go back until several days later, and then the circumstances weren't exactly what we had expected. At some point one of us had managed to get more weed, and I was at Mike's house because we were going to get high. We stood in his driveway for a few minutes bullshitting about nothing, and then I was like, "You want to go back to that house?" And he immediately said, "Yeah, let's go." It was so quick that it was like he was thinking of it all along just like me. At this remove of time it's stupid to speculate, but I strongly believe that neither of us had thought of anything else since the day we first saw it, and as repulsed as we were, we also knew that we had to go back to that place and see what the situation was.

We turn toward my car, I flick my cigarette out into the street and start fumbling for my keys, and then Mike's mom sticks her head out the door and says, "Michael. Phone." So, he goes inside. I stand outside and light another cigarette, which I promptly have to flick into the street, too, because I can see Mike through the door glass motioning me in. He's on the phone—an old-school landline with the long curly cord. It's Lacey. Turns out that she had called my house first, and when she found that I wasn't there, she called Mike's looking for me, and now that she knows what we're doing she wants to go, too, can we come get her? I say yeah. She says she has the booze. Park somewhere a street or two over, and she'll come and find us. Mike grabs his tape player and a stack of tapes, and I already had the light in the trunk of my car, so we head out.

Lacey lived twenty minutes away, in the opposite direction from the house, so I'm flying at some ridiculous speed up Route 72, trying to cut down on how long this whole operation is going to take. But we get there and now we have a problem because she said to park two streets over, but she never said which direction "over" is, or where on the street, so obviously I guessed wrong. We waited forever. Mike finally said let's just leave, but I didn't want to go without her, so we ended up driving around and found her sitting on a curb, shivering and angry with me. We pick her up, and she has a backpack with the stolen booze, and now I'm flying down 72 in the opposite direction, and none of us are talking. Here we are, silent, on the way to an abandoned house at what must now be around 9:00 p.m.—and remember that the stated purpose for going back is to fucking party and get drunk. We have Mike's tape player with batteries, a bunch of tapes, a bunch of weed, a bunch of booze, and we're going to make a night of it. It's a big thing, and we should all be excited about it, but here we are saying nothing, like we're all nervous or something.

So, finally we get back to the right section of Old Baltimore Pike, which is hell and gone from Lacey's house, and we're flying down it, literally downhill toward 273. We get there, no one's around so we pull right in, and then we all sort of realize how fucking awesome this is going to be. Like, whatever spell was over us has now been canceled entirely, and we're happy to be there. I'm carrying Lacey's backpack and the light we stole from one of our dads, so I'm going first, down the exterior steps into the basement, up the steps into the kitchen, up the main stairs, and into the room—the master bedroom or whatever that still has glass in the windows—and we're talking about dumb high school shit—school, our parents, other people, and so on, which all makes the atmosphere seem more appropriate. We were there to have a good time, and it finally sounded like it. Even if it didn't quite feel that way, it was starting to. So, we get to the room, and the light fills it, and we start arranging stuff. It was way colder in there than we thought it would be, but that's relative—it was only October, so it wasn't like we were freezing. It was just that there was pretty much zero difference between the temperature in that room and the temperature outside. But whatever. We had music and light and weed and booze and privacy and each other, and we had all that at the same time, which was more than we were used to.

None of us had brought anything to sit on, even though Lacey had specifically mentioned that the first day we were there, so we sat on the floor with the lantern in the middle, and we started passing around booze. First was a bottle of some terrible, super-sweet wine that we all hated. I don't know if it was port or sherry or what, but it was awful, and we all made those horrible faces you make when you're young and you're not used to drinking. Then at some point we quit drinking that and opened the other bottle she had, which was Beefeater gin. I remember Mike at one point saying something like *What the* fuck *is a beefeater?* and none of us knew. Drinking straight gin seemed fucking impossible to us, but somehow we did it for a little while before we gave up on that, too, and started smoking weed out of one of those pipes that's made out of glass that looks like it has colored ribbons in it. I don't recall whose pipe it was, but probably Mike's. But things went on like that.

We sat there for I don't know how long smoking weed, smoking cigarettes, talking nonsense, laughing our asses off, and occasionally taking a quick drink off one of those horrible bottles. I guess we didn't yet know how to pace ourselves because we wound up just astonishingly fucked up. Like, the kind of fucked up where you start thinking you're in trouble, and eventually we all passed out. I only remember a few other things before that happened. I remember Lacey peeing in the hallway because she didn't want to go into the bathroom for some reason, I remember trying really hard not to throw up in front of her, which I didn't, and that at one point we were listening to Metallica's *Ride the Lightning* and it had an extra layer of tape hiss because it was a dubbed copy, and Mike was irritated because the sound was so bad. And then at some point we were all three completely out. I can only speculate about the time. Could have been eleven or twelve, but it probably wasn't much later than that. And then at some point we all three seemed to wake up together, or at least it seemed to *me* that we were waking up at the same time, and when we woke up, things were very different.

When we woke up, the lantern was gone, and I don't think I realized that we were still in the same place. The room was dark, but there was a wedge of light coming from the partially opened door, and we could hear a conversation going on downstairs. The house was warm now, and it smelled lived in. Before we had fallen asleep, the house essentially had no smell, or had the same smell as the woods around it. Now it smelled like a house. You could smell food and laundry and leather and water and somehow even the fabric of clothes—it was a living place. Mike and I looked at each other, and he said something like,

Dude, we have to get the fuck out of here. Lacey was silent, but her eyes were wide, and her arms were crossed like she was holding onto herself. The voices downstairs got louder. I couldn't make out what was said. I could only tell that it was a man and a woman arguing, that the man was very angry, and that very abruptly the voices stopped. There was the sound of vigorous movement, a brief scream, then racing footsteps, which soon reached the stairs and became louder as they ascended. A woman bolted into the room, turned around and tried to push the door closed behind her, but the man, her pursuer, reached it before she could get it closed and flung it open violently. The doorknob must have slipped out of her hand or something, because the door came swinging around so fast it was like there was nothing resisting it, and it hit her right in the face. She screamed this muffled scream and fell on her knees crying with both hands over her mouth. The man turned on the lights. When the lights came on, Lacey screamed, and Mike and I jumped to our feet, like we were going to fight this guy, but we both just stood there. The man and the woman who I assume was his wife did not react to our presence at all. The man went over to the woman, punched her in the side of the head, and when she fell over, he knelt on her chest and started strangling her with both hands. This whole time Lacey was screaming louder and louder, just over and over again, and I remember having the weirdest thoughts at that moment. It was almost like a part of me lifted right out of my body, and was experiencing it from above, and was completely indifferent to everything that was happening, even while my conscious self was horrified.

This woman is on her back being strangled, her whole face is covered in blood, and you can see the giant gash on her top lip from where the door had smashed it against her teeth, and the whole scene is fucked. Mike and I go over to try to stop this dude from killing his wife, but we can't touch him. We can see him, but our hands pass right through him like there's nothing there but air, nothing solid, so we just back up against the wall. Pretty soon the lady stops moving, and then the guy lets go. I remember that moment very clearly because his hands were frozen in the pose they were in while he was strangling her—his fingers were long and thin, and his hands were shaking and bent at all three knuckles and looked like claws. Then, in the new silence—Lacey is silent now, too—we realized that there was noise coming from outside the room.

We look over at the door, and there's a little kid standing there. I'm not good at figuring out what age a kid is, but let's say three? Like, the kid was old enough to walk but still seemed more like a baby than a kid, and I wouldn't have guessed that the kid could talk very well yet. The kid was holding a pillow really tightly and crying in that way that only little kids cry, where it's like a low, continuous *ooooooooo*. I never had any kids of my own, so I don't get affected like some fathers I know, but it was really upsetting to see that kid looking into that room, the circumstances being what they were.

The man backs up, and the kid looks past him and sees his mother, and suddenly the kid seems to both regress and to age a hundred years. He starts crying in the way that newborn babies cry, where it's this sorrowful screech or wail that's distorted and ugly and makes you wonder whether something is seriously wrong. More than anything else, the man looks embarrassed. He says something like, *It's OK, son. Your mother's OK. She's just resting,* or *she's just sleeping,* or something equally absurd that you might expect a desperate man would try to fool a kid into believing. The man takes his son and lays him down next to his wife, who we all at this time think is dead, and then he puts a sheet or blanket over the two of them with their heads poking out the top like they really are just asleep on the floor. The kid curls up into the fetal position and goes silent. The man goes into the closet, reaches up to a shelf above the clothes hanging there, and now he's got a chrome pistol—a revolver. And then in the new silence we can hear a distant crying. And then we hear the only name—the man says, "Carrie. Carrie, it's OK, baby," and his footsteps recede, and we can hear him talking low to his daughter. Then there's a pistol shot. Me and Mike look at each other like *what are we going to do?*, but we don't actually do anything, and then the man comes back. He goes right up to the kid and pulls the sheet back a little. The kid is still in the fetal position, sucking his thumb, and he's got some of his mother's blood on him. The man puts the pistol to the kid's temple and fires. After that, the kid's head just doesn't exist anymore. Not like it did. There's, like, a spray of red and a gaping hole and just ... fuck.

Let me tell you this. I'm an inveterate fan of horror of all kinds—ghost stories, slasher flicks, *Evil Dead*, *The Haunting*, *Texas Chainsaw Massacre*, all that shit. Even, like, Poe. Horror is something I love, and after being immersed in it for a while nothing affects you. You don't cringe when Ash gets his arm cut off with a chainsaw or when that possessed woman keeps trying to get out of the basement screaming "Dead by dawn!"—it's just another scene in another movie, and you literally laugh. But it's *different* to see something real. Like, the hole in that kid's head wasn't filled with shredded latex and corn syrup dyed red. There was a brain in there. I don't really know how to say it, but the stuff that makes your head work—the muscles, skin, bone, teeth, *real things*. When you see that stuff inside a bloody hole in a human body, all horror movie effects look ridiculously fake by comparison. It's affecting, and powerfully sad, and it makes you realize that your own death is coming. It's *momentous* that this once-living being lost its life and that you are bearing witness to it. And that feeling has always stayed with me because of that kid. Seeing that kid get shot like that was the most disturbing thing I've ever experienced, and I still think about it.

The pistol report is so loud in the closed room that I go almost deaf for the next few minutes. And I wasn't the only one affected by the noise—the woman, the wife, who seemed dead, starts moving, like she was just passed out and the shot startled her awake, and she starts choking on her own blood. She's coughing and spitting up blood and gasping for breath, but then the guy shoots her, too, and she's definitely dead this time. Her head also sort of dissolved, or sort of collapsed a little, and it was just too much. I can't even tell you about it.

So, then the guy gets this look on his face, and at first I think he's going to try to cover this up—he's changing his shirt because it has blood on it, and wiping his hands off on the bed sheets—but then I realize that he's planning on running. He starts gathering up clothes, he takes a box of shells out of the closet, and I start to get the impression that he's going to set the place on fire, but something stops him. I don't know what it was—whether he could hear sirens that we couldn't hear, or whether he just decided that he wasn't going to be able to live with this, or what—but at some point he just sits down on the bed, looks at his hands for a few seconds, looks dispassionately at his dead wife and son, then lays on the bed for a few seconds and sits back up. It seems like he can't decide what he's going to do, but then very abruptly, almost like he was trying to make himself do it without having time to think his way out of it, he just stands up, puts the muzzle in his mouth, and blows his own brains out.

And that's it. We watch as the light in that room fades away and turns into the now very dim light of the electric lantern. All the furniture is gone, and it's just us and our bottles and tape player and some cigarette butts. Everything is back to the way it was when we were drinking, except that we're all looking up at the hole in the ceiling right above where that man had been standing.

So, at this point, we all think it's over. Mike sits down like he's exhausted, and I stay leaning against the wall, and the three of us are there in the lantern light for a few seconds. Then something even stranger happens—the lady appears. The room doesn't change back to how it was, but she's there with us, and she's just like an outline, and there's no sound. There's just this form, and it's walking around to each of the three of us, and the outline is so thin. It's like, if you wear glasses and you see an electric light at night, and that light is the only light, there are these weird kinds of reflections, ghosts of light that appear somehow *inside* the lenses—the lady was like that. If I had turned my head away, I wouldn't be sure if it was the lady or just one of those weird ghosts of light. But I didn't wear glasses back then, and I didn't turn my head, and I saw this lady walking around to each of us, making these gestures, like *imploring* gestures, like she was trying to get us to do something, but we couldn't hear her. And this I remember very clearly because I never saw anyone do this in real life—it's the kind of thing you only ever read about in *the Bible*—she starts tearing at her own hair, ripping it out with both hands, and her mouth was wide open like she was screaming even though it was dead silent in the room. It was the strangest thing I ever saw.

So, then we hear a car and, being stoner kids, we immediately think it's the cops. We look toward the window, but there's no light, and I realize it's a car out on 273 or Old Baltimore Pike. Then I turn back to look at Mike and Lacey, and the lady is gone. It's just the three of us. Mike picks up the tape player and the tapes. Lacey picks up her bag and puts the bottles in it. I take her by one hand and pick up the light with the other, and the three of us make our way down the stairs and outside without saying anything.

When we get outside, we all stop by my car and look back at the house, but it didn't show us anything else. It looked as black and dead as if there had never been anyone in it. I light a cigarette but Lacey takes it from me, so I light another one, and we're all looking at each other but no one wants to say anything. I didn't have a watch, the clock in my car had stopped long before I bought it, and I don't remember looking at the clock after I got home, so I don't even have an estimate of what time it was. I just know that it was very late or very early because it was so quiet. There was almost no traffic, no white noise, not even a dog barking. I felt like people a mile away might hear us if we said anything. Finally, real low, Lacey says something like "I have to get home," so we get in the car and pull out of there. I hit the road, tires spinning, and that was that. I never went back there, and I would bet money that Mike and Lacey never went back there again either. But that's still not quite the end.

At some point in the forty or so minutes it takes me to get Lacey home, I hear her sniffing in the back, so I know she's crying. I mean, she was well within her rights to cry as much as she wanted after what we saw—if she and Mike weren't with me I might have been crying, too. But me and Mike don't say anything. I look in the rearview to try to see Lacey, but she's laying down out of sight. So, then I look at Mike—I guess because I'm a fucking bigmouth, you know? I have trouble sitting still for things. I need to say something about everything, and I want to say something about this. So, I'm driving, and I look over at him and see him look at me, but we don't say anything. I look over again and he looks at me again, but it's like he's annoyed, and I get this vibe like *Quit fucking looking at me*, and then he reaches over, turns Danzig back on—"Until You Call on the Dark"—turns to his right, and just looks out the window.

I finally turn into Lacey's neighborhood, and she just says, "Let me out here," right at the entrance of the place. I don't argue. I stop the car and let her out. She stashes her bag with the gin and wine in the trunk of my car, asks me for another cigarette, which I give her, and then I give her a light. In the light from the lighter I can see that her face is all shiny and red, but before I can say anything she looks at me real quick and says, "See ya," and walks away.

I get back in the car and drive Mike home. Neither of us says anything the whole time. And I keep dwelling on the silence, or the Danzig, because *why weren't we talking?* Inside I was screaming and fucking crying and running around in circles yelling *holy shit, holy shit, holy shit*, you know? But I can't get any of my friends to talk to me, and it's driving me fucking insane. We get to Mike's house, and I pull up out front and shut off the car. We sit there. More silence—not even Danzig now.

And finally I can't take it anymore and I just go, more loudly than I meant to, "Dude, did you fucking see that shit?"

And Mike doesn't hesitate or anything. Immediately he goes, "Fuck yeah, I saw it. I didn't know if *you* saw it."

So, then there's like a flood of fucking talking. Like, *what the fuck was that? It was like a movie. I guess that happened there. I wonder if people who lived there after them saw crazy stuff inside the house and that was why it was abandoned.* All kinds of obvious talk. The one thing that bothers me now is that we took for granted that we saw the same thing—we never discussed exactly *what* we saw, we just assumed it was the same thing and speculated about what it meant or what were the possible reasons for it or whatever. I just wish we had had a more explicit or descriptive conversation. But I guess it doesn't matter that much. I think they *must* have seen what I saw.

After a while we stopped talking, and I was smoking, and Mike was like, "Are you going to tell anybody?"

I said, "Fuck no," because who the fuck would believe me? He felt the same, and he probably never did tell anyone. But like I said, I have a big mouth. I wanted and intended to keep quiet about it—I never wanted to be the idiot who tells this tale—but here we are.

At that point, there is nothing else to say, so he goes inside, and I drive home. It was a long drive, north, or northwest on Telegraph Road, and then north on 213, and the whole time I keep looking behind me like I'm going to talk to Lacey or something, even though I know she isn't back there. But somehow the urge to turn around, or to my right, like turning toward someone, is always with me.

Finally I get home, and obviously everyone is asleep. At that time, we rented this awful house that looked like the seventies—everything was earth tones, burnt orange and brown, and the living room carpet was that carpet that looks like mashed potatoes, and it was this dirty pale green color. The whole place smelled like what I now recognize as the smell of water damage, and it was always cold unless it was hot outside, in which case it was hot. The walls were paper thin, too, so I couldn't even put on music. Jesus, I *hated* it, and after a night like that I couldn't take it without some help, so I steal some of my stepmom's vodka, and replace it with water. I took too much, but what the fuck was I supposed to do after literally seeing a ghost murder some other ghosts? And I just felt weird. I felt off, like something was wrong. I kept getting chills up my spine, and I kept turning around as if to see someone or talk to someone, but of course no one was there. And I couldn't shake it, it *would not stop*. So, I steal the vodka and drink it down—still a little drunk and high, or at least burned out, from our little party—and, thank God, it puts me right out.

I don't know what I dreamed about, but I was tossing and turning all night—it felt like a physical struggle just to stay asleep. In the morning my alarm goes off, and for the next couple hours I'm half awake, half drunk, and feeling like I had just been in a fight or something. I spend most of the day drifting in and out of sleep and smoking cigarettes out my bedroom window. And all that time I'm ignoring something. You know how sometimes you know something but you just choose to look the other way? Choose to pretend it isn't happening or it isn't true? Usually when you do that it starts to feel like it really isn't happening or isn't true. But not that day. I kept the act up, like whistling through the graveyard, you know? But I knew, I was absolutely *certain*, that that lady had followed me home.

Nothing happened after that, and that's really the end of the story, but I think that should be enough to keep you awake if you believe me. And if not, I guess good night.

9

UNPLEASANTNESS

In 2001, Todd was twenty-four years old, five feet and nine inches tall, weighed 285 pounds, and made $8.25 an hour at the Mobil station that was right in the center of I-95, where he worked at least forty hours a week. The Mobil station was on what Todd thought of as the south end of the service plaza but was actually the west end, as he would have known if he ever considered why the sun set pretty much directly in his eyes every day. Though the signs said I-95 NORTH and I-95 SOUTH, the freeway actually ran east and west around here. But he never did consider that. He just sat there smoking Marlboro menthol lights, coughing, and spitting out the door of the little booth where the cash register was.

Although he was only twenty-four, several months ago he had started having searing chest pains that reached out like long, sharp fingers, or like a forked lightning bolt, up through his shoulder and into his left arm. During these events, he also felt dizzy, like he was going to pass out. Knowing that chest pains were a sign of heart trouble, and knowing that although he was young he was also really fat and drank and smoked way more than a normal person, he assumed he was having a heart attack or something like a prelude to one. The insurance offered to him and his fellow employees at the Mobil station was known to be a very expensive joke. Ann had to get it because she had a daughter, and everyone followed her experience as a sort of test case. Once she had signed up for it—and there was no getting out of it for a full year after signing up—she found out that the closest doctor who accepted that insurance was across the state line, somewhere in Pennsylvania, and that the copay was thirty-five dollars, so she couldn't even use it. After watching Ann sign away a ton of money from each paycheck for insurance she couldn't use, everyone else was glad they had waived it. But now, altogether without insurance, Todd's situation prevented him from going to a doctor until he could save up sixty dollars. That wouldn't have been too bad but for the fact that before he could even start saving, he actually passed out at work during one of his episodes, and John and Jason had to call an ambulance.

The ambulance drivers were really nice guys. They asked him if he could walk out to the ambulance, which he did, and then they put him on a gurney. Once they got him to the hospital, they wheeled him in and left him in a hallway, where he waited—glad to be lying down—for three and a half hours before the doctor actually saw him. The doctor hooked him up to an EKG machine and left him sitting there for quite some time but ultimately said that there was no sign that he had had a heart attack, that his heartbeat was regular and normal, and that in all likelihood what he had actually had was a panic attack. He gave Todd a small brown prescription bottle that had three little blue Xanax pills in it and said to take one the next time this happened. Which he did, and did again, and again. They sort of helped. But once they were spent, he couldn't afford to refill the prescription, and he didn't know anyone who could get them from a dealer. And anyway, he had never heard of a panic attack, and the pains he had were not in his head—they were in his chest, and they were *very* real—so he couldn't bring himself to believe the doctor. The doctor hadn't even seen him until three and a half hours after the attack, so, Todd reasoned, his heart could have straightened out during that three and a half hours, and he could have *seemed* fine to the doctor when in fact something really bad had happened. He was sure he was going to have heart attack and was essentially helpless to fight it.

Todd had seen a commercial, though, for Bayer aspirin, and the purposely vague claim it made was that taking a Bayer aspirin before a heart attack could save your life. He couldn't afford to see a doctor yet, but he could afford aspirin, so he started carrying a bottle of store-brand Bayer-lookalike aspirin around with him. Whenever he would start feeling dizzy or get chest pains, he took one. But that didn't make it stop. Nothing changed at all. So he started taking two, and then three, and then four aspirins at a time. That was several months ago—probably six or more—and now he couldn't stop coughing and spitting. Phlegm would come up, as well as little hard white things, which scared him. The hard white things could be pieces of a tumor, for all he knew. Whenever he ate now, he felt sick, like he was going to vomit, and no matter how much he ate, or what it was, it felt like it got caught somewhere between his throat and his stomach. No amount of water would wash it down. Water actually made it worse. There seemed to be nothing he could do, so he just sat and smoked and coughed and spit out the door of the booth while Jason changed all the trash bags in the cans between the pumps.

He and Jason worked the two-to-ten shift together almost every day, and the arrangement they had was that Todd ran the register and Jason did all the shit outside the booth—manned the full service pumps when they were open, cleaned the bathrooms, changed the trash bags. Though it seemed unfair to outsiders, it suited them.

It was nearing 5:00 p.m. on a Sunday in July. The rickety little air-conditioner in the side of the booth hummed steadily, but the temperature inside never got below seventy-eight and often hovered around eighty-two, as it was doing right now. They were both sweating patches through their scratchy, rented, Cintas uniforms, and condensation was running down the walls. Todd lit another cigarette. "It smells like a summertime blow job in here."

"Yeah."

"Wish we had some weed."

"Yeah."

"You have any whiskey?"

"Yeah. Not much left, though." When he could afford it, Jason kept a pint of whiskey in his backpack for the stated reason that it helped with his toothaches, which was originally the truth, but more and more frequently it was for drinking at work. "I thought you couldn't drink it because of your stomach."

"I just have to have something. I just have to. If you don't mind. Between the two of us, we'll probably kill it."

Jason got the bottle out of his pack, took a hit from it,

and passed it to Todd, who hit it too. Now the whiskey was caught between his throat and his stomach. He swallowed hard several times, but his mouth was dry, and he knew that no amount of saliva or water or anything was going to stop this. He felt a kind of desperation. He had no idea what was wrong with him, physically or mentally. He hated this place but couldn't bring himself to quit, and anyway it was a bad idea to quit because this was the best-paying job he had ever had. He sometimes thought about walking out into traffic.

"How's your stomach? That shit tear it up?"

"Little bit." He coughed and spat out the door, then got up to change the CD. He took out *Undertow* and put *Static Age* in, but the minute it started playing he remembered that they had listened to it already today and switched it out for *Walk Among Us*. As much as he loved the CD, it did not improve the situation.

About this time on Sundays it was usually intensely busy. Everyone was coming back from the beach, and the traffic on this stretch of 95 was worse even than it was during weekday rush hour. But today it was comparatively dead. It had rained four days in a row, starting Thursday, so, they supposed, fewer people had gone to the beach on Friday, and consequently fewer people were coming back today. Whether that was the real reason, they didn't know. Traffic was only partly predictable. They were just glad to have a relatively calm Sunday. There were twenty-four pumps here, and on a typical Sunday it was normal for sixteen of them to be in use at once, for them to have to sell oil and cigarettes, and to have to answer the same goddamn questions ("Where's the bathroom?" "How am I supposed to pay first if I don't know how much I need?") over and over to at least seven of those sixteen. And because the traffic jam on the freeway would last at least four hours, this number was constantly replenished. There was always a line, and the people in the line had been in traffic all afternoon and were looking for someone to spit on. It was a hateful place.

Things started to pick up a little bit around 8:00 p.m., which was when the sun started to set, and Jason had to lock the bathrooms and clean them. The story was that years ago a girl had been kidnapped from back there by a trucker, and after the police caught the guy and she was free, she tried to sue the franchisee for gross negligence because there was zero oversight of that area. Ever since then the owner had insisted that the bathrooms had to be locked as soon as it started to get dark, which pissed the customers off even if they were told the story, because the story, everyone had to admit, sounded like a lie.

"I'm going to go up," Jason said, meaning go up to the garage, lock the bathrooms, and clean them. "You gonna be OK?" He was referring to Todd's heart issue, or panic attack issue, or whatever it was.

"Sure." Being alone here with the customers, whom he viewed as his enemies, did not comfort him, but the alternative was that *he* clean the bathrooms, which he flatly refused to do. Jason took the keys and went up. Todd felt the muscles in his back and shoulders tighten and checked his pulse—in his own way. He didn't actually know what doctors or nurses were doing when they checked a pulse rate—what they were timing, or for how long, or what was normal. He just put his two fingers on his jugular and just sort of . . . checked. Not too fast, not too slow, not too hard, not too soft? Whatever. It felt OK right now. He was satisfied and lit another cigarette, coughed, and spit out the door. He was starting to notice that whatever was wrong with his stomach also came with wicked heartburn. He swallowed hard to no effect, then decided to take two aspirin just as a precaution.

THE NEXT AFTERNOON when Todd woke up, he was covered in sweat, the inside of his mouth tasted like battery acid, and his esophagus burned all the way from his throat to his stomach. He rifled through his grandmother's medicine cabinet for something that might stop it. He stumbled onto some Rolaids that, from the packaging, looked like they were from the eighties, but he chewed them up anyway. They tasted like metallic chalk with a hint of mint and were definitely from the eighties, but they did the job for a few minutes. During that few minutes, he thought he may have found a solution to this whole situation until he realized that even the Rolaids got stuck in his esophagus. He coughed, lifted the screen of his window, and spit outside. His grandmother had turned off the air-conditioner early in the morning to try to cut down the electric bill, and she wouldn't turn it back on until after he went to work. She had some kind of complex reasoning for that, but he felt like she did it to spite him, or drive him out. He was sweating through his shirt, and his sheets were damp with sweat. He believed he could feel heat radiating down from the ceiling in waves. "Fucking sun."

He stumbled into the kitchen to try to find something to eat. He didn't understand why milk was so damaging to him, but he knew better than to have any. When this started, the first solution that came to mind was to drink milk, so he did, and he never felt worse. The pain was needle-sharp and seemed to be everywhere. It came up from his stomach and shot branches out all over his chest like a tree of fire. It was so intense he didn't even consider that this might be some kind of stomach ailment. He thought there was something wrong with his nerves themselves. So, no milk. He settled on a cheese sandwich. Then a second and third. And about six Chips Ahoy! cookies.

It was nearly 1:00 p.m., so he needed to hurry. He took a quick shower, got out on the freeway, and was immediately in a traffic jam. There had been an accident, and they were only letting traffic through the left lane, where he already was. As any traffic savvy person knew, that meant he would get through more slowly than all the fucking assholes from the other lanes who were cutting in line. "Fucking assholes." He would be late again, but he didn't care. His job was not in danger. There was so much volume at this station, and so many of the customers were helpless whining assholes, that they had trouble keeping employees for more than two or three weeks. The last new hire had only worked four days before he quit. Todd had been there for more than a year and always showed up for his shift, so within reason he could do whatever he wanted. But now he had to wait. He rolled his window down and spit onto the shoulder of the freeway. Then he had a coughing fit and spit again, prodigious amounts of hideous phlegm with hard little white things. "Please fucking God," he said, breathing deeply, and meaning something like *please god let that be the last of this shit I have to spit out today*. He took a couple of deep breaths that felt good and cool before the discomfort started building toward pain. He winced and shook his head, and then a hard rain started. He rolled his window up eighty-five percent of the way, lit another cigarette, and blew thin streams of smoke out of the crack. But soon there was too much water coming in, and he couldn't stand it anymore.

This had once been a nice car. It was an eighty-eight Trans Am with a high output .305 and T-tops. It could still fly, provided it was cold outside, but it suffered in the heat and was prone to stalling when it was humid or raining like today. Keeping it running in these conditions was a complex operation. He had to put one foot on the gas just a tiny bit to keep the engine idling high and then hold the brake down hard with his other foot to keep the car from moving forward. Any failure or subtle change in this balance would cause the engine to stall. All the weather stripping was dry rotted too. The passenger side window was OK, but the driver's side leaked, so water dribbled down the inside of the glass, and when it rained a lot, like it had been doing recently, the driver's side floorboards would be wet all the time. The T-tops leaked as well. Mostly toward the back of the passenger side, which kept the floorboards and the back seat wet, too, but he didn't care about that. What pissed him the fuck off more than anything else was the drip from the front corner of the driver's side. It dripped right onto his left knee, so the knee of his pants would be wet all day at work. And it dripped irregularly, so just as he was starting to forget about it, it would drip and piss him off all over again. The cigarette he had been smoking eventually went out from the rain that hit it when he flicked ashes out the window, so he flicked the butt outside, rolled the window up, and just waited. During the time it took him to smoke that cigarette, he had moved forward maybe three or four car lengths, just inches at a time, as asshole after asshole, in SUVs and minivans and a thousand other types of cars that were all newer and in better shape than his, cut into the fucking line and kept the left fucking lane from moving almost at all. All this time and he wasn't even at the Churchmans Road exit.

Obviously, the air-conditioner in Todd's car didn't work, so with the windows up it was horribly hot, and he was sweating through his scratchy Cintas uniform. The T-top dripped on his knee. "Fuck." His stomach hurt, and little razor pains were starting to work up his chest. He coughed, rolled down the window, spit onto the shoulder of the road, and put the window back up. Sweat from his forehead was starting to soak the band of his Mobil hat, which already felt loose and moist from yesterday. He watched the brand-new cars ahead of him cut in line. "Fuck." Drip. "*Fuck.*" He had a nervous habit of working his fingers into the cut-out of the steering wheel. The steering wheel of the eighty-eight Trans Am had a big square cut-out right in the center that, he had discovered because of this habit, would slide right out and reveal a roughly cube-shaped cavity perfect for hiding weed or a pipe or any other small object he wanted to hide from cops. At the bottom of the cavity were the contact wires for the horn and his sleek black anodized aluminum pipe. He, like a lot of stoners, had a sentimental connection to his pipe. It had been with him all through high school. Had been to all his classes with him. Every one of his friends, most of whom he had now lost touch with, had smoked from that pipe many times. Its age showed in the scratches and scrapes that shone silver through the black coating. It was his favorite possession, and he would have loved to use it right now, but there was no weed to be had. And he couldn't have afforded it anyway. He even considered taking the pipe out of its hiding place in the steering wheel and stashing it somewhere in his bedroom. You never know what the cops know. Maybe some slick cop had pulled over a guy in a Trans Am before and found something in the wheel. If a cop like that pulled him over and thought to check his, he'd be fucked. He left it there for some reason, though.

When he finally got to work it was 2:47, and by the time he clocked in it was 2:52. He couldn't even make that lost time up because the shift was set from two to ten. When Mike came in to work graveyard, that was it, he had to clock out. So that hour, or fifty-two minutes, that he had spent watching rich SUV drivers actively slow down the people with the presence of mind and common courtesy to get in the correct lane cost him money that he couldn't get back. Nearly eight dollars and twenty-five cents. His left knee was soaked. Sweat had wicked through the back of his shirt pocket, so now the back of his cigarette pack was moist and concave. The cigarettes inside were a little bent, and he felt like an idiot smoking bent cigarettes, so he tried to straighten one, lit it, and coughed and spit as he walked down from the office to the booth. Without even coming inside, he walked around to the back of the booth, where he had a serious coughing fit, and spit prodigiously.

When he opened the door, the shift change was over, and only Jason was inside. Mark and Ann were long gone.

"Where the fuck were you, man?"

"Traffic. There was an accident by the mall."

"Fuck. I was wondering what happened."

Per their understanding, Todd took Jason's place in front of the register, and Jason went outside to move the orange cones away from the full service pumps. There was a line of customers.

"Lemme git seventeen on . . . that one over there and a pack of Marlboro reds." He gave the man his smokes and his change.

"Newport box." He gave the man his smokes and his change.

The next combatant in line had the fighting look on his face, as if he were planning to make an unassailable argument and expose an injustice that couldn't possibly be justified. Todd knew to show no emotion whatever and to refuse to even change the blank expression on his face.

"How am I supposed to pay first if I don't know how much I'm going to get?"

"You have to pay first." It was best not to engage.

"But I want to fill it up."

"You have to pay first."

"That's what I just said, how am I supposed to pay first if I don't know how much I'm going to get?"

"You have to estimate or use a credit card."

The guy dropped a credit card in the metal drawer.

"You have to put it in the pump."

"I don't want to put it in the pump. I saw on TV they can steal your credit card information from those pumps." This was untrue in 2001. The report that had been on TV was based on a misunderstanding.

"Then you have to pay first." This was untrue. He could have just taken the guy's card, let him pump as much as he wanted, and then run it. He just felt it was important not to make concessions to customers. The overall attitude of this station was that no one should allow the customers to create unnecessary work for you. They all considered the kind of confrontation that was currently going on a principled stand. The customers should be putting credit cards in the pumps, pumping gas, and driving away. If they wanted cigarettes or oil, that was fine, but there was no excuse for complicated fussiness of this sort except being old or a flat-out asshole.

"They said on the news that if you don't want your credit card stolen, you have to use it *inside*."

"OK. How much do you want?"

"*I want to fill it up!*"

"You have to pay first."

"You're a fucking asshole, man." This was clearly true. "I want to talk to your supervisor."

"He's not here." Also true. There effectively were no supervisors at this location.

"Then I want his name and phone number."

Todd put a business card in the metal drawer and slid it out to the other asshole.

"Asshole," the customer said as he took the card and walked angrily back to his car. The number was a corporate number of some kind. No one who worked there had ever bothered to call it, but they also never heard back about complaints from customers who said they were going to call, so they gave the card out freely. In truth, people who called just got lost in a series of dialing options and gave up, or if they did get through, they didn't know the location number, address of the station, or the name of the person they had gotten angry with, so it all came to nothing.

"That guy was a fuckin' asshole."

Jason said nothing.

"Seriously, *fuck* that motherfucker."

Jason continued to say nothing. Jason's opinion was that it was foolish to start fights like that, but he also had started his share of them out of a similar type of anger, so he wasn't in a position to judge.

"Fucking *cocksucker*." Todd's lungs felt tight, and he was a little short of breath. He swallowed three aspirin with some warm, flat Mountain Dew. About twenty minutes later, he was behind the booth, vomiting uncontrollably.

TODD'S GRANDMOTHER saw how much he was suffering and gave him a break on the rent so he could see a doctor. Over the last three months it had become so difficult for him to hold down food that he lost just over forty pounds, and he felt nauseous at all times. He had started carrying around a bottle of thick, allegedly cherry-flavored syrup called Emetrol, which was supposed to relieve nausea. He sipped it whenever he felt a heave coming, but it did nothing. Maybe it made him feel like he had some measure of control over whether he actually vomited or not, but it didn't prevent him from vomiting any more than simply swallowing or taking tiny sips water.

Doctor Syed Khanna's waiting room was tiny and dark and smelled like fresh paint, though Todd didn't see any paint that was identifiably fresh. The walls were a dark shade of beige that wasn't sharp enough to be tan, and the baseboards were a shade of brown that was just barely lighter than black. It seemed like it had last been painted in the late seventies. Even the vinyl chair he sat on—burnt orange with silver duct tape covering the cracks in the vinyl, little hairs of polyester filling caught in the gum—seemed like a relic that there might be pictures of him sitting on as a baby. The office itself was in a house that had been converted to an office when the real estate on Main Street got too expensive to justify simply living in. Todd wondered when they would knock it down to build more template-designed storefronts leased by businesses he couldn't afford to patronize.

A fat nurse with frizzy black hair brought him back and took his vitals, and when the doctor came in, he took them again himself. Todd told him everything about his heart, the emergency room trip, the aspirin, the vomiting.

"Why didn't you come to see me before this?" Doctor Khanna had a deep, velvety voice and spoke with a combination of Indian and English accents that seemed both comforting and foreboding. He used the language with what seemed an almost too-precise precision, a too-formal formality. He guessed Doctor Khanna had been trained that way, but it made Todd feel both soothed and censured at the same time, like the doctor was going to help him but also considered this illness Todd's fault.

"No insurance. It's expensive."

The doctor looked exhausted after hearing that. "Yes. But it will be more expensive now. As to your heart." Significant pause. "You do need to lose weight. You do need to stop smoking and drinking. But for right now there is nothing wrong with your heart. Even at your weight you are too young for heart problems of this kind. What you are having are panic attacks, which are caused by anxiety. I understand that it feels real to you and that the symptoms are physical, or seem physical to you, but they are created by your mind. This conclusion is supported by the fact that the Xanax worked. It took away these feelings, whereas the aspirin did not. Xanax will not prevent a heart attack, so if you had been having one and took a Xanax, the heart attack would have continued. The likelihood is that these feelings are due to panic.

"The first thing you must do is stop taking the aspirin. The aspirin caused the stomach and esophageal discomfort. It caused the coughing and spitting and is now causing the vomiting. Immediately stop taking it, and do not take it for any reason in the future. Once you do that, the vomiting may go away on its own, but I do not think so. I think that the aspirin, which is very acidic, has damaged your esophageal sphincter. This damage is permanent."

"I have to have surgery?"

"Without insurance, this is not possible. Nor is having such a surgery likely to help you very much or for very long. But there are drugs that can help you." Doctor Khanna took out some sample packets of Xanax and Nexium out of a drawer and handed them to Todd. "When you get this anxious feeling, take one of these"—he held up the Xanax—"just like before. But be careful. These pills can be habit-forming. You can become addicted quite easily, so you must only take this drug when you *need* to. *This* drug"—he held up the Nexium—"is very effective. It should make your stomach issues go away within twenty-four hours. Possibly less than that. Take one right now," he said and gave Todd a paper cup of water. "And take *no more aspirin*."

"So, once I finish these pills, my stomach will be ok?"

Doctor Khanna looked exhausted again. "Unfortunately, it will not work that way. You will need to take these pills perhaps for the rest of your life. This vomiting is not caused by an illness that might be cured. By taking so much aspirin, you have injured your body permanently. Even if at some point in the future you obtain health insurance, the surgery to correct this injury is often not covered because it can reverse itself. What is done by the surgeon can come undone, and then you will need to have the surgery again or else take this medicine or one like it. You will need to take one of these per day from now on. I will write you prescriptions for both of these drugs."

Todd took the Nexium but was not relieved. Nexium was a drug that he had seen commercials for on TV. He didn't know whether that meant that it would be very cheap or very expensive, but he guessed expensive. And he already knew that he couldn't afford to fill the Xanax prescription, but he didn't bother to say it. The doctor wasn't there to pay Todd's way through life. And anyway, Doctor Khanna seemed to know it—the stack of sample boxes he had given Todd amounted to far more medicine than he had expected to come away with. He thanked the doctor, took his pill boxes and prescription slips, and left. When he got to his car, he took a Xanax with some near-boiling Mountain Dew that had been in his hot car all day and headed to work. He decided that he would wait to see whether Nexium actually worked before he would worry about trying to fill the prescription, but almost to his disappointment, by the time work was over he felt so much better that he knew he would have to try.

He told his grandmother the news when he got home, but he withheld from her the fact that he couldn't afford the new drug and that he had spent some money that he should have given to her on a pint of whiskey. She had trouble, as he did, understanding why he would feel like he was having a heart attack when there was nothing wrong with his heart, but she was glad for him and glad that his stomach felt better. "Oh, that's great, honey. You want something to eat?"

"No thanks. It doesn't feel good enough to eat yet," he

lied, avoiding her eyes, "but it will by tomorrow, I think." She had said it was great and pretended to smile, but he could see on her face that she knew he would soon run out of pills, and that he couldn't afford to buy any more. And he knew she couldn't help him. She would have to watch him suffer.

When he closed his door he took off his scratchy Mobil uniform shirt, hung it on the hook on the back of his door, being careful not to disturb or bend the corners of the CD covers he had carefully thumbtacked there—they were cheaper than posters, and more of them would fit. He took off his hat and hung it on the same hook, fished around in some laundry piles for a T-shirt to put on, sat on his bed, took his boots off, kicked them under the TV stand in front of him, fished the pint of whiskey out of his bag, unscrewed the cap, took a hit, turned on his tiny TV, and lay down. There wasn't much else to do in a room this size. From the door to the outer wall was eight feet, and from inner wall to inner wall was six feet. But the bed was about three feet wide and about six feet long, so for practical purposes the bed took up more than half the space. The only things, other than clothes and clutter, that were in the room were a small TV on an upside down milk crate in the corner, a floor lamp, a small CD player, a crate of CDs all the covers of which were tacked to the walls—most recently A Perfect Circle's *Mer de Noms*—and his bed. Virtually nothing else would fit. His options were to sit or lie on the bed and either watch broadcast TV or listen to music while he drank. He had been upright and listening to music all day at work, so TV and lying down were the only viable options. He had to lie on the bed with a pillow under his left arm and the blanket all bunched up because he always slept in the same position, which had caused the mattress to thin out there. If he didn't cushion it properly, he could feel the wooden slats under the bed, and they bruised his arm and elbow. He took another hit of the whiskey and closed his eyes.

Even though it had only been about ten hours since he had taken the pill at the doctor's office, it had taken effect some time ago, and his stomach felt virtually perfect at this point. After about six o'clock that evening he had stopped coughing and spitting out the door. He had even considered having lunch that day but decided against it. He had gotten used to eating nearly nothing, and weight was falling off him. He hadn't been down to 240 since his sophomore year, and he was afraid that if he let himself eat lunch at work he would start eating like he used to and gain it all back, so he had elected not to eat at all that day—he had survived on three Mountain Dews and two, but now three, hits of whiskey.

Tomorrow he would have to find out how much money it would cost him to fill this prescription and then think up a way to get it. He had almost hoped that the drug wouldn't work at all and that he'd either die or the solution would be something else entirely—he had no idea what, but something other than having to take expensive pills forever. His paychecks usually worked out to about two hundred and twenty dollars, and he had to hand one hundred per paycheck over to his grandmother and then live on about four hundred and eighty dollars a month. Cigarettes, gas, car insurance, food, CDs, and booze were his real expenses, and those costs ate up everything at a surprising rate. He usually ran out of cash between three and four days before pay day, and during that time he had to steal sodas and cigarettes, when possible, from work. The sodas were easy, but they had to count the cigarettes at the beginning and end of every shift and account for every pack. It was tricky to live like that. Every cent he earned was spoken for. There was no room for a pricey prescription. He took another, much bigger swallow of whiskey and coughed a little, but nothing came up.

For a while he thought about breaking into the pharmacy, but he knew he never could. There were cameras everywhere. And the pharmacy was set up to keep people from seeing back where the pharmacist was, so he didn't know what he would be dealing with. He knew they locked opiates in a vault or something, but he didn't know if the stomach pills would be locked up too. And he had no way to open a vault if they were locked in there. And there were probably silent alarms. The cops would probably be there before he even got out of the building. Maybe a real burglar could do it, but not him. He took another hit of the whiskey and picked up his alarm clock. He set it for half an hour earlier than normal—eleven forty-five—took another hit of the whiskey, and stopped thinking for the night. Eventually he got trashed and went on a Slayer binge, listening to *South of Heaven, Seasons in the Abyss,* and the record of all records, the unholy of unholies, *Reign in Blood.* The end of the CD, "Postmortem" and "Raining Blood," always moved him, but with the addition of whiskey it was a religious experience. At the end, when the rain cut off dramatically, he breathed a long sigh of relief and soon he passed out on his back. Due to his weight, he had sleep apnea, so his grandmother could hear him snoring all the way on the other side of the trailer.

The next morning he was not rested at all. He was angry and sad and irritated, and more than anything he really wanted to get into a fight with someone. But only his grandmother was there, and he couldn't stand being mean to her. She was the only person who ever actually loved him. He felt that strongly and would never want to upset her or be unpleasant or unkind to her in any way, if he could avoid it. He didn't realize how unpleasant and unkind he actually *was* to her, but if he ever *had* realized it, he would have been mortified.

"You want some coffee, honey?"

"Yes, please."

She sat it in front of him as he sat at the table, his head in his hands, trying to figure out why he felt so terrible. He just wanted everything to stop. He wanted life to be over. He had taken his Nexium as soon as he woke up. It was a beautiful drug. Whatever was wrong with him—he couldn't remember exactly what Doctor Khanna had said—this drug would effectively cure it as long as he took it. He knew how to play around with drugs and make them stretch, but experience told him he wouldn't be able to go more than two days without it, if even that long. For a second he wished he could crush his skull with his fingers. There was no way that he was going to be able to afford this drug. There wasn't any question about that. It was obviously out of his reach; the question was how far.

On his way to work, he stopped at the Rite Aid across the highway. He secretly loved drug stores because they were full of junk food. Big inviting bags of candy and chips and freezers full of ice cream. He hadn't had anything like that since the vomiting started, and he eyed it all avidly as he drifted back to the drug counter. There were people in line, and their transactions were going very quickly. *Picking up? Name? That'll be 26.99.* That kind of thing. All these people had insurance. They all wore nice clothes. They all smiled. They drove the new cars in the parking lot. They probably all lived in the new housing developments that were springing up all over Route 40 and making traffic so awful. *Where do these fucking people get their money? What do I have to fucking do to get this kind of money?*

"Dropping off?"

"Uh, well, no. Sort of. I don't have insurance. Can you tell me how much it would cost to fill this without insurance?"

"Just a minute."

He wasn't sure he was talking to a pharmacist. This person was a tiny, very young-looking blonde woman, but she had a confidence about her that made him wonder what kind of degree she had or whether she was training to be a pharmacist. She looked up from her computer. "Um, it would be two hundred forty," she said in a low tone with a sheepish smile of apology. She could see that he couldn't pay. He was the only person there dressed like that, looking like that. "Sorry," she almost whispered. Her confidence had disappeared. She was embarrassed, and sad for him.

"It's OK. Thanks," he said, and walked out.

DOCTOR KHANNA HAD GIVEN Todd five little boxes that each contained a purple plastic bottle that had five purple Nexium capsules in it, which gave him less than a month's worth of medicine. After experimenting to find how long he could go without but maintain himself at a non-vomiting level, he managed to stretch those pills out for almost two months, and after that, now knowing the nature of the problem, he was able to keep the symptoms at bay using over-the-counter drugs like Tagamet. But it wasn't the same.

Tagamet kept him from vomiting but left him in constant discomfort. The biggest benefit was that he still couldn't eat very much, so he continued to lose weight. At this point he was down to 230 pounds. He couldn't remember the last time he had weighed so little. But the constant almost-pain in his stomach and esophagus, and the relatively severe pain he felt for hours after he ate anything, were making him miserable and angry, which wasn't great given his line of work.

He coughed and spit and blew smoke out the door of the booth. It was Monday, dark, and nearly 8:00 p.m. He had been trying to be nice today in order to avoid having to fight while he felt so bad, but the little annoyances always expanded when he was nice to customers. They were like dogs or children. If you didn't treat them badly, they would ask for more and more and more until you reached your threshold and *did* treat them badly. If they saw he was in a decent mood, they'd milk him for everything they could get and keep at it until they made him mad enough to turn on them. They had done this to Todd several times in the last few hours, and now while he was coughing and spitting and blowing smoke out the door, he was also wishing for death.

The phone rang. Jason answered, said a few yeahs. "I can't." Long pause. "No." Long pause. "I can't." Long pause. "No." Long pause. "Todd." Jason handed the phone to Todd.

"Yeah." It was Vern.

"Mike can't come in tonight. Can you stay and work his shift?" Todd hated this place more than he hated life itself, but it very abruptly occurred to him that if he wanted more money he had to work for it, so he blurted out, "Yeah."

As soon as he said it, he was mad at himself. He hadn't even been here for eight hours yet, but he was already tired and hungry, and fast food or the type of stuff he could get delivered hurt his stomach. The more grease or dairy something had, the worse it was for him. And working one night of overtime wasn't really going to get him any nearer to two hundred and forty dollars. He didn't know how to calculate what he made after taxes, but he knew that $8.25 times eight hours was sixty-six dollars, and that sixty-six times 1.5 for overtime was ninety-nine dollars. Then taxes would be taken out. And he had been late several times this week, so he wouldn't even get a full eight hours of overtime. Even if there were no taxes, he would still need more than another one hundred and forty-one dollars to fill his prescription. But he couldn't back out now. He was stuck. Vern made the rest of the conversation as short as possible because he sensed what was going on in Todd's head, and once he hung up it was done. Todd was sentenced to another eight hours in this shithole. He tried to make the best of it in his mind. It wouldn't get him his prescription, but maybe a couple of CDs he couldn't otherwise afford. Or maybe he could save toward the prescription. *Some* money was better than *no* money.

"I'm pretty fucking shocked you're staying. I mean, what if you have a panic attack or whatever the fuck in the middle of the night or something?"

Todd hadn't thought of that. Since the vomiting had started, the panic attack or heart attack thing had sort of gone off his radar. When he couldn't hold down food, how he was feeling otherwise got ignored. He had stopped taking aspirin as soon as Doctor Khanna had told him to, and he had quit carrying the bottle around with him. He gripped each side of the register as hard as he could. "I don't know. If I have one, then I have one."

When Jason went up to clean the bathrooms, Todd started thinking about how he was going to get something to eat. In addition to discovering which particular foods and drinks hurt him, he had also recently discovered that going *without* food for too long could hurt him nearly as much as eating the wrong things, so he really couldn't starve himself for sixteen straight hours. The station's store was contained entirely within the booth, which was bigger than his bedroom by only maybe two or three feet in length and width, and because the air-conditioner and heater didn't work very well, it held nothing perishable. All they had was oil, transmission fluid, antifreeze, windshield washer fluid, maps, ice scrapers, fuel treatments, cigarettes, and BiC lighters, so there would be no surviving on snacks the way he might at a normal gas station. He could steal soda from the palate in the garage used to stock the machines, but that idea didn't thrill him either because, again, now knowing the nature of his condition, he found that doing without soda was helpful. He supposed that he could give Jason four dollars and ask him to go to McDonalds real quick. He would feel bad asking, and the grease would kill him, but he had to have something to eat. The four dollars was all the money he had until he got paid on Wednesday, but the extra hours he was picking up would make it worthwhile in the long run.

 He was trying to psych himself up, to tell himself that tonight wouldn't be bad, that the place would mostly be empty—it was almost entirely empty now—when a brand new red F-150 crew cab hauling a thirty-foot boat on a trailer pulled up to a diesel pump on the southbound side. The boat was white, as they mostly were, and he could see that the steering wheel was on top and that there was a cabin below it, like that boat in *Jaws* but without the mast or whatever that Roy Scheider was clinging to at the end. *This asshole has a two-story fucking boat.* And at this point it was nearly winter, so he almost certainly wasn't just going down to Rehoboth. He was probably driving down to South Carolina or Florida or some fucking place like that and staying at a hotel, or maybe he had a second house down there.

People started getting out of the truck. The driver wore jeans, a plaid flannel shirt, a full salt-and-pepper beard, and shiny black shoes. His hair was thick and wavy, but controlled. The passenger was clearly his wife. She was petite, very pretty, his age, wore a dress that somehow managed to show off every contour of her body without being tight or slutty, and she carried a tiny hand bag by a very thin and proportionally way-too-long strap. Their daughter was in an awkward stage. Braces, hair that didn't look like it had been brushed, jeans, white sneaks, white jacket that was striped down the arms, mild but dark-colored acne, no discernible attitude or personality, probably thirteen or fourteen and definitely not advanced for her age, little pink patches of nail polish here and there—the rest had all peeled off. She just stood there waiting for some kind of cue from her mother while her father went about his business, oblivious to both of them.

Todd didn't know what to make of the man. He was like some kind of rich person–redneck hybrid. Small business owner? Todd didn't know anyone who had been to college, so he couldn't spot the professorial type unless it was a cartoonish TV version, but he felt that the man wasn't in his element in that truck. It was like he was playing dress-up. Some of Todd's earliest memories were of his father wearing a cowboy hat even though they lived in the mid-Atlantic. It seemed to Todd like this was the same kind of artificial thing.

He could see on the cash register's LCD that the man had put his credit card into the pump. This happened from time to time. People with gasoline engines would accidentally fill their tanks full of diesel, then have to sit there for an hour waiting for a tow truck. All of this station's employees hated the customers, but this was such a huge problem, one that they themselves would hate to have to deal with and would cost hundreds of dollars to fix, that they made every effort to save the customers from it. Todd shut the pump down and waited for the guy to realize the problem. The message on the LCD out on the pump, he knew, said PLEASE SEE ATTENDANT, but like every single customer who made this mistake, the guy just looked over at the booth and waved his arms like a fucking asshole. Todd looked intently down, pretended to be counting the money in the register. He just wanted the idiot to realize the situation on his own. It was a situation that it was almost impossible *not* to realize anyway. On top of the pump was a green sign that said DIESEL in yellow letters outlined in black; there was only one pump handle; there were no buttons for choosing octane; the pump was only half as wide as every other pump in the station; the handle had a bright green plastic coating on it, unlike any other pump handle in the place, and there must have been fifteen pump handles visible to the guy right that second. In Todd's opinion it took a deep and abiding stupidity to fail to realize that there was something about that pump that wasn't right. An intelligent person would at least investigate. But the guy just stood there angrily waving his arms. Finally he started toward the booth. As he pretended to count the ones in the cash drawer, Todd could see the guy out of his peripheral vision and could tell by his aggressive walk that the guy intended to vent.

"Turn that pump on!" the guy said, halfway to the booth. Todd pretended to be counting until he couldn't anymore, then looked up at the guy with fake confusion.

"Turn that pump on!"

Todd pointed to his ear and mouthed *I can't hear you.* He was lying. He *could* hear. The guy closed another half of the distance between them. He was now three quarters of the way to the booth. Todd pointed to his ear and mouthed *I can't hear you.*

He was not actually trying to start a fight with the guy. On principle, when they were alone in the booth at night, employees did not open the door except to smoke and spit. Also on principle, they refused to let lazy customers draw them outside the booth and potentially expose them to danger in the form of people who might then rob or otherwise assail them. They weren't actually afraid of that because it hadn't happened in recent memory, but the principle was the thing—they couldn't let customers jerk them around, have them running all over the place to tell them that they were on a diesel pump and ask them did they *want* diesel? So the game they played was to try to force the customers to figure out for themselves the things that were clearly marked and obvious to anyone who looked. They didn't go outside. If the idiot needed a clearly indicated fact spoon fed to him, he was going to have to come over here. And finally he did.

In a tone designed to sound like someone who was

trying to hide his feeling of superiority, the man said, "Didn't you hear what I was saying?"

Todd turned on the intercom. "I'm sorry?" He had heard well enough.

With more fake patience, more slowly, "Didn't you hear what I was saying?"

"No." Lie.

"Why didn't you turn on this intercom?"

"I wouldn't be able to hear you from that far away. You have to be right here. Otherwise it doesn't pick it up." Another lie.

The man sighed the fake TV sigh of someone pretending to have decided to be the bigger man and let his anger go. "I put my credit card in that pump. It was working for a second, but then it stopped. Presumably because you, or the computer, or something else, turned it off. Would you please turn it on again?"

"You want diesel?"

The man was now acting like someone pretending that he wasn't mad before but had been pushed too far. *"If I wanted diesel, I would have asked you for it!"* The man's shout was genuine—the first genuine thing about him that Todd had seen.

Fake-guilelessly, at a totally normal volume: "That's a diesel pump."

The wife was now walking over, the girl trailing behind her. "Walter. Walter, what is going on? Why are you raising your voice to that . . . man?"

"This . . . fat idiot is fucking with me, Alison. *That's* why."

Alison gave Walter a disapproving look with a slightly

cocked head and an open mouth. The girl was shocked. She stood with widened eyes, grasping the tips of the fingers of her left hand with the tips of the fingers of her right, mouth slightly open. Todd lost track of everything past "fat idiot." Later, he didn't quite know why. He had never before been particularly sensitive about either his weight or being called stupid (he accepted and acknowledged to his friends that he was both fat and stupid), but there was something about this guy that enraged him. He came here with his brand new F-150 crew cab and his thirty-foot fishing boat and his pretty wife to whom he was utterly oblivious, dressed like a working man when he was clearly a rich idiot in class-drag, acting like he owned the place, talking down to Todd and calling him an idiot when *he* was the idiot—maybe not in life, but in this particular situation—and it blinded Todd with rage, made him angrier than he had been in the last five years. He felt like he had done a line of meth to brace up for a fistfight. Unfortunately, it also paralyzed him verbally. He had often told customers to fuck themselves and their mothers and grandmothers and whoever else —he was not afraid of laying into the errant customer when the situation called for it. But right now, he had nothing. Just rage. And his inability to speak made him angrier and angrier, second by second. He wanted desperately to say anything to this person, but was completely blank.

The man walked back toward his truck. The wife and daughter followed, the girl still clutching her fingertips, ponytail bouncing, jogging to catch up with her mother. Walter backed the truck and trailer up so it was even with the gas pump behind the diesel pump. Todd could have and should have let it go at that, but the rage was too much. Walter put his credit card in this pump. Todd watched the LCD. Waited for the blinking to stop, for the margin above the pump number to turn solid black, indicating the card was authorized. Waited for Walter to put the pump in his truck. And then with a keystroke he shut it off. He could see Walter squinting to see the message on the pump's LCD. He looked, read it, looked at Todd, and raised his arms in the universal sign for *what the fuck?* Todd raised both fists, middle fingers extended, in the universal sign for *fuck you* and mouthed it slowly and dramatically. Walter and Alison were agape. The girl was out of sight but presumably shocked as well.

Walter came back angrily. "I want to fill up on that pump."

"*Fuck* you, you fucking redneck!" Todd knew Walter wasn't a redneck but figured that if Walter wanted to wear the uniform, he would have to hold the title.

Walter was clearly exasperated and just wanted the thing to end, to be on the road, away from here. "Look. I apologize for what I said. Will you please turn the pump back on?"

"*Fuck* you, you redneck piece of shit! Get the *fuck* out of here!"

"I'm not a redneck, I was born in New Jersey." As if there were zero rednecks in New Jersey.

"Then go the fuck *back* to New Jersey, you fucking redneck piece of shit!" His rage was visible. Voluble. Implacable.

"You can't refuse to sell me gas. I'm calling the cops."

"Good. That means you're leaving, you fucking redneck piece of shit!" Walter, who no longer had enough control over his anger to spin it to look like sarcasm or superiority, started walking back toward his truck. Todd ought to have noticed that his heart was both racing and pounding, and that he was just fine, but he didn't quite notice. He was focused on hating the man on pump three, hoping to God that he would fucking leave. But there was no such luck. Walter sifted through the console of his new truck for some quarters and then made his way to the small bank of pay phones about a hundred yards behind the booth, near the restaurants.

Todd had not been in this exact situation before but assumed this was one of those things that idiots believed but wasn't really true about the law, like when people say that if you're buying drugs or something and you ask someone if they're a cop, they have to tell you. That's not actually true—they don't have to tell you anything—it's just something that dipshits repeat to each other because they heard it somewhere. Todd assumed this "you can't refuse to sell me gas" bullshit was the same, but he didn't know, so he started preparing for the possible presence of police. He took Jason's pipe out of his bag and tossed it onto the roof of the booth. It wasn't irretrievable there—the booth was only about three feet taller than he was, and he had hidden drugs and paraphernalia there before. This was the standard *police are coming* procedure. He made sure there was nothing else illegal in Jason's bag, and just to be thorough he went and got his own pipe out of his Trans Am and tossed it up on the roof too.

In a few minutes, Jason came down from the bathrooms and was looking over at Walter's truck and wife and daughter, neither of whom noticed Jason. They had apparently gotten sick of being in the truck cab and were standing on the far side of the truck so as not to be seen by the angry fat idiot.

"Fuck's with them?"

"I kicked the guy out, and he wouldn't leave. Cops are coming."

"For what?"

"The guy says I can't refuse to sell him gas. Says he's calling the cops."

Jason started fumbling around in his bag.

"Pipe's on the roof. Mine too."

"I'm trying to think do I got any other shit on me."

"I don't think so. I looked through your bag just in case and didn't find nothing. I wouldn't normally have gone through your bag, but... the cops."

"I don't care. I'd rather you go through the bag than the cops come and me not be ready for it. I'm not opening full service again."

"I'm down with that."

Walter reappeared near the truck. Todd turned on the intercom and listened carefully as Walter talked to his wife. The first thing he could make out was, "They said they're not coming out here for that."

"Of course they're not coming out here for that, you fucking redneck idiot, now get the *fuck* out of here!" The sheet metal canopy overhead actually made Todd's voice echo through the station. Walter got into his brand-new truck with his pretty wife, his daughter who presumably loved him, and pulled out of the station, towing his two-story, thirty-foot fishing boat, defeated. In one way.

"Damn," Jason said.

"For real. *Fuck* that guy."

"What'd he do?"

"He was on a diesel pump and he was embarrassed, so he called me a fat idiot."

"Fuck him. I hate these fucks who can't fucking read."

"Want me to get your pipe down?"

"I'll get it. Yours too. With all these fucking pipes it's a shame there ain't no fucking weed. We could probably scrape out a decent ball of resin."

"Nah. That shit just makes me tired. And I have to stay awake for another fucking nine or so hours."

IT WAS ONLY after the shift change that Todd recalled how hungry he was, and in the residual excitement he forgot to ask Jason to pick him up something before he went home. Now he was stuck with four useless dollars and zero food. *Fuck.* He walked up to the garage and stole a warm Mountain Dew and a warm iced tea that he thought would get him through the night. He drank about half of the iced tea all at once, waited about fifteen minutes, and then drank the other half, believing this would give him the caffeine he would need to make it through the first half of the shift. But by eleven thirty he was already tired, and whatever the fake lemon flavor in the tea was made out of, it must have had real acid in it because his stomach was hurting badly. It was burning with a peppery sensation that he knew he could partly abate with something like bread or crackers, but there was also that awful feeling in his, esophagus like something was stuck in it, and it was burning more and more urgently. He guessed it was time to take another Tagamet.

There was no proper faucet in the garage that was really usable. The faucet in the bathroom was one of the ones that hung over at an angle, and the basin was very shallow, so there wasn't enough space to fit a soda bottle under it. He could stick it in the sink at an angle and fill it up about three quarters of the way, but the mouth of the bottle had to touch the faucet, and it made him sick to think of people taking a shit in that bathroom and washing their hands in that sink and that his bottle had touched it, so he had to use the sink in the garage itself. The sink there was a big plastic basin that had been used to find leaks in tires back when they actually did repairs here. The water from it tasted horrible, like rust, or dirt. The thought of it made him almost as sick as the water from the bathroom sink, but he was hurting bad enough that he couldn't risk drinking any of that Mountain Dew yet. He choked down the Tagamet with the metallic water that was probably coming through lead pipes, then coughed in disgust. He lit a cigarette and spit on the garage floor.

When he was back in the booth, his mouth still tasted like metal, so he stood at the door, blowing smoke outside and spitting. Eventually he did open the Mountain Dew, not knowing what else to do with himself, and began to drink it. It had been eleven hours since he had eaten anything, and he thought that even if it hurt his stomach, the sugar would give him some energy.

Around midnight, customers started coming in. Late night customers were easy. They were relaxed because there was no traffic, and pretty much none of them were just getting off work. Most often they didn't even come to the booth. They used their cards at the pump and were gone. And there was no specific type that was out late. There were teenage girls and elderly men, all races, all degrees of car from '79 Honda to '01 Porsche. One night he saw Allen Iverson in a Mercedes with purple headlights. And it was definitely him too—he didn't come to the booth, but Todd had checked the tape on the printer. The name on the card was Allen Iverson. It was the only celebrity sighting at the station, except the time Motörhead's tour bus stopped there —but nobody actually saw Lemmy. Tonight they were all nondescript men. Mostly white and black. He watched them come and go, listening to the printer record their transactions. One loud smooth screech when the card was approved, a second staccato screech when they hung the pump back up, recording the final amount. Then they disappeared. He didn't even hear that printer during the day, but at night it was deafening.

The worst thing was when he saw other people his age. Guys his age in brand-new cars. Sometimes groups of dangerous-looking drunk guys came in together and exuded a team vibe, like a gang. Sometimes couples. No one remarkable, but they all—even the '79 Honda types— seemed infinitely better off than he was. He was ashamed just being there in that fucking uniform. He looked like a fucking clown in that white and blue striped shirt with tiny red pinstripes. He wished he could disappear.

Other than the class-drag redneck, no one particularly hateful to him had come in tonight, but he never forgot encounters with people like him. He didn't know how long ago, but one time a bunch of kids from the university came in during the day, before he and Jason had made their arrangement, so he had to go out and serve kids who were only two or three years younger than him and just plain *better*. None were fat. All were beautiful and had perfect skin and nice clothes, and they were driving a Camry that was only three or four years old. They had enough money that when he explained that full service was twenty cents more a gallon, they still wanted it. And then he made a mistake. He had pumped a reasonable amount of gas when the pump shut off. The kid driving insisted that the car wasn't full—which it wasn't—and then he got out of the car to show Todd what he thought was the reason the pump had shut off.

"You see this metal flap? The pump has to be in there far enough to push that down. Otherwise it won't work."

"You think I don't know that?" he shot back.

The kid wasn't being an asshole. Not intentionally. He was just trying to show Todd what he thought the problem was, and it came out as horribly condescending. Or at least Todd, in his mortification, took it as horribly condescending. First of all, Todd knew that—no one who worked at a gas station could possibly *not* know that—and second of all, that wasn't actually the problem. But Todd was so angry and humiliated he couldn't even begin explaining.

"Alright," the kid said submissively and got back into the car. But Todd hadn't won anything. It wasn't the submission of a person who felt defeated, it was the submission of a person who cared so little about this, who had so much else in his life, that this battle meant nothing. The kid won because he didn't care. Todd stood there like an idiot, pumping a penny at a time, angry over nothing and humiliated in front of four kids who clearly had more important things to do. The girls in the car shot Todd occasional glances through the window. They were tiny young women. They weren't movie-star beautiful, they were average girls, but pretty in the mysterious, aloof way that upper-class college girls were. They made Todd feel so far away from them, like they could casually, effortlessly, argue with him about anything and win. But here they were with this kid who didn't even seem particularly happy to be with them. He seemed to feel entitled to it, like it was no big deal to be with them, like he might drive around with any number of girls anytime he wanted. They were so different from the trailer park girls he had been with. His girls were heavy, with that sloppy nasal accent that sounded like Joe Genaro from The Dead Milkmen, except they had nothing funny or clever to say. They smoked and wore too much makeup and low-cut shirts. They had ragged hair. It was like they were a different species. These girls' skin looked smoother even though they weren't wearing makeup, and their hair looked prettier, cleaner, thicker. They spoke carefully, reasonably, clearly, and knew a thousand things Todd had never heard of. If they had been at a bar, these girls wouldn't even have accepted a drink from him. That was the last time he ever worked full service.

He coughed and spit out the door. He hated this place. He hated his life. He hated this feeling. It was one thirty. The Tagamet he took had either started to wear off or the Mountain Dew he had no choice but to drink was canceling out its effects—or the Tagamet didn't work because it was not the right drug for his condition. Even if he started picking up extra shifts, it would take months for him to save up two hundred and forty dollars, and he wasn't sure they would even fill the prescription after all that time. Do new prescriptions expire or something if they aren't filled right away? He didn't even know. And now he had the added expense of paying for the over-the-counter stuff to stave off the vomiting until those months went by. He looked around the booth. There were brown stains on the walls where condensation had leaked from the air-conditioner in the summer. The shelves were dusty. The floor was covered with dirt. The floor pads were ripped. He didn't think anything in the booth had been cleaned in all the time he worked there. Everything in his life was just like this.

The obvious thing was to try to steal some money from the gas station. Here he was, alone in the booth with a cash drawer, and no one could see what he was doing. There probably wasn't even two forty in the drawer. He counted, just to see, and he was right. Only one thirty-eight. Even the fucking cash drawer couldn't afford Nexium. Just for the fuck of it, he decided to keep a running tally to see how long it would be before he had two forty in the drawer.

Mostly this was a game. He didn't actually intend to rob the gas station. But Todd had a bitter streak in him, and he liked to have facts to shore up his bitterness. He liked to have imaginary conversations with imaginary people he could crush with what he thought were water-tight arguments, or to throw the enormity of the injustices against him into the face of his imaginary opponent to underscore how much he would have to overcome to pull himself out of the hole he was in. He knew there was shame in this, that it was guilty self-pity. But he figured it was fine for him to let off steam if he kept it to himself. No one would ever hear the arguments he had in his head with imaginary opponents late at night when he was completely alone. No one would hear the occasional lines he said out loud or even know he was preoccupied. People did it all the time and didn't feel ashamed of it—look at Dylan's "Like a Rolling Stone"—all that song did was self-righteously rip some imaginary girl a new asshole, set up straw man arguments to make her look horrible, and he heard on TV that it "defined a generation." So, he thought, fuck it. He kept that running tally to prove a point, and he cultivated his argument around that point.

The station where he worked didn't even take in enough cash in a shift to buy his medicine, and even that money wasn't profit—there were costs, electricity, overhead, his wage—so how could a pharmaceutical company justify charging one person that fucking much? It was wrong. Fuck research and development. Fuck *their* overhead. They were making fistfuls of cash every second—they even had TV commercials for this fucking pill, so they *had* to be making metric fuck-tons of cash. There was no way around that. And of course those metric fuck-tons of cash came from charging people sickening amounts of money. He guessed insurance paid for almost all of it for most people—for the rich fucks with new cars he saw at Rite Aid—but how the *fuck* would he know that, not having insurance, and when, if he took the insurance offered him, he'd have to go to Penn-syl-fucking-vania to see a doctor? Not to mention pay a giant copay and then somehow find the money in his check to pay for the fucking prescription, too. It was a good argument. It *felt* good. He liked it. It would put him in a good position to win, in his head.

By two 2:53 a.m., he had two hundred and twelve dollars in cash in the register. Twenty-eight dollars short. He could get twenty-eight dollars in a week or two. The station was empty, dead quiet, and had been for forty minutes. "Fuck it," he said out loud. He took all the bills out of the till, walked back to his Trans Am, and put the cash in the steering wheel cut-out with his pipe. He didn't close the car door right away. He stood there panicking for a few seconds. But his stomach hurt. He needed that money. It was already in his possession. He could feel the Mountain Dew in his throat, in his stomach, burning. He slammed the car door shut, ran out to one of the black plastic trash cans that stood between the pumps, and dove into it head first, like Pete Rose stealing second. The can slid a few feet before it capsized and spilled its contents—garbage, windshield washer fluid, and a battered squeegee with a fraying edge went clattering to one side. He had a good bloody scrape on both his palms and his right elbow, and there was a small tear in the knee of his scratchy Cintas uniform.

He went back inside the booth and kicked the rack with the quarts of oil. They all thudded to the ground. *The guy pushed me into it.* He opened the register, pulled the cash drawer out, dumped the coins on the floor, and threw it down. Then he stood there looking.

It wasn't permanent yet. He could get all the money back—pick up every coin, get every dollar out of his car. But his stomach was boiling, and he couldn't stand another swallow of rusty water, or Mountain Dew, or iced tea with that fake fucking lemon acid. He picked up the phone but put it down again. Who to blame? Black guy. The police would believe that. Or would they be more suspicious if he just said black guy? Who would do this? He pictured a wiry man who looked like the seventies. Long blonde hair, scraggly mustache and goatee. Then he realized that he wasn't inventing anything; he was remembering. That was pretty much a picture of his father as a teenager. A trucker. There were twenty rigs parked behind the booth. But they might go through them all, keep him here all night. Maybe the guy wore a mask. For two hundred dollars? A person who would rob a shithole like this for two hundred dollars wouldn't have planned that far ahead. Then he remembered Mark. He knew a guy named Mark who did a smash-and-grab at a liquor store once. He wore a hoodie and had an old T-shirt wrapped around the lower part of his face so the security cameras couldn't see him. That was the appropriate formula for robbing this shithole. Half-ass disguise, totally believable. He picked up the phone again.

Half an hour later the police arrived. He told them he had gone outside to change the trash bags and a guy came up behind him, knocked him down, and threatened him with a gun that he kept in his pocket. He wasn't sure the guy really *had* a gun in that pocket, but he wasn't going to find out. The guy made him go back into the booth—pushing him into the rack of oil—and open the register. The guy grabbed the drawer, took all the paper money, threw the drawer down, and ran off. He was wearing faded blue jeans, a gray hoodie with the hood up, and something wrapped around his face. A bandana? No, it was just, like, cloth. He didn't know what, just cloth. Maybe it was an old T-shirt or something. He was white, had black eyebrows—so probably black hair—but that's all he could say. The cops called Vern, and Vern came in. Both the cops and Vern seemed to think he was really shaken up. He was tired and weak from not having eaten in so long, and something about lying to the police, knowing he could go to jail, knowing where the cash was, worrying that they saw right through him, freaked him out bad. So, in a sense, they were right. They all appeared to believe him. The cops asked if he wanted medical attention. No, it was just a few scrapes and bruises. He was fine. Vern sent him home and worked the rest of the shift himself. As Todd pulled out of the parking lot, he saw Vern starting to clean up the trash. "Fuck you, Vern." And he drove off with Vern's money. Mobil's money. Someone's money that wasn't his.

When he got home it was four forty-five or a little after that. He didn't bring the money inside. He felt sure that all the guys who might break into his car were long since asleep. And anyway, if the cops came to talk to him or something, the money was safer there in the steering wheel. He made sure his car was locked and went inside to eat a cheese sandwich and to figure out where he was going to get twenty-eight dollars.

Printed in Great Britain
by Amazon